Praise for the Love

"Hallee writes with such authentic detail that I felt the sweat drip off my brow, heard the buzz of the African jungle, and ran for dear life with Cynthia and Rick. A rich story of courage and seeing the world with new eyes. Riveting, this book will get under your skin and into your heart. Absolutely fantastic."

Susan May Warren, *USA Today*
bestselling author, on *Honor Bound*

"What a fabulous story with perfectly crafted characters who grab your heart from the opening page. I loved everything about it—from the witty dialogue to the breath-stopping suspense to the tender romance. Once I started, I couldn't put it down. I highly recommend this book and can't wait for the next one."

Lynette Eason, award-winning, bestselling author
of the Extreme Measures series, on *Honor Bound*

"Hallee Bridgeman weaves a military suspense with romance for a fast-paced adventure. *Word of Honor* kept me turning pages all night long."

DiAnn Mills, author of
Concrete Evidence, on *Word of Honor*

"This book has something for everyone—action, adventure, romance, and true-to-life sadness and grief. Hallee crafts a complex story infused with spiritual truth, wrapped around intriguing lead characters with complicated personalities and backgrounds. Phil and Melissa will have you rooting for them the whole way through."

Janice Cantore, retired police officer
and author of *Breach of Honor*, on *Honor's Refuge*

BOOKS BY HALLEE BRIDGEMAN

LOVE AND HONOR

Honor Bound
Word of Honor
Honor's Refuge

LOVE ☆ HONOR
BOOK 3

HONOR'S REFUGE

HALLEE BRIDGEMAN

Revell

a division of Baker Publishing Group
Grand Rapids, Michigan

© 2022 by Hallee Bridgeman

Published by Revell
a division of Baker Publishing Group
PO Box 6287, Grand Rapids, MI 49516-6287
www.revellbooks.com

Printed in the United States of America

Library of Congress Cataloging-in-Publication Data
Names: Bridgeman, Hallee, author.
Title: Honor's refuge / Hallee Bridgeman.
Description: Grand Rapids, MI : Revell, a division of Baker Publishing Group,
    [2022] | Series: Love and Honor ; 3
Identifiers: LCCN 2022001731 | ISBN 9780800740221 (paperback) | ISBN
    9780800742300 (casebound) | ISBN 9781493438907 (ebook)
Classification: LCC PS3602.R531375 H667 2022 | DDC 813/.6—dc23
LC record available at https://lccn.loc.gov/2022001731

Baker Publishing Group publications use paper produced from sustainable forestry practices and post-consumer waste whenever possible.

22 23 24 25 26 27 28   7 6 5 4 3 2 1

This book is dedicated to the EMTs and paramedics who are on our streets every day—first responders who go into unknown and at times dangerous situations with the single mission to help those in need. Thank you for your dedication to your calling.

PROLOGUE

Missy huddled with three-year-old Lola between the night-stand and the bed, praying her little sister would stay asleep. Her father's fist hit her mother's face with a sickening thud, and Missy's stomach rolled. She really shouldn't have let the macaroni and cheese burn. This was all her fault.

Her mom landed on the floor, clutching her big round belly with the new baby. Her father yelled and kicked her with his boots. Her mom reached forward, and for a moment, Missy was terrified that she was grabbing for her. Instead, she grasped the cord of the telephone. It landed next to Missy as her father stomped on her mom's arm.

She stared at the phone. 911. She'd learned that on *Sesame Street* yesterday. In case of a fire, call 911. Even though this wasn't a fire, maybe a fireman would help her mom. She reached out, pressing the buttons very carefully.

"911, what's your emergency?" a woman said.

Missy trembled, afraid her father would hear her speak, so she said nothing. Pulling Lola closer, she kissed her curly black hair. Her sister started to struggle against her, and she worried she would start crying. Just as Lola broke free, her father stormed away and slammed the bedroom door.

Eyes closed, Missy waited for him to come back. Her mom gave a long cry, and Missy cracked open one eye to make sure the door was still shut. She shifted out from her hiding place. Her mom lay with her arms around her stomach, panting. Lola walked over to her and knelt down, patting her on the head. Her mom let out another long moan.

With a loud bang, the door slammed open. Missy's whole body froze in fear. Her hands tingled and her breath wouldn't move past her chest. Her father filled the doorway. He looked at Missy, then at Lola, and walked toward the bed. Missy ducked out of the way, grabbed Lola's hand, and ran to the door.

Her father picked the phone up and stared at it. "What did you do?" he shouted at her mom. He bent and grabbed her by her hair, putting his face close to hers. "What did you do?"

Her breath ended on a hiccup, and she panted, "You better run. They're coming and they'll find it all."

Missy clung to Lola's hand and crouched in the hall, trying to decide what to do while her father hung up the phone and then dialed a number. He turned his back on them and spoke in Spanish. "Cops are coming." After a pause he said, "Whatever you think is best." He looked over his shoulder at Missy and narrowed his eyes at her. "Yes, sir."

Missy's heart leapt into her throat. She kept a firm grip on Lola's hand and ran down the hall and through the living room. In the kitchen, she could still smell the burned macaroni and cheese.

"Come on, Lola," she whispered, pushing open the dog door.

Lola hesitated, giant tears sliding down her face. "Mommy said no," she said, pushing her hand against the door.

"You have to go!" Missy looked over her shoulder. Her father must still be on the phone. Thinking that Lola would follow her if she went first, she pushed her hands and head through the small door. Little pebbles on the patio dug into her palms, and the front of her leg scraped against the metal frame, but she didn't cry.

Outside, she lifted the flap and motioned for Lola to follow her. Her sister's lip trembled, but she crawled through.

On the back porch, Missy looked around. Where to hide? He'd look in the fort by the swing set. She took Lola's hand and ran around to the front of the house, to the big bush by the mailbox. If they sat on the curb, he probably couldn't see them. The bush would hide them.

Lola covered her ears with her hands and closed her eyes. "Mommy," she said.

Missy put her arm around her. Her leg stung where she'd hit the dog door. She poked at the bloody scrape as tears fell down her face. "Be quiet, Lola. Let's wait for the firemen."

Instead of a fire truck, though, a police car came. Missy didn't know what she'd done to make the police come instead of the firemen, but she was so happy to see two officers get out of the car that she couldn't even speak.

The woman spotted them and knelt next to them by the mailbox. She had nice eyes and smelled like peppermint. "It's not safe out here by the road," she said, putting a hand on Lola's head. "Where are your parents?"

"Mommy," Lola cried, then looked over her shoulder toward the house.

Missy's lower lip trembled. "Mommy's hurt."

"Is your dad here?" the policewoman asked.

"Daddy's bad," Lola said. She covered her ears again.

As the policewoman stood up, she talked into the radio on her shoulder, using words and numbers that Missy didn't understand.

"It's okay, Lola," Missy said as the officers walked toward the house. "We'll be okay now."

CHAPTER

★

ONE

When Melissa Braxton eyed Phil Osbourne's black truck turning into the parking lot, she snatched up her book and opened it. She settled back into the booth to give a false appearance of relaxation. She didn't want him to think she'd sat here just anticipating his arrival, watching every car that drove by. He didn't need or want that kind of attention.

She didn't put the book down until she felt him slide into the booth across from her. She intentionally looked startled at his arrival. "Oh, hi," she said with a grin. "Glad you made it."

Phil had dark blond hair, gray-green eyes set on a square face, and a mouth that didn't smile often enough. Normally, he wore his EMT uniform to their Thursday morning breakfasts, but today he had on a light-blue T-shirt that stretched across his broad chest and emphasized his healthy tan.

"You ever going to finish that book?" he asked as he settled into the booth.

She found the gumption to blink in innocence. "I beg your pardon?"

"You've been reading that same book for a couple of weeks now."

She should have given his observation skills a little more credit. She kept the book in her car for the "reading, not waiting" ruse. She shrugged. "I only read it here."

The diner owner, Delilah Pérez, arrived with a pot of coffee. She was Phil's mom's best friend, and Phil had grown up around her. She usually waited on them instead of one of the waitresses.

"Morning, Phil," she said as she set a container of cinnamon next to his coffee cup.

He smiled up at her. "Delilah. Good to see you."

"Regular?"

"Yes, ma'am."

Delilah looked at Melissa. "What about you, hon? What's this morning's story?"

The Cuban diner had all the flavors she remembered from her grandparents' kitchen. "Hmm, how about plantain and corned beef hash?" she asked.

"You want spice?"

"Oh, yes, ma'am." Melissa pulled her braid over her shoulder and toyed with the end of it while she redirected her attention to Phil. "I don't see how you can eat oatmeal day after day. This place could bring so much flavor to your life."

"I like flavor. Just not at eight in the morning." He rested his forearms on the table, linking his fingers. "How are you?"

How was she? She didn't think "desperately in love with you and wishing you'd notice me" was the answer he sought. So she went to where he would follow. "Rough night. A woman with three kids called at two. The police took her husband, but she was afraid he'd come back before morning, so she wanted to get out of there as fast as possible."

Melissa operated a domestic abuse shelter. Everyone kept the location mostly a secret. She and her partner had spread the contact information to doctors' offices, hospitals, therapists, schools, and emergency services. She gave the victims a safe home, provided family and individual counseling, and helped them start new lives—usually away from Miami. Phil provided medical care whenever she couldn't convince someone to go to the hospital.

"How old?" He sprinkled cinnamon into his coffee.

"Four, five, and seven."

He shook his head as he stirred the rich brew. "Poor kids."

"I know. They're shell-shocked right now."

He held up the cinnamon as if asking if she wanted some, but she shook her head.

"I didn't get a lot of time to speak with her," she said. "I have a meeting with her during lunch to start the initial counseling."

As Phil took a sip of his coffee, she studied his face. Normally at breakfast, he had a hint of a beard and tired eyes from working the night shift. This morning, he looked rested and groomed, and she could smell the hint of his aftershave. "Big plans today?"

He put his cup down and smiled. "Actually, I have a couple of friends coming to town."

"Friends?" She knew his parents and brother from church,

but she had never met any of his friends. "Where are they coming from?"

"Alaska and Virginia."

"From the service?"

He nodded.

"That will be nice. You going to play tour guide?"

Another smile. Wow, two in one morning! "Nah. Drumstick is helping me with a project. Pot Pie is his business partner."

With raised eyebrows, Melissa repeated, "Drumstick and Pot Pie?"

"That's what we call them. Those were their nicknames on our team."

He sounded animated, almost happy. She loved that his friends generated this kind of energy in him. "Let me guess, your nickname was Ozzy Osbourne."

"No. Close, though." He took another sip of coffee. "Doc Oz."

"Right! Of course. Because you're a doctor."

"I was the medic. When they first named me, they didn't know I was actually a doctor. Eventually they did, but I thought Doc Oz fit perfectly. Though, in tight situations, Ozzy took less energy to say, and they often just reverted to that."

She stared at him in awe. Those had to be the most words he'd strung together in all the time she'd known him. Before she could reply, Delilah arrived with the food. Melissa smiled as the woman slid her hash onto the table. The spicy smell of the peppers wafted up with the steam. Phil glanced at his oatmeal and thanked Delilah, then looked at Melissa. She bowed her head and listened to his voice soften as he spoke to God.

"Father, we thank You for the way You constantly bless us. Thank You for this meal, and we ask that You bless it to the nourishment of our bodies and bless our bodies to Your service. Amen."

Delilah set a hot sauce bottle on the table before Melissa could ask for it, then winked at her as she walked away. Melissa doused her hash liberally while Phil sprinkled sliced almonds and raisins over his oatmeal.

"So, I'm going to guess Pot Pie's name is probably Swanson," she said, "hearing how it works."

He looked surprised. "Well done."

"I'm stuck on Drumstick, though. Let me think about it some more."

"I have no doubt you'll be able to deduce it."

They ate in silence for several minutes before she asked, "How long are they here for?"

He shrugged one shoulder. "Until they're done."

"What's this project?"

He paused, looking at her for several heartbeats. "Something for a friend."

"Another elusive friend? Well, you're just building a village, aren't you?"

He ignored her like she knew he would. Disappointment tried to cloud her contentment at spending the morning with him. She wanted more, and she wanted him to want more. She'd made the initial step in asking him to breakfast the first time. He'd suggested lunch the next Sunday. That was where it all began and exactly where it all ended.

She'd made up her mind today to just ask him about it. Did he want to see her beyond this? Was he attracted to her? Should she give up?

Not when he had friends coming to town today, though. Seeing how animated he'd become filled her heart. She didn't want to risk infringing on that.

She took a sip of her coffee and washed down a bite of plantain. "My abuelita used to make this," she said to fill the silence. "My uncle has always corned his own beef for his deli, and whenever he had some left over, she'd make big batches of hash. She said potatoes made her sneeze, so she made it the way her mom made it in Cuba, with plantains."

"Oh, right. Your family owns that deli. I still haven't been there. Work seems to keep me on this side of Miami."

"Yep. My great-grandfather opened that deli in the late sixties. It's been handed down from son to son since."

He chewed on a raisin. "What will happen if there's not a son?"

"You take that back," she said with a laugh.

"Did you ever work in the deli?"

Images of customers lined up out the door and meat slicers and giant vats of pickles ran across her mind. "Yes."

"I'd like to have seen that."

She couldn't stop the little tug on her lips in response to his interest. "I worked there all through high school and college." Her smile faded as memories from her childhood filtered through her mind and her thoughts turned to her sister. Would she ever find her? Her smile faltered as the memories assailed her, but she pushed them aside and said, "So, friends in town today. Will I see you Sunday?"

He ripped a piece of toast in half and spread orange marmalade on it. "I will see you Sunday." He reclined against the bench while he ate. "I may have my friends with me, but I'll be there, regardless."

"Good. I'm speaking." She finished the last of her hash and took a final sip of her coffee. "I have to run. I have a mom who needs a ride to the bus station at ten."

As she slid out of the booth, he reached out and touched her forearm. She immediately stilled. "I'm sorry I was late. It's good to see you."

Unsure of what brought on the intenseness emanating from him, she stared into his eyes for probably a second too long. Finally, she said, "Drumstick is Sanders, right? For Kentucky Fried Chicken?"

A slow grin covered his face. It made her heart flutter. "Impressive," he said.

Heat filled her face, but she couldn't help smiling as she left the diner.

With Melissa gone, the room felt so much emptier. Phil stirred his oatmeal, then dropped his spoon and let it clatter against the bowl. He kicked himself for being late. He'd gone to a Narcotics Anonymous meeting first thing, then hit traffic getting to the diner.

He looked forward to every single moment he could snatch with Melissa. The first time she'd smiled at him, her brown eyes shone with a light that had stripped his ability to speak. When she'd asked him out to breakfast, he couldn't believe she could possibly have an interest in him. The next Sunday he found her in church, where she wore a yellow sundress that glowed against her dark tan skin. Her black hair fell in thick curls down her back, and she smelled like summer peaches. Somehow, the invitation to lunch had rolled off his tongue before he could talk himself out of it. And now, for over a year, he'd tortured himself by snatching a couple of meals a week with her. Every time he asked her how she was, he tensed up, waiting to hear that she'd met some really great guy and was desperately happy and couldn't meet him for breakfast or lunch anymore.

Even though she deserved to meet some really great guy who made her desperately happy.

He tossed his napkin over his bowl and pulled his wallet out of his shorts pocket. He'd worn shorts this morning, displaying the prosthetic leg he always kept hidden, but she'd had her nose buried in a book when he got there. It wasn't like she didn't know about his injury, but he wanted to see her reaction anyway because she'd never actually seen it.

Why? Why continue to put himself through this?

Because you're in love, you idiot.

He just needed to stop. If Melissa deserved anything, it was a whole man. Not someone who'd gotten addicted to narcotics in medical school, walked out on a career because he couldn't stand to have all sorts of access to drugs in his office, and joined the Army to run away from everything Miami could offer him. And that was just the beginning of the end of him.

Delilah slid into the booth across from him. "Why do you put yourself through this?"

He stared into the rich brown eyes of his mother's best friend, who had eerily echoed his own thoughts. "She needs someone who is whole."

"You're a whole lotta something, but it ain't smarts." She tapped the table. "She pines for you. I watch her. As soon as she sees you coming, she snatches up her book and pretends to be reading, but she'll watch for you the whole time."

18

Something inside of him started to bloom with hope, but he quickly doused it. "No. Look, Dee, I love you, but you need to stay out of this. I'm in as deep as I'm able. End of story." He took a twenty-dollar bill out of his wallet and set it on the table. He had quit trying to make her give him a check for breakfast and just figured what it should be every week.

She ignored the money and pointed at him. "If it's the end of that story, then it's time to start a new page. Brand-new." She slid out of the booth and stood over him. "Just to warn you, there's a mom with three kids behind you."

He let out a deep sigh and steeled himself for the stares. Adults pretended not to see, but children didn't know how to be subtle. As he slid out of the booth, the metal on his prosthetic leg caught the red lights shining behind the counter. Finding his balance and getting to his feet, he turned and made eye contact with the kid in the booth behind him.

The little boy's eyes widened, and he whispered, "Mom!" more loudly than some people shout.

Knowing the attention his leg—well, his lack of leg— received, he kept his head up and his eyes forward as the kids in that booth whisper-screamed among themselves. Relieved to get to the door, he pushed it open and stepped out into the heat of the late October morning.

The farther he walked away from the diner, the lighter he felt. Aunt Dee needed to mind her own business.

His phone chirped. He scanned the incoming call. "Well, if it ain't Drumstick Sanders. How are you, my brother?"

"Finer than a frog hair split three ways," Bill Sanders said. His Alabama twang made Phil grin. "We're on the tarmac headed for the terminal."

Phil glanced at his watch. They'd arrived much earlier than expected.

As if reading his mind, Bill said, "My flight from Alaska changed, so we were able to push up travel all the way across the board."

"With the traffic, I'm about twenty minutes away."

"Ain't no thing. I'm sure by the time we get to the gate and then to baggage claim, we'll be twenty minutes."

"Sounds good."

Even though he'd never admit it out loud, he was a little nervous about Bill and Daniel coming. In the almost two years since he'd gotten medically released from the Army, he'd had plenty of phone conversations, group messages, video conferences, and the like with the men he'd served with in the military. He'd seen them at an awards ceremony in Washington, DC, but he'd not been in a good mental state. Since then, he'd attended two weddings. However, both times he'd made his travel arrangements super tight so that he'd have an excuse to leave as soon as possible, limiting his exposure.

He'd needed to distance himself from the warriors in his life. Being with them did nothing but remind him of everything he'd lost the day that a bullet from a Chukuwereije soldier in the jungles of Katangela, Africa, had pierced the femoral artery in his left leg.

Still, while he battled nerves, he also felt very anticipatory. These were his brothers-in-arms, closer to him than his actual brother only because they'd served together in a Special Forces A-Team for five years. The things they'd seen, the things they'd done, the way they'd watched each other's backs for years, had burned into his heart and soul in a way that made them family in his mind, despite the close core family he himself had.

As if on cue, his phone rang, and his brother's name appeared across the screen. "Yo, Winston," he said as he unlocked his truck.

"Hey. I have those tickets you wanted." His older brother was an attorney in the state attorney's office. He could always get his hands on Dolphins tickets.

"That's great, man. Thanks."

"I forwarded you the email confirmation."

"You're still planning on going to the game with us, right?"

"I wanted to, but I have a last-minute conflict. I do want to meet your friends. I'll be by in the morning with the keys to my boat if you still want to borrow it."

"I do."

Winston's voice was muffled, then he said, "I have another call. Love you."

"Love you too." Before Phil pulled into traffic, he put a reminder on his phone for next Friday to have dinner with Winston. That would give him a week to take care of the business with Daniel and Bill.

As he pulled up to the loading zone at the airport, Daniel came out the door. The tall Black man carried an air of authority around him that made him stand out in a crowd. Right behind him was Bill. He had a closely trimmed dark beard and a red baseball cap covering his black hair. The last time Phil had seen him, he'd had a dark tan, but clearly, the Alaskan autumn had faded that away.

Phil pulled up right next to them and rolled his window down. "Looking for a ride, soldier?"

Daniel rested his forearm against the truck's frame and

leaned into the open window. "Ozzy, my man. Good to see you."

Bill tossed their suitcases into the back. Daniel opened the cab door. "I'm calling shotgun so I don't have to fold myself up to get into the back seat."

"Fair enough," Bill said in a drawl. "No judgment." As he slid into the back seat, he leaned forward and slapped Phil on the shoulder. "Good to see you."

"Thanks for coming."

As Phil pulled out into the airport traffic, contentment he hadn't felt in a long time settled into his soul. He needed these men in his life. He needed to know people who had been there and done that, people who understood without requiring an explanation.

He glanced over at Daniel. "How's civilian life?"

His friend grinned as he pointed to the back seat. "Well, other than starting a company with that jackal, it's perfect. Food's good, mornings are relaxed." He paused. "How are you?"

Phil smiled as he merged onto the interstate. "Better now, man. Better now."

CHAPTER

TWO

Melissa signed the receipt for a two-hundred-dollar disposable credit card and handed it over to Amanda Markle. Amanda pulled out her wallet, the cast on her left hand making her fumble. She slid the card into place behind her new ID.

"Your job interview is Monday at three," Melissa said, handing her a manila envelope with the optometrist office's information. "And the sister shelter in Dallas has a bed for you and Jeremy. They have someone picking you up at 10:05 tomorrow night. Here is her cell number. Just text her when you arrive."

Amanda's eyes filled with tears. In the two weeks she'd stayed at the shelter, this was the first sign of real emotion that Melissa had seen. "I don't know how to thank you."

Melissa took Amanda's uninjured hand with both of hers and looked her in the eye. "Stay away. Be solid and secure before he gets out of jail, and don't let him manipulate you back. That's how you can thank me."

Amanda hesitated before nodding, then pulled her hand free. "Jer, time to go to the bus station."

The ten-year-old boy got up from the little table where he was putting a puzzle together and quietly stood next to his mother. Melissa smiled at him but didn't reach for him. He didn't like touch. "You have a fun trip," she said. "Relax. Every minute on that bus will be another mile between you and here."

He nodded but didn't speak. Amanda held her hand out. He hesitated, looking at it for a moment before taking it.

"You all packed, Son?" Amanda asked.

With a nod, he rested his head against her side. Melissa had to keep herself from grabbing him in a bear hug and promising him that now that his father was no longer in the picture, he would gradually learn to relax and one day smile again. She knew because it had happened for her.

The two picked up their backpacks that she had helped pack with items from the thrift store, and they all walked out to the parking garage to Melissa's car. As she waited for Jeremy to get settled in the back seat, she looked back at the three-story building. It had been an old college dormitory prior to World War II. When the college closed down, the building was bought and converted into a hotel. It changed owners' hands several times and at one point was a halfway house.

Tall hedges and a fenced entrance provided security for the comings and goings of their clients. The parking garage hid vehicles from street view. Everyone who came promised to never reveal the location, and as far as they knew, no one had.

Melissa and her partner, Sharon, had converted half of the bottom floor to counseling rooms, a large recreation room, and a commercial kitchen with an attached dining room. On the other half of the floor, they'd added two full-sized apartments for themselves. The other two floors each had nine units. Some units had a separate bedroom, others had one common room, and they all contained a tiny kitchenette. The apartment off the inner courtyard, originally used by the college president, was home to the housekeeper and her husband.

Coming back to the matter at hand, Melissa glanced over at Amanda. "Have you ever been to Dallas?"

"No."

"Well, this will be an adventure."

The guard in the shack at the front of the drive waved at her and lifted the gate.

"Why do you do this?" Amanda asked.

Inevitably, someone always asked her that question. Aside from Sharon and what she'd allowed herself to tell Phil, she'd never talked about her own past with anyone. "It's the passion God gave me," she said. "I couldn't imagine not doing this."

"Is this what your life plan was?"

"I knew I wanted to counsel abused spouses. Everything else brought me to here."

Amanda looked behind them as they drove down the street. "There's a lot of money tied up in what you do."

"There is. We're thankful for the generous donations we receive from the community. My partner is brilliant with that kind of thing."

"It's good that you're there. Thank you for helping us."

"You're welcome."

Amanda was silent for the rest of their drive. Melissa knew she was steeling herself to leave everything she had ever known and start over. Glancing in the rearview mirror, she caught a glimpse of the excitement on Jeremy's face. She was glad he could feel that way about the trip.

She dropped them off at the entrance to the bus station. She used to take her residents in, sit with them, make sure they got on the bus. Eventually, Sharon reminded her that they were capable adults. It wasn't up to her if they got on a bus or not. She just helped provide the route to escape.

"God bless you, Amanda," Melissa said. "I'll be praying for your journey."

On the way back to the shelter, Sharon called. "Can you go to the St. Ignatius church? The priest has someone there."

Melissa calculated the time. "I have our new resident at lunch. I need to start her initial counseling."

After a moment, Sharon asked, "Which one can I do?"

"Start the counseling. I'm much closer to the church than you are. Then set up a time for us both to meet with her."

"That works."

Melissa drove to the sprawling church three blocks away. It served a large Cuban community, offering Spanish-speaking services a couple of days a week.

Father Ferretti had sent them women before, so she knew her way around the back of the church building to the side door in the alley. She tapped on the door, and Sister Elizabeth opened it almost immediately. She wore a white shirt, a khaki skirt, and a veil that covered her black hair. Her dark brown skin provided a striking contrast to the veil.

"Melissa, please come this way."

She followed the nun down the hall and to the priest's study. Sister Elizabeth opened the door and stepped aside. "I'm going to make sure all is well in the front of the church," she said to Father Ferretti.

He nodded as he crouched next to the gray couch that sat under the only window in the room.

Melissa walked into the room and saw a woman on the couch. One of her eyes was completely swollen shut, and her lip was split and puffed up. Blood covered the front of her shirt, likely from the obviously broken nose. When Father Ferretti saw Melissa, he shifted and stood. He was in his early thirties with light tan skin and black hair.

"Melissa, she's refusing an ambulance. I didn't know who else could help her the way you can."

"How did you find her?"

"She was in the vestibule this morning."

Melissa set her purse by the door and crossed the room. "What's her name?"

"I don't know. If I've ever seen her before, I don't recognize her."

She knelt next to the couch and touched the woman's wrist. Her good eye widened in fear. "It's okay," Melissa said softly, her heart twisting in response to the woman's distress. "I'm here to help. Can you tell me your name?"

She mumbled something, then closed her eye. Melissa looked up at the priest. "I can't take her like this. She needs medical attention."

He clasped his hands in front of him. "What am I to do?"

Biting her lip, she pulled her phone out of her pocket. Should she? Phil said he had friends coming into town. Maybe they weren't here yet. On impulse, she hit his number. He answered on the first ring. It sounded like he was in his truck.

"Hey," she said. "I'm sorry to bother you. I know you have friends coming."

"It's not a problem. What's up?"

"Can you help me? I'm at St. Ignatius. There's a woman hurt badly."

"I'm five minutes away."

Relief pushed away her worry about calling him. She hung up and looked at Father Ferretti. "Do you know Phil Osbourne?"

He frowned in concentration. "Paramedic? Yes, I know him. Good man."

"Yes. He'll help."

When Phil saw Melissa's number, his heart skipped a beat. Even though Bill and Daniel were in the truck, he answered, wanting to hear her voice, not wanting to miss a call.

After he hung up, he glanced at Daniel. "Sorry for the detour."

"Sounds important."

He gestured at the phone. "She's the reason I need your help."

"I saw her name on the screen," Bill said. "I didn't have to come from Alaska to get you a date, did I?"

Phil's cheeks flooded with heat, and he shook his head. "I can handle that on my own. Thanks, though."

At the church, he pulled his medical kit out of the back seat of his truck and led the way to the door on the side of the building. It felt good to walk next to his friends again.

Bill looked up at the blue sky. "Ah, October heat. I've forgotten about that after living a year in Alaska."

"Alabama getting leeched out of you?" Daniel asked.

"Apparently."

Before Phil could even knock, Sister Elizabeth opened the door. She looked over his shoulder. "Not like you to bring backup."

"Sister, I love you. Does that help?"

She didn't respond to that comment but opened the door wide. "They're in Father's study."

Phil led the way down the long hall. He tapped on the door and opened it without waiting for a reply. Melissa was kneeling on the floor next to the couch.

Father Ferretti crossed the room toward them. "Phil, thank you for coming," he said in a quiet voice, giving Bill and Daniel a curious look.

"Father, these are good friends of mine. Bill, Daniel, Father Ferretti." Phil could read the concern in the man's face. "I didn't know if we'd need muscle."

As he shook their hands, Father Ferretti said, "If you're with Phil, I trust you to be strong and discreet." He gestured at the couch. "She won't let me call an ambulance."

"She's not going to appreciate me, then."

"No, I think she's afraid of being found."

Tingles of rage danced between Phil's shoulder blades. If her abuser was in front of him, he didn't know what kind of control he'd have over his actions. He anticipated that Daniel and Bill felt very much the same way.

His friends waited out of sight while Phil walked up to the couch. Melissa looked up at him, worry covering her face. "I think a broken rib has punctured her lung," she said.

He put a hand on her shoulder. "Let me see."

She glanced toward the door, then back at him. "I'm sorry to pull you away from your friends."

He knelt on his right knee and kept his prosthetic foot on the ground. He could see the caramel streaks in her brown eyes. "You never need to apologize for calling me," he said.

She shifted out of his way. He pulled a stethoscope out of his bag and slipped it over his shoulders. "What's her name?"

"We don't know."

As he put on gloves, he said to the woman, "Hi, I'm Phil. I'm a doctor." Her good eye flew open. The fear etched in her face made his stomach twist. She whispered something that he couldn't hear, and he shook his head. "If it's okay, I'm just going to check you right now."

He listened to her chest. Her heart was pounding, her pulse rate way above normal. As he moved the stethoscope down her rib cage, he could not hear breath sounds on the left side. He kept his voice even as he pulled the stethoscope out of his ears. "You have a punctured lung. I'm guessing from a broken rib. Will you let me help you?"

A tear escaped her good eye. After searching his face for several seconds, she finally gave a brief nod and closed her eye.

He glanced up at Melissa. "I need to put in a chest tube."

"Can you do that here?"

"I have what I need." He looked over at the priest.

Father Ferretti crossed his arms and gripped his own shoulders. "I don't know what the correct answer is. Is this a place where you can perform that?"

They had several options, and Phil mentally ran through them. "Without an X-ray, I don't know the severity of the injury. But I can treat the symptoms here." He glanced at Melissa. "Would you take her this injured?"

Her hesitation told him how much she wanted to say yes, but she shook her head. "No. I don't have access to the proper kind of care or resources."

Father Ferretti lowered his arms. "Treat her. Sister Elizabeth has a sister under her care who is a nurse. We'll take care of her here."

Phil returned his attention to the patient. He grabbed the chest tube kit out of his bag and pulled fresh gloves out, then picked up the pre-filled syringe. "Okay, you're going to feel a stick, but it's just going to numb the area. I'm going to help you with your breathing." He took a towel from a stack on the table next to him and looked at Melissa. "Can you help me with her shirt?"

He shielded Melissa with the towel while she unbuttoned the woman's shirt. She took the towel and laid it over the woman's chest, then he felt along her rib cage. The woman winced when he found the fracture.

"I know," he murmured, giving her the shot of local anesthesia. He grabbed a spare pair of gloves out of his kit and held them out to Melissa. "I'm going to need an extra set of hands." He prepped the tube and clipped the clamp onto it, then held the clamp out to her. "Hold this."

He cleaned the area with efficient movements, covered it with a paper drape, then prepped the area with a scalpel. He held his hand out, and Melissa set the clamp in it. Without hesitation, he inserted the tube.

The woman gasped and moaned. He pointed with his chin to the open kit. "Hand me the suture and that clamp, and see about more light."

Bill stepped forward and handed Melissa his phone with the flashlight on. She held it up while Phil added a couple of stitches around the tube. Then he took the gloves off and put fresh ones on while he checked her for other injuries.

"I'll come back tomorrow. I want to check her eye." He looked up at Father Ferretti while he ran his hands along her jaw. It didn't feel broken, but he'd prefer having an X-ray to make certain. "What will you do if the man that did this to her comes here?"

Father Ferretti held up a finger and spun his hand in a circle. "This is a secure building. We have phones and a relationship with the police."

After cleaning up, Phil said, "Keep her still. Call an ambulance if she gets worse than this." He put a hand on the priest's thin shoulder. "I mean it, Father. Call an ambulance. Then call me. I'll meet her at the hospital and keep her safe from whatever she's afraid of. In the meantime, I'll see you tomorrow."

Melissa followed them out. He stopped beside her at her car, and she glanced up at him. The sunlight caused red streaks to shine in her dark hair. "Thank you for coming."

"You're welcome." He gestured at his friends. "Daniel Swanson, Bill Sanders, this is Melissa Braxton."

With a smile, she held out her hand. "Pot Pie and Drumstick, right?" she asked as she shook their hands.

The men laughed, and Bill said, "I feel like we've been the topic of conversation."

"Only briefly."

Bill gestured toward the truck with his head. "We'll head over there. Y'all take your time." He slapped Phil on the shoulder as he walked by.

Phil looked down at Melissa. "Anytime you need me, you call me." He glanced at the church and back down at her. Shadows had crept into the corners of her eyes. "You okay?"

"I am now." She smiled and the shadows fled. "I am. See you Sunday?"

He glanced at Bill and Daniel, who waited by his truck, watching them without pretense. "Definitely."

As he walked away, she called out, "Hey, Phil?"

He spun and kept walking backward, taking careful steps. "Yes?"

"Nice shorts."

A pleasant rush flowed through his chest. So she had noticed his prosthetic. They could finally move past the elephant in the room.

When he got back to the truck, Daniel said, "You know, man, if she'd called me, I'd have come running too, regardless of my friends in the vehicle."

With a laugh, Phil stored his kit back on the floorboard of his truck. "Shut up, Pot Pie."

"I'm just sayin'."

CHAPTER

★

THREE

Melissa added the money she'd given to Amanda to the column on the spreadsheet, then stamped ENTERED on the carbon copy of the receipt. She glanced down at the bottom line and smiled at the number.

At her desk, her partner, Sharon Clark, hung up the phone and turned in her chair. She had white-blond hair that fell in waves down to her shoulders, giant blue eyes that glowed against her porcelain skin, and a model-thin body. During her fifteen-year marriage to the founder and CEO of one of the biggest tech industries on earth, she'd been a favorite of the paparazzi.

When Melissa worked as a family counselor in a megachurch in Fort Lauderdale, Sharon had come to her for help. Sharon's husband regularly mistreated her, especially those times when she objected to his liaisons with other women. She felt trapped by her wealth and her husband's position of power, by the constant media coverage, and by the judgment she regularly faced on social media. Melissa helped her detach herself from her marriage and her public life and seek a divorce.

After her divorce, Sharon had had cosmetic surgery to alter her appearance just enough to prevent facial recognition. Melissa had tried to dissuade her from such drastic measures, but Sharon hadn't felt safe from the eyes of the world until she'd done it. In hindsight, Melissa was glad she had, even if it offered Sharon nothing more than peace of mind.

Over the course of months of treatment, the two became best friends. Neither remembered who had the idea to open the domestic abuse shelter first. It just became a conversation that eventually turned into a plan.

Five years later, they ran this shelter together. Without Sharon's financial investment coupled with Melissa's vision and training, the hundreds of women and men they'd helped over the last couple of years would have had no place to go.

"How's it looking?" Sharon asked now.

"Good," Melissa said. "The fundraiser we did last month supplemented your stipend perfectly."

Sharon smiled. "God is good." She picked up a paper off her desk. "My investment guy called me. One of the stocks that I use to fund us split."

"What does that mean?"

"Something like a twenty-five percent increase in value. I'm not entirely positive. It's why I pay him an extreme amount of money. But the bottom line is that he's increased our budget."

With a grin, Melissa said, "As long as the market holds."

Sharon winked. "I have faith." She stood. Today she wore a white jumpsuit with a bright-red belt and red heels. "I'm off to dinner with my church women's group."

"Have fun."

On her way out of the office, Sharon paused and tapped the top of Melissa's desk with her red fingernail. "You go to bed. I'm on call tonight. Turn your phone off and relax."

"I will. I'm just waiting for Aaron."

After Sharon left, Melissa called St. Ignatius church. Father Ferretti answered on the first ring.

"Hello, Father, this is Melissa Braxton."

"Melissa, hi. Our friend is resting comfortably, according to Sister Elizabeth. Nothing new to report."

"That's great. Thank you." She ended the call and looked up when someone tapped on her office door, then smiled at Mrs. Horton. "Hi."

Mrs. Horton had blond hair streaked with gray that she normally kept back in a severe bun and wore short-sleeved dresses that fell to her knees. She and her husband were the backbone of their operation. She handled the housekeeping, managed the residents who volunteered for various housekeeping and kitchen tasks, and did the cooking six nights and five mornings a week. Mr. Horton took care of the maintenance and the grounds. He served as their in-house chaplain and was a lay minister at a local church.

"Evening, Miss Braxton. Mr. Horton and I are headed to bed. I left Aaron some meatloaf in the fridge. I know how much he likes it."

"How was choir practice?"

"Christmas is coming." Mrs. Horton grinned on her way out the door. "My tambourine was ringing!"

Twenty minutes later, Melissa heard the notification of the side door opening. She glanced up at the monitors that streamed the activity from the security cameras and saw Aaron McIntyre locking the door behind him.

He used to play semipro hockey, but a head injury caused some diminished functioning, and he could no longer remember how to skate. Melissa had met him when he rescued a neighbor from her husband. They'd called Melissa from his apartment, using the phone number he'd taken from his church bulletin board.

He had a heart for protecting women in tough situations. She'd hired him away from his grocery bagging job to be her night security officer, and he'd thrived in that position. Melissa thanked God regularly for the way that He put people into place to help her ministry.

She locked her desk and switched one of the monitors to Aaron's favorite classic movie channel. As he filled the doorway, she smiled up at him. "Mrs. Horton put leftover meatloaf in the fridge for you."

His bushy red eyebrows rose in joy. "I like meatloaf."

"I know. That's why she always saves you some."

He held up a paper bag. "I packed peanut butter."

"I'm sure if you put that in the fridge it will be good for tomorrow." She stretched her arms above her head. "I'm off to bed. Twenty-two took her six-year-old to a movie. She's due back about 8:30." Aaron insisted on knowing the residents only by their unit number. He felt like that anonymity kept them safer.

"Got it." He checked the board that showed what units were occupied. "Thirty-six left today?"

"She did. It was hard to see her go. She was here for so long."

"Six point four weeks. I liked the boy. He'd come down here and watch John Wayne whenever it wasn't too late for him."

With a warm smile, Melissa said, "It's good that he had a positive experience with a man while his mom was here recovering."

"I agree." He pulled out her chair and sat down. "See you in the morning for pancake Friday."

"I can't wait."

She locked the office door behind her, then walked down the long hallway to her apartment. As she walked in, she kicked her shoes off, then threw the dead bolt on the door.

Her apartment had frosted pinewood floors. She'd accented them with a lighter gray throw rug and a gray couch with an orange-and-yellow throw pillow. A white island separated the living area from the kitchen. Nickel-plated appliances and darker gray cabinetry kept the color scheme flowing. She had white barstools pulled up to the island and a big red bowl of apples in the center of it.

She'd decorated her bedroom in whites and greens. It had an exterior window that overlooked the enclosed patio area. Giant elephant's ears right in front of the window gave her some privacy but still allowed light in and a view of green out.

She went into the bathroom, turned on the bathwater, and added some lavender foaming bubbles. She pulled out her journal and sat on the edge of the tub.

Phil introduced me to his friends today. That was big. He also wore shorts. No hiding his leg. Why do I feel like that's a major step?

I understand the psychology. I just don't know how to break through. How do I convince him that I'm a safe place? What do I need to say? And how many times have I written those questions in this journal over the last year or more?

She wrote about the woman at St. Ignatius and finished with,

I've seen Phil with abuse victims several times. Too many times to want to count. But this one was different. He didn't just assess and bandage. He performed a medical procedure that a doctor would. Because he is a doctor. It was so impressive. I wish that telling him that would make him realize that having a leg or not doesn't affect anything about my perception of him. Oh, God, please hear my prayer.

She soaked in the bath until the water turned tepid. As she got ready for bed, she thought again about the woman at St. Ignatius. She'd seen fear like that before. The last time her father beat her mother, Melissa had seen her mother's face. With one eye open, she stared at Melissa, her mouth opening and closing, terror covering every feature.

The police came first, responding to Melissa's 911 call. Not long after, the ambulance came. She'd never seen her mother again.

Until she touched her cheek, Melissa didn't even realize her tears were falling. She thought of her sister, wishing she knew how to find her, praying that God would bring her back into her life.

★ ★ ★

Phil didn't launch right into the reason he'd asked Bill and Daniel to come, because Bill had traveled from Alaska to Miami, nearly a twenty-four-hour trip. Instead, they spent all of Thursday afternoon catching up. Phil heard about Bill's wife, an FBI agent stationed in Anchorage. Daniel talked about loves lost, and Phil reminisced with them about prior deployments and anecdotes from when they'd served together.

They went to the Miami Dolphins football game, and it was after eleven when they got home. No one stirred until almost nine the next morning.

Bill and Daniel joined Phil just as he finished grilling thin steaks and scrambling eggs. After a leisurely breakfast, Bill finally asked, "Does Melissa know why we're here?"

Phil felt the tightness in his chest that always appeared when he thought of Melissa. "No."

Bill stared at him, his face perfectly expressionless.

Phil stared back for a few seconds, then relented. "I didn't want to say anything until we knew for sure."

Daniel stirred cream into his coffee. "Whatever. Give us the background."

Phil frowned. He'd given them some background in the beginning, but he had a feeling Daniel had a specific reason for asking. "Why?"

His friend stared at him. "It's important."

"Her father beat her mother when she was pregnant. She bled to death when Melissa was five. He went to prison. Melissa went to her mom's family, to a sister. Her three-year-old sister went to the father's side of the family. Melissa doesn't know for certain who. She's been looking for her since she could remember. Always examining faces of anyone who might be her sister."

Daniel pursed his lips. "She never asked her family?"

He shrugged. "Her aunt wouldn't talk with her about it. After she died, Melissa lived with an uncle. She didn't know how to approach him with it. She has no access to her father's side."

Bill got up, grabbed a folder out of his backpack, and held it out. When Phil opened the folder, his breath caught in the back of his throat. The woman staring back at him in the driver's license photo could have been Melissa if the jaw was just a little narrower and the eyes slightly closer together.

"We didn't have a problem finding her," Bill said.

Phil stared at the photo for several seconds. "Wow. Melissa wouldn't be able to deny her, would she?"

Bill shook his head. "That's what surprised us yesterday. We thought for a minute you'd already found her."

Phil flipped a page and saw an aerial photograph of a mansion on the coast. "What is this?"

"Her address."

Daniel tapped a shadow on the roof. "Armed guards." He ran his finger along the stone wall surrounding the compound. "High-tech security."

This made little sense to him. "Does she work there?"

"No, man. Her husband is a cat named Hector Molina." Bill opened his soda and poured some over the ice in his glass. "Seems like he's tied to a cartel out of Colombia."

"Her husband?"

"Yes. And the father of their two children." Daniel turned another page. "Your friend's father? He went to prison and

41

was killed there. But before that, he was deeply embedded in the cartel. Far as we could tell, he wasn't anyone in charge, but he did a lot of the muscle work for them."

Phil set the folder aside and absently rubbed the bridge of his nose. "Thanks. Thanks for this." He got up and crossed the room to look out his window. Down below, he watched a mom play with a toddler on the edge of the swimming pool.

How did he process all of this information? What could he possibly tell Melissa, if anything? Maybe he should leave her in blissful ignorance.

Bill joined him and, after a few silent moments, asked, "How are you doing?"

Phil pressed his lips together. He knew Bill was asking about his life as a whole and not his reaction to this information. "Mostly good. I go to meetings at least once a week. That helps. I have a good church."

"And Melissa?"

"We have lunch after church on the Sundays I'm off and breakfast most Thursdays."

"Is this relationship serious?"

Phil cut a glance at his friend. "No. You know that's not an option."

Bill's eyebrows shot up. "Hogwash. I know nothing of the sort."

"Dude, she deserves a whole man."

Daniel got up and walked to the kitchen to refill his coffee. "I'm seeing a whole man from this angle."

"Then you're not looking hard enough."

"Does she not know about your leg?"

He knew Daniel was being facetious, but he replied anyway. "Of course she knows."

Daniel chuckled. "It apparently doesn't matter to her."

"You don't even know her."

"No, man, but I saw the way she watched you yesterday. I can assure you, she's looking at a whole person too." He batted his eyelashes. "All goo-goo-eyed and everything."

Phil's jaw muscle ached, so he relaxed it. "It's not just about the leg."

"Seems to me if someone has been sober for seven years, he ought to give himself some grace," Bill said, walking across the room to sit on the couch.

"Sure," Phil said, choosing the recliner. "I would agree. Only, it's not been seven years. It's been less than two."

"You can't count that." Daniel sat on the couch and put his coffee cup on the table next to him. "You were shot. In the thigh. You'd had vascular surgery performed in a nearly primitive location by a doctor who didn't do that kind of specialized work."

"Then you had to trek across the jungle only two days post-surgery," Bill said.

Daniel reiterated, "You can't count that."

"I have to count that," Phil said. "It's the way it works. I had to start back at zero. 'Hi, I'm Phil and I'm an addict. It's been one year, eight months, and seventeen days since I last had opiates flowing through my veins.'"

Bill shook his head. "Dude."

"It is what it is." Phil rubbed the bridge of his nose. "I'm not proud of it, but I can't do anything more about it either."

After a long pause, Daniel asked, "And does Melissa know about it?"

He couldn't keep eye contact. Shame made the back of his throat burn. "No."

"So, it's not the leg holding you back."

He looked at Daniel. "It's the entire package, man. And I'm seriously done with this conversation."

One heartbeat passed, then two. Finally, Daniel said, "Fair enough." He took a sip of his coffee. "So, let's get back to the matter at hand."

The picture on the driver's license crossed his mind. "I'd like to know more about Hector Molina. I was expecting you to give me an address of a girl somewhere in suburbia America. I was not expecting a Colombian cartel."

"At least it isn't boring," Bill said. "I'd hate that."

Phil chuckled. "Yeah." He thought about it. "Let me check with my brother. He was going to let me borrow his boat today anyway. I'll see what he knows."

Phil opened the door and stepped back to let Winston in. He gestured at Bill and Daniel. "Winston, Bill, Daniel. Men I served with."

Bill shook his hand. "Thanks for the tickets."

"Sorry they lost last night." Winston tossed Phil his boat keys. "Can I have a word?"

"Sure." Phil led the way to his office and shut the door. "What's up?"

"Why are you asking about Hector Molina?"

He'd anticipated this being the reason Winston wanted to speak to him. He explained about looking for Melissa's sister. He gestured toward the door. "Bill and Daniel have a security company. They were able to track her down."

Winston slipped his hands into his pockets. "I am going to tell you something that can't leave this room."

"Okay."

"I've been working with state and federal agencies. We've been trying to infiltrate the Vibora cartel for months and cannot get in. They're extremely closed off to any outsiders, so placing an agent in there has proven to be impossible. We have wiretaps, we listen with directional mics, we monitor comings and goings, and we still have nothing. They're too careful."

"And?"

"And you need to stay away from them. They're seriously hard-core. I don't want to find you dangling from some bridge one morning in some messed-up kind of message."

"If Melissa's sister is inside that compound," Phil said, "then—"

"Then she cannot be trusted." Winston crossed his arms over his chest. "Her husband is a teniente to the cartel capos."

"A lieutenant?"

"High enough ranking to get his own security and compound. He's located on the water so he can handle the drugs smuggled in. They have shipments that get dropped with boats and we think submarines. He uses divers to collect them."

When Winston paused, Phil said, "Don't stop now, Brother."

"Let me think about it some. If there's a way the information your buddies have gleaned can work with what we know to be true, then maybe it will all come together after all." He looked at his phone. "Can we talk about this again tomorrow?"

"Of course." On their way out of the room, Phil said, "Melissa doesn't know I've been looking for Lola. Please don't mention it to her."

"That's rough. If I was looking for you my whole life, I'd hate to find out you were married to some cartel teniente."

"I would hate to find that out too." Phil nodded, his voice low and serious.

Winston laughed, then stopped in the front room to chat with Bill and Daniel. When he was gone, Bill asked, "Was that about the information we found?"

Phil nodded. "Yes, but he asked me to keep it quiet."

"What can we do?" Daniel asked.

"I think we'll know more tomorrow. But in the meantime, we can probably do some intel gathering."

The bright Florida sun shone down on the water. Even though the calendar claimed late October, the temperature pushed toward ninety degrees. The brilliant blue sky stretched out behind the green-and-blue parasailing canopy. The early-afternoon sun lit up Mid Beach and the houses stretched along it. From Winston's boat, Phil could see only the rooftops of some of the taller buildings, but Daniel could see the entire shore from his vantage point.

As Phil brought the boat around, Bill tightened the winch. Phil glanced up at Daniel, who was suspended about four hundred feet in the air, the sail stretched above him.

Through the earpiece he wore, Daniel gave him directions. "On point. Keep me here for a minute."

Phil drove the boat about ten more yards, then slowly swung it around while Bill made sure the tow rope kept up with the boat's movement. A gigantic wave sent them up and back down hard.

Bill groaned. "Dude, we aren't in a race."

"That's right," Phil said with a smile. "I forgot you don't like the water much."

"I don't mind the water. It's sinking in it that I hate."

Phil grinned, feeling lighter, like his soul had been trapped and was now released. Working with Bill and Daniel reminded him of what life used to be like. For the last two years, he'd existed in some sort of stasis, as if waiting for the next thing instead of seeking it out.

"Give me one more pass," Daniel said.

"Roger," Phil said. "Anyone notice you?"

"No visible activity."

Bill used binoculars to peer toward the shore. "If they did, let's pray they don't have a sniper on staff."

Ten minutes later, Bill worked the winch that gradually brought Daniel down to the deck. Once they had everything secure, Phil turned the boat and headed toward Winston's dock.

"Do you have a way we can print these pictures?" Daniel asked over the sound of the boat's motor and the rushing wind.

"Yeah." Phil slowed down as he entered the harbor's no-wake zone.

Bill came forward and stood behind them. "Any thoughts?"

Daniel nodded. "Remember the time we had to invade that ISIS compound outside of Mali?"

Bill snorted. "Like I remember my meemaw's biscuits and sorghum."

Phil chuckled. Bill's colloquialisms fascinated him. It was like he stored them up to use whenever the situation required.

"Well, that was an easy in compared to what I just saw." Daniel glanced over at Bill. "Fortress would be a mild term."

Phil whistled under his breath. "If we have to go in, sounds like we'd need a solid plan."

47

CHAPTER

★

FOUR

Melissa raised her fingertips to the azure sky and twisted her body, loosening her lower back as she and Sharon stretched before their morning run. The tropical sun beat down on them, but the breeze coming off the water felt wonderful. Above them, a seagull squawked as it looked for its morning meal.

"My ex wants to meet," Sharon said almost casually.

That made Melissa pause. "Why?"

"I was wife number one. You know he always calls me when things are getting rocky with his current love."

"First, I didn't realize he had a current love."

Sharon snorted. "He never doesn't have a current love."

Melissa went on as if she hadn't spoken. "And second, I can't imagine why things get rocky when he likes to pinch and demoralize."

Sharon sighed. "Right? I'd say that to him if I was willing

to speak to him. My attorney always acts as a good buffer, though."

Sharon's ex-husband believed that if he could get Sharon alone, he could convince her to come back to him. So far, in five years, she'd stayed strong and refused to see him.

Once they finished stretching, they took off at a jog. They never spoke while they ran. Melissa enjoyed the company, but she also liked being in her own head. She had a playlist going in one earbud and left the other ear open to listen to the sounds around her.

Even on a weekday in late October, people flooded the beach. Her mind wandered and settled on the empty room in the shelter. Her stomach twisted when she considered what might bring someone to fill it. She understood the pain and terror that future resident lived under and prayed for them, asking God for wisdom in her relationship with them. Then she mentally went through her speech for church Sunday morning, making sure she covered everything she wanted to say and that God stayed in the center of it all.

As she dodged a toddler running with a green plastic shovel, her phone rang. "Hang tight," she said to Sharon and slowed to a walk while she answered it. "Melissa Braxton," she said, panting.

"Our friend is awake and aware," Father Ferretti said.

She put her hands on her hips and looked up at the blue sky. Sweat slid down between her shoulder blades. "Is she needing help?"

"She's refusing to seek help. Can you come talk to her?"

She spun her finger in the air to signal to Sharon that she was turning around. "Sure. I'm two miles from my car, though. It will take me a little bit of time."

"She's not going anywhere with a chest tube."

Sharon turned with her after she disconnected the call. "Father Ferretti?"

"Yeah. I'm going to go counsel the woman, see if we can get her some help."

"I'll come with you. She might get more out of a team."

Melissa glanced behind her. "Sorry to not get your five miles in."

"Bah, it's okay." Sharon huffed out a breath. "This is entirely more important."

Melissa sat in a wood chair at St. Ignatius and leaned forward. Sharon sat next to her. They'd taken the time to go home and shower before coming to the church.

"I'm so sorry about what you've been through," Melissa said to the woman. "How can I help you?"

The woman's left eye was still swollen shut, and she lay still because of the chest tube. The swelling in her lips had receded some. "You can just let me go home."

"If you leave, it needs to be under medical care," Sharon said in a soft voice. "You have a chest tube."

"He's supposed to come take it out today, according to the priest."

"Good. I'm sure that will be a relief." Melissa studied the woman's face, watching for pain or some emotion that would help her know how to act. "When he clears you, it will be safe to leave." She looked at Father Ferretti and back to the woman. "I'm the director of a shelter for abused women. Would you like my phone number?"

"No." She closed her eyes and held up her hand. "Please

leave me alone. I don't know you and I don't want to know you."

She slowly let out a breath. "Okay. I'll leave. But I know that someone did this to you. If it wasn't your spouse or partner and you aren't in a domestic abuse situation, then maybe you should consider asking Father Ferretti to call the police. The person who did this to you is a violent offender who needs to be put off the streets." She stood because she wanted the woman to see that she was actually going, but she set her card on the table next to her. "Here's my card if you change your mind."

Sister Elizabeth came in carrying a tall glass with a wide straw. She held it up. "It hurts her jaw to chew. So I've been putting high-protein shakes together for her."

Melissa smiled and touched her shoulder. "That's very kind of you."

"I just feel so horrible for the poor lamb."

Sharon spoke quietly to Father Ferretti, then joined Melissa at the door. She pulled Melissa against her in a hug. "You can't win them all."

"If this was a domestic partner, she'll die next time. That beating was so violent."

"True." Sharon put a hand on her shoulder. "Listen, it's not your responsibility. You made the offer. You're available. She has to be the one to take the step."

"If it's domestic."

Sharon crossed her arms over her chest and leaned against the doorframe. "If it's criminal, then it might not be safe for her to leave here."

"I don't know why she's so afraid of hospitals."

Sister Elizabeth appeared in the hall. "Your Phil Osbourne is here."

Without warning, Melissa's pulse quickened. Sharon met her eyes and gave a knowing smile, making her face flood with heat. Melissa stepped out into the hall in time to see Phil walking their way. His friends followed.

"How's she doing?" he asked.

"She's aware, and a little belligerent." Sharon lifted her chin. "I tried to talk with her, to empathize, but she shut me down. Same with Melissa."

Phil looked from her to Melissa. "What do you think?"

"I think she's terrified. And I think that whoever did this to her isn't done."

A muscle ticked in his jaw. He gave a brief nod, then went into the priest's study.

His friend with dark hair and a dark shadow of a beard looked at her. "Bill," he said. "We met yesterday."

She smiled, even though she wanted to be back in the room with Phil. "Yes, hi. Have you had a good time?"

"We have. We went parasailing this morning."

"Really? Was that fun?"

He shrugged. "I once jumped an MC-6 off the shore of Antigua. That was better because I wasn't strapped to the back of a boat. I didn't like that lack of control."

She examined his face, trying to get a read on his mood and failing. "I've never done it."

"I think we're headed to Mid Beach today."

She couldn't imagine why anyone would want to go to the area dubbed Millionaires' Row. "Why?"

"We're going to scope out a property."

"There are some beautiful houses there. Estates, really."

"Yeah. Ever been there?"

She frowned. "Me? No. My business partner, Sharon, used

to live there. I think her ex-husband still owns a place, but she never goes."

He stared at her with intense eyes, and she couldn't pinpoint exactly why she felt like she was under interrogation.

"Who's her ex-husband?" he asked.

With a raised eyebrow, she said, "Not any of your business."

As if he understood he'd crossed a line, he smiled warmly. "I apologize. Miami's nuances are all new to me. I'm from Alaska."

Melissa studied his face. His voice was Southern and sweet. She had a feeling he understood everything and simply was trying to charm her. She wondered why he'd asked and what exactly he wanted to find out.

Phil appeared at her elbow. "I've talked her into letting me drive her to the hospital. I convinced her they won't ask her name." He looked over at Bill. "Sorry, dude."

"No worries." He gestured to Melissa. "Why doesn't she drive you? Daniel and I can run that errand."

She watched the hesitation come and go from his eyes. "Yeah, sure." He looked at her. "Do you mind?"

An excuse to be semi-alone with him in a car? "Of course not." She cleared her throat. "Happy to help."

"Great." He tossed Daniel his key fob, then put a hand on her shoulder. "I'll go get her ready for transport. I want to move before she has a chance to change her mind."

As he started to turn away, she grabbed his hand. "Phil, what will happen if they find out you put a chest tube in?"

He stared down at her. "I'm a doctor and a paramedic, Melissa. I'm fully capable and, dare I say, legally allowed to place a chest tube."

Her face heated as he went back into the study. Pushing aside her discomfort, she said to Sharon, "Do you want to ride with us?"

Sharon glanced at Bill and Daniel. "Do you mind giving me a ride?"

Daniel stepped forward with a smile. "No, ma'am, we certainly do not."

Watching the change come over Sharon as she stared at Phil's handsome friend amused Melissa. Sharon brushed her hair off her shoulder and smiled up at him in a helpless yet totally competent way. "That would be wonderful. Thank you for the rescue, sir."

Melissa shook her head. She'd never pull off anything like that. She looked into the study. Phil leaned close to his patient and talked to her in a low voice.

"Which would be better—your truck or my car?" Melissa asked.

He glanced in her direction. "Probably truck."

She pulled her keys out of her pocket and held them out to Daniel. "Sharon can take you back to Phil's or you can borrow my car to run your errand."

Bill glanced at Daniel then at Sharon. "If you don't mind, we'll borrow your car."

"Of course." She swapped keys with Daniel. "I'm going to go move the truck to the back door."

She walked outside, and the muggy air enveloped her. Parasailing would be so much fun. When was the last time she took a day for fun? What would Phil say if she asked if he wanted to go parasailing with her? She'd never even considered that he might be able to do something like that.

Silly to think that. What would stop him?

She got into the truck, and as she turned toward the side door of the church, the sun shot into her eyes. On reflex, she put down the visor.

She slammed on the brakes and stared at the picture on the inside of the visor. She recognized the setting—a church picnic this past summer. She was sitting next to Phil, and the church historian had taken their picture. Phil had put his arm across the back of her chair. For a better camera angle, she'd leaned into him.

And he'd put that picture on the back of his visor.

Feeling like she'd invaded some private space, she closed the visor with a snap and stared at the church door. "Okay, Melissa, just pretend like you never saw it."

Like that'd ever happen.

She carefully pulled up to the door just as it opened. Sister Elizabeth supported the woman on one side, Phil on the other. Melissa scooted out of the truck and opened the back door, then stood aside while they helped the woman into the cab.

Phil walked with her to the other side of the truck. "I'm going to sit in the back with her. You okay to drive?"

"Sure."

They were pretty close to a trauma center, so Phil directed her to go there. She pulled up to the patient drop-off area and idled the truck while Phil ran in and grabbed a wheelchair. When he came out, a nurse followed him. They carefully helped the woman from the cab and into the chair.

As the nurse wheeled her in, Phil tapped on the glass. "If you want to go park, I'll get her settled. It might take a few minutes."

She glanced at the clock on the dash. "I'll go down to the cafeteria and get a cup of coffee."

He smiled quickly. "Perfect. I'll meet you down there."

She headed for the hospital's main garage. She didn't want to think about the many times she'd come here, at all hours, to pick up a woman to take to the shelter. A couple of times, she'd even had to get men who were seeking shelter from an abusive spouse.

She couldn't understand the hearts of people who intentionally hurt others. It physically hurt her when she allowed her mind to go down that path.

Phil stood in the back of the treatment area as Jane Doe refused to answer any of the questions from Mary, the charge nurse. He'd convinced her to come get treated, but it was only after he realized that she didn't want to go to a specific hospital. Knowing the system and how billing and corporate ownership worked, he'd explained that this particular hospital and trauma center were independent. No one here worked for a corporate organization that shared files and doctors. The doctors worked for the hospital, many of them for a fraction of their worth, as a way to serve the community. She'd finally consented to come.

Once Mary gave up on Jane Doe, he followed her out. She glanced at him. "Another rescue, Phil?"

"You know me."

"Nice job on the chest tube."

"It can come out today."

"I'll let her doctor make that determination." Mary looked toward the closed curtain. "Any information?"

He shook his head. "I got nothing. And Melissa Braxton couldn't get anything out of her either. She's very scared."

She put a cool hand on his arm. "We'll take care of her."

"Thanks, Mary." He pointed at her. "I owe you one."

She shook her head. "Not yet. I still owe you like four hundred and thirteen."

He chuckled and turned to go through the trauma center doors and into the main hospital. He'd met Mary at an NA meeting. They'd crossed paths a few times over the last almost two years. One night, her drunk ex-boyfriend showed up as they left a later meeting. Phil had to step between them and extract her.

He found Melissa easily in the nearly empty cafeteria. She had her head down while she focused on the pad of paper she wrote on. Before approaching the table, he studied her. He felt like he could be content just sitting to the side and watching her all day. His fingers itched to brush the strand of hair off her cheek.

Shaking his head to ward off those thoughts, he walked up to her. When he pulled out the chair across from her and sat down, she jumped and looked up.

"Hi," he said with a broad smile. "Fancy meeting you here."

She put the lid on her pen and shut the tablet. "I was making a shopping list. Aaron is getting low on his chocolate milk." She propped her chin on her hand. "Parasailing, huh?"

He relaxed a little further. "I am a paratrooper." Then he remembered. "Or, I was."

"I read a book once about a woman who was a spy for the Resistance in occupied France."

"Oh yeah?" He raised an eyebrow. "Do tell."

"She lost her leg. She was there as a spy, got injured, got

out. A few months later, she parachuted back into France with her leg strapped to her back." She sat back, picked up her coffee cup, and decided to restart the conversation. "So, parasailing, huh?"

He grinned. "Do you imagine that I strapped my leg to my back to sail?"

"No. I think you did your own amazing thing that was unique to you and your situation." Her cheeks flushed endearingly, and she cleared her throat. "Anyway, when your friend told me about it, I realized that it has been years since I've just taken the day and had a fun, touristy kind of day, you know? Windsurfing, parasailing, eating from a food truck. And in two years, I've never seen you take any kind of downtime. If you're not working, you're at the church doing. So I thought, maybe one day soon, we could help hold each other accountable, you know?"

Accountability. One of the tenets of his meetings. Did she somehow find out or was she just projecting her own training as a counselor?

"Say, 'Hey, it's been a few weeks. We should go to the beach,'" she continued. "What do you think?"

He had a quick mental image of Melissa in a swimsuit and shook his head. "Sorry. The only reason we went was that the guys wanted to go. When they leave, I can go back to my norm of working and volunteering."

A disappointed look crossed her face. He wanted to tell her why they'd gone parasailing and the recon they'd done pertaining to her sister, but now wasn't the time.

"But you should definitely plan something fun into your schedule," he said.

She lifted her chin. "So should you."

"I do. Every available Sunday after church and Thursday morning. Meals with you, remember?" He looked at his watch. If Bill and Daniel had gone ahead without him to photograph and observe the compound, they would probably be another hour.

When he looked at her again, she was staring at him, emotion clouding her eyes. "Why?" she asked.

"Why what?"

"Why do you have lunch with me every Sunday and breakfast every Thursday? Why sit with me at events at church?"

She'd never been forward or demanding. She'd always just accepted his limitations. But he'd always known that one day his limitations wouldn't be enough. "Because I enjoy your company."

"Then why limit it?"

He looked around, scoping out the environment, his eyes skimming over the other people in the room before coming back to her. "Because that is all I have, Melissa."

Tears filled her eyes. He could see her consciously push them back as she steeled her face. "And if someone comes into my life? What will you do then?"

His knee-jerk reaction was to say he'd find a way to fill the gaping hole in his chest because she would have ripped his heart out. Instead, he said, "I'd miss you. And I'd understand."

"What if you meet someone?"

Not a chance. "I'm not looking to meet anyone. At all." He ended the conversation by looking at his watch again and saying, "Ready for me to drive you home?"

"No." Despite her words, she tossed her notepad and pen into her purse with abrupt movements. They both stood, and on their way out the door, she tossed her cup into a trash can. "I'll find my own way home."

He put a hand on her elbow. "Don't be ridiculous."

She ripped her arm free and took a step away from him. "I'm not being ridiculous. I'm establishing my own personal boundaries, and I can get home without your help."

"My friends have your car."

"I have numerous ways home. And I loaned them my car free and clear. Have a great afternoon."

She spun on her heel and went back into the cafeteria, pulling her phone out of her purse. He felt like he ought to go back in with her, force her compliance. Instead, he watched her for a moment, then turned and walked out of the hospital.

He stopped at his truck and leaned against the door, covering his face with his hands. "God," he whispered, "please help me let her go."

CHAPTER

FIVE

OCTOBER 22

Phil examined the whiteboard propped up against his balcony door. The compound where Melissa's sister lived was heavily guarded, more so than seemed reasonable. Six guards walked the roof, and Daniel had identified three more armed guards on the ground.

Why?

Did this teniente have a price on his head? Or was this location ground zero for their entire operation? If it was, why did the man's wife and kids live there? Why not keep civilians away from the main action?

"You seem distracted," Bill said. "Everything go okay taking the woman to the hospital?"

Phil frowned and looked at Bill. "I beg your pardon?"

"I said you seem distracted."

He huffed out a breath and turned his back on the outline of the compound. "Sorry. I don't mean to be."

"It wasn't a condemnation, brother. It was a simple observation."

He focused on Bill. "Everything went okay with taking her to the hospital. We never found anything out about her. I'm sure we'll never see her again."

Daniel carried three bottles of water from the kitchen and handed them out. "Would be nice to know who did that to her."

Phil shook his head. "You say that, but then you see that it happens so often to so many. We'll never be able to stop it all, and then you get disheartened and pray you never get used to seeing it."

Daniel stared at him for a moment. "Sounds like the voice of experience."

"Yeah. Sounds like." Phil paced to the window and looked out at the pool. He glanced at his watch. In five minutes, he needed to leave for work. "Melissa asked me to go to the beach with her."

After a moment of silence, Bill said, "You two *are* dating, right?"

"No." He sighed. "Well, I mean, we do eat together a couple of times a week, but not under the heading of date."

With a raised eyebrow, Daniel asked, "So, what do you call it?"

"Breakfast." Phil gestured at his leg. "She doesn't need broken. She needs whole."

"Perhaps you ought to let her decide that." Bill stood in front of the whiteboard and took a sip of his water. "Why six on the roof? If I was manning this, I'd do two. Maybe three on a tense night."

Daniel stood next to him. "Do you think they're just keeping people busy?"

Phil turned. "It wasn't shift change?"

"Nah. We thought maybe, so we hung out an extra ten minutes just in case. Nothing changed."

"Okay." Phil rubbed at his temple, trying to put together a plan of action. "Somehow, I need access to Melissa's sister. I just don't know if knocking on the door is going to be welcomed."

Bill chuckled. "It might be if they were looking to feed some sharks."

He snorted. "They probably use alligators. It's cleaner." His phone vibrated and he glanced at the screen. Winston's face appeared. "Hey," Phil said as he answered the video call.

"You still wanting access to Hector Molina?" It looked like Winston was calling from inside a surveillance van.

"No. I'm wanting access to his wife, Lola."

Winston looked over his shoulder and then back at him. "Can you get an ambulance?"

He glanced at Bill and Daniel, who were listening to the conversation. "Yes. In fact, I have a shift starting in a few minutes."

Winston sighed and pinched the bridge of his nose. "I'm not calling you in an official capacity."

"Spill it."

"Molina has a way with his fists and his wife's face. Usually, he calls his own doctor when he's done with her, but it takes him a few hours to decide he needs to. Maybe you can get there before he does that."

"Now?"

"Yes. He just started. It'll be a few minutes."

Phil ended the call and looked at Bill and Daniel. "I'm going in."

They looked at each other, then back at him. "Got spare uniforms?" Daniel asked.

Melissa tried to shed yesterday's confrontation with Phil from her mind. She should have let him drive her home, but she'd felt like she needed to make a point. Still, she doubted he got it.

Should she keep waiting for him? What if he never got himself emotionally and mentally to the point that he was ready for a relationship? Was she willing to wait with no promise of a future?

She knelt next to her bed and rested her forehead on her crossed arms. "God, please, show me the right direction. I know I said I'd wait. But that was me saying it. What do You want me to do? Wait? Force his hand? Love him anyway?" A tear slipped out of her closed eye. "Because I don't think I can help myself with that last one."

At the ding-dong sound of a doorbell, she raised her head. Sharon was out, so Melissa had to handle whichever resident had pressed the button at the desk. She scrubbed her hands over her cheeks and rushed into the bathroom to splash water on her face and quickly dry it.

She left her room and hurried down the hall. At the desk stood the high schooler Terry Quinn. He and his older sister, Rowena, had arrived a week ago. Sharon had started the process of securing Rowena a job in Detroit.

"Hi, Terry."

"She's going back to him." The pain etched into his face made her stomach hurt. She wanted to grab him and hug him, but she could see that he wanted to stay strong.

"I'm sorry."

"I turn eighteen in five days. Can I stay here?"

She had rules she had to follow for minors. "Are you emancipated?"

"No. She's my guardian."

With a sigh, Melissa said, "You can't legally stay here without her. She's your guardian. Are you in fear for your life? Should I call social services?"

He fisted his hands and held them up like a boxer taking a stance. "No, man. I'm in fear for his life. If he touches her one more time, I'm going to kill him. And he ain't worth my entire future." Suddenly, the angry man fled and left behind the hurt boy. "Please. Make her stop." Anxiety radiated off him.

"I'll go up. Stay here, okay?"

He nodded. Melissa rushed to the stairs and took them two at a time to the second floor. At room 23 she knocked on the door.

Rowena opened the door. She had fresh braids in her hair and bright red lipstick on. Her dark skin contrasted beautifully with her light-pink tank top. "Hi, Melissa," she said. "I was just coming to see you."

From the doorway, Melissa could see paper bags on the bed. Rowena had arrived with nothing—not even her purse. Melissa had taken her and Terry to the thrift store to supply them with clothes and sundries. "Hi, Rowena. What's going on?"

She smiled broadly. "Anton is taking me back. He forgives me."

How many times had Melissa heard those words? "Can I come in?"

Once inside, she spotted the cell phone on the nightstand. The night Rowena arrived, Melissa had helped her disable the tracking app and turn off all location settings. She wondered if Rowena's husband had convinced her to turn it on again.

"Terry came to see me," Melissa said. "He's a little upset."

Rowena's face turned hard. "He's just lazy. He doesn't want to go back home to school and responsibilities."

Melissa sat on the edge of the bed. "Rowena, he has been doing school, and he takes his responsibilities very seriously."

"You don't know what you're talking about. You need to stay out of my business."

Melissa pressed her lips together and thought about what angle she could use. "I'm thinking about hiring Terry as one of the night guards. He'd need to stay here, of course. You live too far away. He's really grown here, and I think it would be good for him."

Rowena's mouth opened and closed. Melissa had a feeling she relied on Terry's physical presence for a modicum of protection. "But I need him to come home with me."

For a moment, she glimpsed the woman who had come here, terrified, beaten, bruised. Melissa reached out and took one of her hands between both of hers. "I know you need him. He needs you too. Way more than the man who hurt you, who wants to keep hurting you. He calls it love, but it's not. Stay here with Terry. Be safe here. Give it another week."

Tears slid out of Rowena's eyes. "I already told him I'm coming home."

Melissa stood and took her into her arms. "How about I take your phone? We'll get it switched over to a new number.

That way, you don't feel like you have to answer it, and if you do feel like talking to him, you're the one who makes that decision. Does that work for you?"

After several long moments, Rowena nodded. "I'm sorry. I'm weak."

Melissa cupped the woman's cheeks with her hands. "You are not weak. You are here, standing up for yourself. You just have to learn how to break free from years of conditioning. Understanding the psychology isn't going to help you as much as time will." She moved her hands to Rowena's shoulders and squeezed. "I'm not going to force you. You're of course free to leave whenever you want. Would you like for me to pray for you? Will that help you?"

Rowena nodded, so Melissa closed her eyes. "God, we love You. Rowena told me that when she first came here. Help her find You, to seek You first when she is feeling most lost. Teach her to discern the people who mean to do her harm. Guide me as I love her and help shield her. Thank You."

They hugged and Melissa stepped back. "I'm going to pick up your phone now, okay?"

Rowena hesitated, then nodded. "Okay."

"Give me a couple of hours and you'll have a brand-new number." She gestured at the telephone on the nightstand. "You have that one if you need it."

As Melissa started out the door, Rowena asked, "Can I still go to Detroit? My cousin is still cool with my going there."

"Of course." Melissa paused. "Detroit is perfect. You can stay as long as you need, though. Don't feel rushed."

The temptation to check Rowena's phone log was real, but Melissa maintained her residents' privacy. She slipped the phone into her pants pocket and went back to the front desk. Terry waited in a chair in the reception area, sitting with his hands laced behind his bowed head. When he heard her, he shot to his feet.

"She's okay now. Coming to me was the right thing." Melissa put a hand on his forearm. "Listen, and don't take this negatively. Right now, she is not going to respond well to aggression, even if that aggression is born out of fear." He opened his mouth, but she shook her head, interrupting what he might have said. "I'm not criticizing. And I'm sure that you didn't start off upset, although the situation is incredibly upsetting."

"Yeah. I just don't know how to . . ." His eyes filled with pain. "What do I say next time?"

"I reminded her that if that man loved her, he wouldn't hurt her. That's what I'd do if I were you." She considered her next words carefully. "I told her I'd like for you to come work for me."

His eyes widened as he looked around. "How?"

"Aaron could use some company at night. Do you think you could do that?"

He already spent many nights hanging out with Aaron, talking basketball and football. She loved that Aaron, the gentle giant, could show Terry some genuine masculine love.

"I'd like that. But what about Detroit?"

Melissa shrugged. "I think I convinced your sister to give it a little more time. If that's the case, then you can make a decision about going or staying when the time comes." She mentioned pay and told him that the position came with a room. "It's one of the smaller rooms across the courtyard. But it's just you, so I'm sure that's suitable."

He hesitated. "I'd hate to take a room from a resident."

She shook her head. "I don't give that one to the residents. Aaron's position comes with a room, but he still lives with his mom. I've kept it for him in case he ever wants to move out." She gestured toward the office, and he followed her in. She unlocked a cabinet, pulled out the set of keys for the room, and held them out to him. "The security company that I use told me the second night guard gave notice. She was just part-time. But I think I'll tell them that I want full-time, let you and Aaron overlap, and you can pick up those two nights a week he doesn't work."

He took the keys and stared at them like she'd just handed him the Cullinan Diamond. "But I'm not eighteen yet."

"Five days, right?"

He looked around before looking back at her, hope replacing the pain in his eyes. "Right."

"Well, I think we can get the paperwork started right away. Your first night is five nights from now." She paused. "Unless you want your birthday off."

With a smile he said, "No, ma'am. Thank you."

"And you have to stay in school, in that virtual program you're in. If that slips, you're out of luck."

He nodded, still smiling. "Yes, ma'am."

After he went upstairs, she went to her office to email the security firm. She wondered briefly if she'd done the right thing. Would keeping Terry here keep Rowena in Miami and eventually put her in danger again? Or would she go on to Detroit and start over without him? She couldn't ignore the need he had for a job, though, and how perfect he meshed with Aaron.

She sent the email, then sat back and looked at the computer screen. "I'm still listening, God," she said out loud, "even if we got interrupted. Thanks for the wisdom with Rowena. Now please let me feel that assurance with Phil."

Phil pulled the ambulance into a gas station thirty-six minutes after Winston called him. He had remained quiet for the entire trip, mumbling or grunting when absolutely necessary. His throat felt dry when he finally said to his partner, Leslie, "We need to talk."

She raised an eyebrow as they opened their doors. They walked over to a picnic table outside the fast-food restaurant attached to the gas station.

Leslie had dark brown skin and curly black hair that she kept pulled back. She was about five two with a thick frame and strong arms. He'd not encountered a patient she couldn't help lift.

Her bright red lips pursed as she said, "What crazy stunt are we about to do?"

With a sheepish smile he said, "Not we. Me."

"I beg your pardon?"

As if on cue, Bill and Daniel approached. Phil gestured at Bill, who wore one of his uniforms. "My good friend Bill here is going to be riding along."

She looked Bill up and down. "Why?"

Phil glanced around, then leaned closer to her. "Because we're going into the home of a Colombian drug lord who just finished beating his wife."

Both of her eyebrows shot up. "Fine," she said, stepping backward. "But if you get killed, they're going to fire you."

"I promise it will be all my fault." He smiled and leaned forward to kiss her cheek. "You're the best."

"Mm-hmm." She looked at Daniel. "What are you going to do while the two of them go in?"

Daniel smiled and raised his arms like he was firing a rifle. "Why, I'm going to be observing from a high vantage point."

"Mm-hmm," she said again. She shifted her attention back to Phil. "We'll discuss terms when you get back."

Phil slapped her on the back. "I love you, Leslie."

She chuckled. "The meter's running. You'd best get a move on."

Daniel got into Phil's truck while Phil and Bill got into the ambulance. "She's a good woman," Bill said.

"She is. Her husband's a cop. I like them both a lot."

Once they got out into traffic, Phil hit the sirens and lights. "Hang tight."

CHAPTER

SIX

Phil drove the ambulance up to the gates of the compound. It had been forty-five minutes since Winston called. He knew somewhere nearby, Daniel sat on the roof of a building, watching the action play out through a sniper rifle scope.

The guard left his shack and sauntered over to the ambulance, both hands gripping his M16. "You got no business here." He didn't even open with niceties.

"We got a call, man," Phil said. "Woman in distress. If I don't go in, cops will come next. That's the only business I care about."

The guard looked at Bill, then met Phil's eyes with a steady look. "Wait here."

When he went back into the shack, Bill let out a breath. "Man, that dude will just up and kill us. Did you see the look in his eyes?"

"Stone-cold." Phil glanced over at his friend. "You still cool?"

Bill winked at him. "Stone-cold."

"Roger."

In his ear, Daniel spoke. "You got them all abuzz, brother. Activity heading to the gate. Two total."

The muscles in Phil's neck tightened almost painfully. He concentrated on keeping his breathing steady even as his vision narrowed and his adrenaline output kicked up a notch. Two men walked through the iron gate in the stucco wall. One of them conferred with the guard and then walked toward the ambulance.

"No one here called you," he said, keeping his hand on the gun in his holster.

"I get that a lot." Phil turned the ambulance off. "Listen, we got a very clear call of a woman in distress. I go in, or cops come."

The man looked back at the other man and then at Phil. "We have a private doctor on the way."

Phil smiled. "Terrific. Let us in to stabilize her, and then when your doctor comes, we'll leave." As the man hesitated, Phil added, "We can even leave the rig here. We'll just come in with our kits." He glanced over at Bill. "Right?"

Bill nodded. "We just want to help the woman."

"Wait here." The man left them and conferred with the other two men, then waved them forward.

Phil took a deep, steadying breath, then glanced over at Bill. "Ready?"

"As ever."

They hopped out of the ambulance and walked around to the back. "Have to ditch the earpieces," Phil said. "They might see them."

"Roger," Daniel replied. "Put them in a pocket. Then I can still hear."

Phil grabbed a duffel bag from the back of the ambulance, and Bill took a cardiac kit. As they shut the doors, the man Phil had spoken with appeared at his side.

"You will stay with me."

Phil nodded and followed the man. The second man who had come with him picked up the rear, keeping his M16 steady in his hands.

They took a cobblestone path past the main house, then walked along the length of an Olympic-sized pool to a large white house on top of graceful arches that gave a view of the ocean. As they climbed the stairs to the door, Phil glanced around to see what he could from this higher vantage point, trying not to be too obvious about it.

The guard in front unlocked the padlock on the door and led the way inside. Phil and Bill stepped into the cool interior. A bright peach L-shaped couch sat on a stone tile floor. A mahogany bar divided the living space from the kitchenette. Arched windows looked out on the ocean on one side and the pool and main house on the other. Phil glanced up and spotted two cameras. He wondered how many he couldn't see.

They walked through the room and to another door. After rapping his knuckles on it, their guard opened it and stepped aside. A woman lay on the bed, curled into a ball. She had her arm around a sleeping girl who was maybe one year old. A little boy about four or five sat on the floor, watching something on a tablet. He didn't even glance up when the door opened.

The woman lifted her head and looked at them. When she saw Phil and Bill, her eyes widened, and she started to sit up but gasped and froze, then moved more slowly.

Phil was struck again by how much she looked like Melissa. Rage boiled in his chest. He fought the desire to grab her and the kids and fight his way out of there. Instead, he stood stoically by until he had permission to approach.

Lola spoke in rapid Spanish, and the man answered. Phil translated as quickly as possible and gathered that she asked what they were doing there, and their guard suggested she'd called them. "No!" she said emphatically. Then she said in English, "How would I?"

The man turned to Phil and Bill. "You will leave when the doctor arrives."

Bill nodded and walked to the bed. Phil glanced around the room as he set his bag on the foot of the bed and observed cameras in three corners.

Bill knelt next to the head of the bed. "We're just going to help stabilize you until your doctor gets here."

Lola had a wild look in her eyes as they darted between Phil and Bill. "Who called you?"

Phil shook his head. "We don't know. We just got the call and came."

The baby next to her stirred, and Bill said, "I can take her while he helps you."

She looked to the man watching them, fear etched into every feature, before she nodded. "Thank you."

Phil prodded at the bruising under her left eye, then ran his fingers down her jaw and across her neck. "Does this hurt?" he asked, pressing into her lower jaw. She shook her head. He continued to run his fingers down her neck and over her shoulders, and she winced as he touched the dislocation in her left shoulder.

He looked back at the man watching them. "I need to set her shoulder. It's going to hurt."

The man looked up at a camera and back at him. "Wait for the doctor."

"The longer I wait, the worse it will be."

After a few seconds, the man nodded. "Fine."

Phil looked Lola in the eyes. "I'm sorry."

She grimaced. "It isn't the first time. Just do it."

She closed her eyes and seemed to steel herself against the pain. When she nodded, letting him know she was ready, he moved as quickly as possible, praying for strength and wisdom. Relief coursed through him when he felt and heard the joint slip back into place. Sweat beaded her forehead, but she never said a word.

He slipped her arm into a sling. "Anywhere else?" he asked.

She shook her head. Without glancing around, keeping his movements normal and natural, he slipped a small piece of paper into her jeans pocket. Her nostrils flared, but otherwise she didn't react.

After examining a cut on her heel, he straightened. "The shoulder was the worst of it. She doesn't need a hospital."

"Of course she doesn't," the guard replied. He gestured at her. "She's clumsy. Always falling. This time, she was holding the baby. She needs to be more careful."

Her gaze flew to Bill, who cuddled the baby against his chest, then back to Phil. "Thank you."

He stood, closing his bag. "Do you still want us to wait for the doctor?"

A second later, their guard pulled a phone out of his jacket pocket and glanced at the screen, then shook his head. "I'll take you back."

Bill set the baby back on the bed, and they left the pool house.

At the door, the man padlocked it again. With Bill's raised eyebrow, he said, "The boy escapes. She needs to not worry about him."

Phil glanced over at Bill and could see the muscle working in his jaw. He felt the same way, but they had no power to effect a change at this moment. Right now, they could only wait for Lola to read the note and reply.

As they walked back along the path, a woman in a red bikini came out of the main house. Phil's footsteps almost faltered when he recognized her from St. Ignatius church. Dark shades shielded her eyes. If she saw him, she gave no indication.

It was a tense walk back to the gate. Phil expected an ambush the entire time, but the man who had never introduced himself just walked them to the door in the stucco wall and opened it for them. When Phil opened the back of the ambulance, he could tell that someone had searched it. He hoped they found exactly what they were meant to find—a fully functioning and normal ambulance.

Back at the gas station, Daniel and Bill got into Phil's truck as Leslie headed to the ambulance, carrying two cups of coffee and a wrapped-up sandwich. She held out a cup to Phil. "I sure hope you were able to do what you set out to do."

He held up his cup and she pressed hers against it, as if toasting champagne. "Figure out what I owe you? Let me guess. Working Thanksgiving for you."

"Your mother will kill me if you work Thanksgiving for me two years in a row."

He didn't deny that. "How about Christmas?"

"I'm already off."

He sighed and put the ambulance into drive. "Fine. What?"

She looked him up and down. "I want you to run the 5K with me next weekend. The one for the children's hospital."

With a scowl, he stopped at the next red light. "I hate running 5Ks. Everyone stares."

"Dude, everyone is going to stare anyway. It's just human nature. 'Oh look, a man with no leg.' Stare over. Life goes on."

Heat crawled up his neck and over his cheeks. A knee-jerk response made it all the way to the tip of his tongue, then he pulled it back. He did owe her. She'd risked her job just now. "Deal."

"Woot!" She clapped her hands and grinned. "You will *not* be sorry."

He glanced at her out of the corner of his eye, certain she couldn't be more wrong.

Lola waited twenty minutes before she got off the bed. Baby Gabriele lay sleeping. Mathias had crawled onto the bed and started sucking his thumb, his way of self-soothing into a nap. She had no idea when food would come, so she encouraged him to fall asleep, promising him lunch after.

Her shoulder hurt enough to make her nauseated, but as soon as Hector had heard the pop when he pulled it out of socket, he'd stopped. Something about the sound had turned him away. If only she'd known it was that easy.

The only reason her shoulder had popped out of socket was because she was trying to put the baby down and get her out of danger. The fact that he'd actually hit her across the face while she held their youngest child in her arms made her realize she needed to get out. How, though?

Whatever the paramedic had slipped into her pants felt

like it was burning a hole in her pocket. She so desperately wanted to pull it out and see what it said, but she couldn't risk being seen by the cameras. Finally, she felt like enough time had gone by. She'd lain completely still, waiting. The kids had fallen asleep for their afternoon naps. This was her chance.

She stood tall, refusing to slump against the pain, and strolled gracefully to the bathroom. The second the door shut behind her, she pulled the paper out of her pocket. Her hand trembled as she read the words.

I'm a friend of your sister Melissa. She has been looking for you. This situation is bad for you. We can help. Work 'It's a beautiful day' into a conversation with someone and you'll be heard. We'll get you out the next time you leave the compound. If it's safe, feel free to call.

A sob escaped. She put a hand over her mouth to stifle any sound. She looked at the phone number, said it over and over again, memorizing it.

She started to destroy the note but decided to hide it instead, wanting to keep it. It felt like proof that someone cared for her, looked for her, and knowing that would give her the strength to go on.

Fumbling a bit with her arm in the sling, she opened a compact of powder foundation and pulled the makeup insert out. She slipped the note in the compact and put the insert back, then prodded and poked but could see no indication of the note anywhere. Unless someone knew exactly where to look, they wouldn't find it.

She went back into the room and sat at the small table,

looking out at the pool and the main house. Thoughts swirled in her mind, and tears burned the back of her throat.

Her sister? Melissa? She had brief snatches of memory of a sister, but no one had ever told her about her. Reading that name brought back the memory of being held in her sister's arms, holding her hand as they walked to the playground, calling her "Sissy." Or maybe that was "Missy."

Melissa was looking for her!

What could she do now? What did the note mean by "you'll be heard"? Was this a way for Hector to trap her? Was it some sick joke?

He'd left for Colombia right after he locked her in here. Time for the quarterly gathering of the tenientes. While he was gone, security lessened a bit. Did she dare risk it?

She went back to the bed and lay down, closing her eyes, praying that they would bring food for Mathias before too long. Could the way out of this nightmare be within her grasp?

OCTOBER 23

Melissa got to church twenty minutes early. Every month, the church picked a ministry to highlight and donated most of the day's offerings to it. Today was her shelter's turn. She'd created a few slides going over budget projections, statistics, and the number of families they'd helped.

She always had a slide about operating expenses because the congregation as a whole was incredibly generous to her. For five years she'd done this presentation, and they deserved to know her stewardship of their money. She hid nothing about the way her business operated except the address of the building and the names of her residents.

She walked into the cool exterior and slipped on the light sweater she'd brought with her. Upstairs, she found Warren Hayes at the computer terminal, loading music slides.

"Good morning," she said, holding out a thumb drive. "There should be seven slides on there and the domestic abuse video I told you about."

He shifted his glasses and took the drive. "Perfect. I'll get it loaded for you. There's a clicker on the podium. Do you remember how to use it?"

"I do. Thanks, Warren."

As she turned to go, he pointed down into the main sanctuary. "Phil's down there. Got here about thirty minutes ago."

Why did she think she wouldn't see him today? They'd never had a disagreement before, but Friday's felt pretty final. "Thanks," she said, then headed back downstairs. With her palm on the door to the sanctuary, she took a deep, steadying breath, then pushed the door open.

Only a few people were here this early. She nodded hello and walked to the third pew in the section on the left, where Phil sat in their normal place, his eyes shut, his head slightly bowed. Not wanting to disturb him while he prayed, she quietly sat down. As soon as she put her Bible on the pew, he opened his eyes and looked over at her.

"Hi," he said.

She swallowed, wishing her mouth didn't feel so dry. "Hi," she said in an almost whisper.

After several long seconds he asked, "Is it okay if I sit with you this morning?"

Was it? Did she want to continue to torture herself, week

in and week out, waiting for him to finally acknowledge that he might be the perfect man for her?

Before she could respond, still unsure of what she intended to say, he said, "After service, I have something important I want to tell you."

She looked around. "Are your friends gone?"

"No. They're here. But they knew I wanted to talk to you privately before service started."

She ran her tongue over her teeth. "Okay. Where do you want to meet after?"

"I have lunch ready at my place."

"Great." Making a concentrated effort to relax the tense muscles in her back and neck, she sat back against the pew. She turned her mind away from Phil and whatever important thing he had to tell her and instead focused on what she'd say to the congregation.

The pastor approached and confirmed she'd given Warren what he needed. They spoke briefly and he went on, greeting people by name, working his way through the growing congregation. By the time the opening song's chords played, the church was full and the overflow balcony doors had opened.

Two songs in, the head deacon greeted everyone and explained the monthly missions offering. "We are always thrilled to have our own local ministry as part of our lineup. Most of you know Melissa Braxton. Melissa runs a domestic abuse shelter in Miami. I think she has a short video for us before she comes to speak."

The domestic abuse video started. Melissa fought the jitters that caused a slight tremble in her hands and a shake to her knees as she walked down the aisle. When she got to the pulpit, she turned and faced the audience of seven hundred.

She didn't need any notes, but she had her Bible in case inspiration called for her to pull up a verse.

"Good morning," she said as the video ended, laying her Bible on the podium and picking up the clicker to change the slides. "When I was five years old, my mom was pregnant with my baby brother." The first slide showed her mom sitting in a rocking chair with her on one side and Lola on the other. They both fought for a place next to her large, rounded stomach.

"My father had always abused her, and one day, he kicked her hard in the stomach. She started hemorrhaging, and by the time the paramedics arrived, she was already dead. My unborn brother died as well. My little sister and I were separated between the two families. I never saw her again."

Murmurs ran through the auditorium. She had five minutes and wanted to use all of them well.

"My passion is to give the abused sanctuary from their abusers. Women, children, and even men come through our shelter at the rock-bottom moment of their lives. They come because they realize they need to make a break. Often, it's because a child is suddenly put at risk.

"Hospitals, clinics, even police stations call us when there is someone in need. We can house eighteen families. I partner with my friend Sharon. One of us is on call twenty-four hours a day, and when we don't have an empty room, we connect with other shelters in the area. Sharon and I are licensed therapists and run personal and group therapy sessions for all our current residents. They are a requirement to stay there. We provide occupational training opportunities to help build job skills. We utilize contacts with other shelters around the country for the many who want to flee Miami but have nowhere to go. And we provide twenty-four-hour security.

"None of that is free." She clicked the button to change the slide. "This screen will show you our output. Security is our largest expenditure but obviously quite important. I take a salary, but my partner does not. She doesn't require it. Food is next on the list. We provide breakfast and dinners. Each unit is also equipped with a kitchenette."

After a pause, she clicked the button again. "Last year, we were able to help one hundred and twenty-three families. Some stayed a few months, some a few weeks. Many of them have gone on to new lives free from their tormentors and abusers."

After the applause died down, she clicked to the last slide. It simply said, "Help us help them."

"You can make a difference," Melissa said. "You can help keep us going. Thank you."

As she picked up her Bible and walked to her seat, the head deacon returned to the podium. "All the offering collected today will go to the shelter. If you'd like your offering designated a different way, please use the green envelopes in the pew in front of you." He paused. "Ushers."

When she sat back down next to Phil, he reached over and squeezed her hand. Her ice-cold skin warmed in his grip. "Well done," he said.

She smiled. "Thanks." Still slightly trembling, she tried to focus on relaxing now that the hard part was over.

It didn't bother her to talk about her past if the result ended up being that she got support for her shelter. But anytime she did talk about it, the memory of the life fading from her mother's eyes brought fresh pain.

CHAPTER

★

SEVEN

The hot sunshine beat down on the black asphalt, making heat waves shimmer and distort the lines of the parking lot. When Melissa turned her car off, the temperature inside felt like it instantly went up twenty degrees. She looked up at the art deco design of Phil's apartment building. Sections of the ivory stucco were painted turquoise, and the windows had coral shades above them. She'd been here only twice before and had gone inside only once.

"Sharon, I have to go. I'm here," she said into the car's mic.

"Well, I'm dying to know what has Phil Osbourne worked up enough that he'd have you meet him at his apartment instead of a safe and public restaurant," Sharon said. "Call me on your way home."

With a chuckle, Melissa hung up the phone and got out of the car. Phil lived on the second floor with a pool view.

In the breezeway, the wind blew her hair, cooling her down. She paused at apartment 24.

Phil had the door open before she could even knock. "Hey," he said, opening it wider.

When she walked in, she could smell meat being grilled on the balcony. She glanced in that direction. Bill and Daniel stood outside with a smoking grill between them.

As she came farther into the room, her eyes wandered over the brown leather couch and matching recliner. A small oval table sat in front of the bar separating the living space from the kitchen. As she slipped her purse off her shoulder and set it on the couch, she noticed a whiteboard leaning up against the window. The picture on it caught her eye. At first, she thought someone had taken a picture of her. But the hair was too long and she didn't have a shirt like that.

Curious, she got closer and bent to inspect it. What in the world?

Her eyes skimmed over the words written on the board in Phil's neat block lettering. LOLA.

With a gasp, she spun and looked at him. "What?"

"I found her for you."

"You found her for me?" She opened and closed her mouth. "I don't understand."

He walked toward her. "Melissa, you are by far one of the most important people in my life. I want you to hear that."

The blood rushed in her ears and her heart pounded. What was he talking about?

"I realize that there's something you think you want from me, and it's something I can't give you. But this—this I could do."

She turned and looked at the board. Her stomach flip-flopped at the face in the photo. Lola looked so much like her. She took in the aerial view of a compound near the water, the photo of a man with HECTOR under it, and several other names and places.

Feeling like she could communicate again, she turned back around. "What does all this mean?"

"Right." He stepped forward. She could almost see the nervous energy radiating off him. "So, this is where she lives." He drew his finger around the picture of the largest building. "And this is a picture of her husband, Hector."

"Husband?" She stared at his photograph. He had a square face with a thin mustache and close-cropped black hair. She didn't like his eyes and hoped it was just a trick of the photography. "Do you have her number?"

"No."

"This is Miami. I can see one of the harbors. Where is this?"

"Listen, I need to talk to you about this." He steered her to the couch, using a little pressure to encourage her to sit down, then turned his entire body to face her. "Your sister is married to a bad man."

Her heart skipped a beat, then picked up speed. "Bad how?" She searched Phil's eyes, wanting to find all of the answers in their gray depths.

He reached out and took both her hands in his. How she'd longed for this kind of contact from him! But she knew he wasn't trying to get closer to her, he was trying to soothe her, likely because he was about to tell her something pretty horrible.

"He's a lieutenant for a Colombian cartel."

The breath escaped her body slowly until even her fingertips tingled with the need for fresh oxygen. He let her process the information. She was thankful he didn't push her to speak. Finally, she asked, "Is she involved in that?"

He smiled and ran his thumbs in circles over her knuckles. "No."

"Then how did she end up . . . ?" She paused, not certain how to ask the question.

"How did she end up married to someone in a cartel?" When she nodded, he said, "It looks like your father's family has always been somewhat involved in the seedier side of life. It seems the family that took Lola raised her in Colombia. I'm not certain, looking at her situation, that she had a choice about marrying Hector, or that she knew she might have a choice. Nothing in the background we pulled up suggests anything different."

"We?"

Phil gestured at Bill and Daniel out on the balcony. "You know we were on the same Special Forces Team. When Bill got out, he started a company offering a select number of special services. Daniel joined him a few months later. They're kind of a cross between private detectives and a security firm."

Thinking more clearly, piecing it all together, she said, "So you hired them to help you?"

"I wouldn't call it hiring. They're refusing payment from me, but that was the intent." His hands stilled. "There's more." He cleared his throat. "She's a prisoner under guard all the time. Her husband abuses her."

"No," she whispered, tears filling her eyes. "Oh no!" She started to pull her hands away, but he applied gentle pressure and she stilled.

"So, Melissa, it's not just finding your sister. We talked about it, planned it, scoped it all out late into the night. They can also help me get her out."

Searching his face, she saw nothing but sincerity, compassion, and understanding. "At what risk?"

It took him several seconds to answer. "Life is a risk. And knowing we could help a woman in need—not just any woman but your sister—we all agreed that it would be worth the risk."

This time when she pulled away, he let her, as if sensing her need to move. She stood and crossed over to the board, then turned to him. "The whole time they've been here, you've been working on this?"

He paused, then nodded. "Yes."

"Did you even go parasailing?"

"Yes." Another pause. "To get a better view of the house from above."

She slapped her hands to her cheeks and laughed. "You must think I'm the biggest idiot in the world. Here I was, thinking you were learning to relax, accept, heal, and you were"—she waved a hand at the board—"not."

"I didn't want to say anything to you until I knew a couple of things for certain."

A bitter taste filled her mouth. "You mean until you discovered whether she was also a lieutenant in a Colombian cartel?"

"Pretty much."

Her mind whirled with so many questions and accusations and so much thanksgiving. She didn't know what to home in on first. "What now?"

He stood and approached her, his hands in his pockets.

"Now—" His phone rang loudly, and she jumped. He frowned as he pulled it from his pocket. "This is Winston. I have to get it." He held the phone up to his ear. "Hey." After a moment, he asked, "And?" His eyes cut to the patio door, then back to her. "Roger." He slipped the phone back into his pocket. "Sorry about that."

She repeated her question. "What now?"

"Now we're going to get her out. And it's up to you whether you want to be part of that or not."

"She might not even remember me."

"You're right. When I talked to her, I didn't get a chance to ask. She's too heavily guarded."

Her breath froze in her lungs. "When you talked to her?"

He roughly cleared his throat. "I, uh, went in under the guise of an ambulance call. I wanted Bill to get a reading on her."

"A reading?"

He gestured toward the patio. "He's brilliant with people. Spot-on. Can size them up without even trying. I knew he'd know about her. When Winston called me, we didn't hesitate."

"Winston?" She put her hands on his shoulders and looked him in the eye. "Can you please start at the beginning and quit making me ask you questions? I'm so confused right now."

He led her to the table, and they sat facing each other. He cleared his throat again and started on the story about his friends helping him locate Hector Molina, his brother calling him to ask why he was looking for Hector, and the state he found Lola in. He told her what he wrote on the note and how they were in a holding pattern to see if she would reply.

He ended with, "Winston just called and said she gave us the key phrase. The next time she leaves her compound with both children, we'll be ready to intercept her."

"Children?" So much information danced through her brain, making her feel almost dizzy.

Phil's smile steadied her. "Yes, two. A little boy named Mathias and a little girl whose name we couldn't find."

Two children? A niece and a nephew! She thought about Winston's steadfast dedication to rules and structure. "Your brother is okay with this?"

"He is if we can convince her to tell us about her husband's operations in the States. He'll get her witness protection for that." He reached out and covered her hands. "Listen to me. Regardless of her ability to cooperate with my brother, you are my priority. I can get her out and hand her over to him, or I can get her out and bring her to you. You tell me."

All of the information clicked into place. Phil had found Lola! Her baby sister—with two children. And she needed rescuing.

The feeling of overwhelming confusion subsided, and Melissa's logical mind kicked into gear. She considered all the angles as she understood them and finally nodded. "Bring her to me. I have an empty room. I'll save it for her."

A grin lit his face up in a way she'd never seen before. "Okay then." He gave her a quick hug, then stood and grabbed a platter off the bar to the kitchen. He paused on his way to the patio door. "If you think about it further and change your mind, that's fine too." He slid the door open and handed Daniel the plate. "We're on, boys. Winston just called. He'll let us know when she leaves."

★ ★ ★

OCTOBER 24

Melissa rattled the locked door of the clinic. Confused, she walked around to the back of the small building. Someone had called her twenty minutes ago and identified herself as a nurse at this clinic, saying she had a patient seeking shelter. But no cars were in the employee parking spaces. If the patient had changed her mind, wouldn't the nurse have called Melissa back?

She pulled her phone out of her pocket and accessed her recent calls. She turned to go back to the front of the building when someone grabbed her from behind and slammed her into the wall.

A startled cry escaped her as the rough brick bit into her cheek. She was pushed so tight against the wall that she couldn't move.

"Explain to me what your card was doing in my woman's pocket," a man said, his mouth close to her ear. She felt the heat of his face against her cheek and smelled tobacco on his breath.

Her stomach rolled in protest. "I don't know who you're talking about."

He pushed her harder against the brick, and a tear escaped her eye. "I know she didn't call you for help, so how did you find out about her?"

"My cards are everywhere. Someone could have picked one up in any number of places."

He squeezed the back of her neck, and little black spots of pain danced in front of her eyes. "You don't get into Vibora business," he said, ending his sentence with a foul epithet. "Understand?"

"I understand." Her voice pitched at the end, fear taking the breath out of her.

He pulled back, then shoved her forward and let her go. She fell against the wall and then down to her knees. She never even saw him leave.

Hands shaking, she fumbled for her phone. As tears streamed from her eyes, she dialed 911.

Phil walked through the emergency room toward the doctor's lounge. As a nurse came out of a curtained area, he caught sight of Melissa's familiar profile. His heart started pounding, and he headed straight toward her. Pulling the curtain back, he saw her lift her hair and gingerly touch the skin on the back of her neck, where there was dark bruising.

"What happened?" he asked.

She jumped and turned. The wrecked look on her face made panic skirt through his system. "Phil," she said, her voice hitching.

"Hey, it's okay," he said, coming all the way into the room. He put his hands on her shoulders and pulled her to him. "What happened?"

"Some man." Her hot tears burned through the shirt of his uniform.

Anger replaced the fear, and he had a hard time keeping his touch gentle. "What man?"

"I don't know. I never saw him." She pushed herself back and looked up at him, then winced. "He set me up. I was called to a clinic, but it was closed and empty. Then he attacked me."

He cupped her wet cheeks with his hands, searching her

face. She had a scratch on her cheek that looked like road burn. "What did he do?"

"Pushed me against the wall. Threatened me. His girlfriend had my card."

"Do you know who he was?"

She gave a small shake of her head, and fresh tears filled her eyes. "Lots of women have my cards. But he said something about staying out of Vibora business." A shudder went through her. "That's the Spanish word for viper. Maybe a gang or something?"

He clenched his teeth hard enough that his jaw ached. Intentionally relaxing, he nodded. "Like the Vibora your sister married into?"

Her eyes widened, and she stared at him with her mouth half open. "Lola? How would she have my card?"

"She wouldn't. But I saw our friend from St. Ignatius at the Vibora compound."

She blinked several times. "She took my card. I left it for her the day we took her to the hospital."

"That explains why she didn't give her name."

"It also explains why she was so afraid of me. She must have thought I was Lola at first, that they found her."

He considered all the possibilities. "Are you sure you want me to bring Lola to you? Winston can keep her safe."

"I'm sure."

He cupped her cheek with one hand and ran his thumb over the scrape there. "You're quite amazing, you know that?"

She pressed her lips together and shook her head. "I was so scared," she whispered.

He gently pulled her to him again and pressed his lips against the top of her head. "I'll wait with you, follow you home."

OCTOBER 26

Phil eyed Lola through an unmounted Sig Sauer Tango4 sniper scope. She sat in the window of a café. Her son sat in a booster seat next to her. She held her baby up against her with a blanket covering her chest. They'd spent the morning at the zoo. Little Mathias looked exhausted. Any minute now, he'd nod off into his grilled cheese.

Lola had said the key phrase on Sunday. It had taken three days for her to leave the compound with both kids. Phil had begun to think she'd lost her nerve . . . or been found out.

Her driver sat with his back to the wall at a table behind her, watching her and eyeing anyone who came into the restaurant. Phil clicked his radio twice, then ran down the stairs of the building and onto the street just as Daniel and Bill pulled up in front of the café with a tow truck. They backed up to the SUV that had carried Lola and her children there, the beeping noise catching the driver's attention. Phil went into the café just as the driver exited, then rushed to Lola's table.

Without waiting for permission, he scooped up the diaper bag and slipped it over his shoulder, then picked up Mathias. Lola startled, looking up at him with shocked eyes. They cleared as she recognized him.

He jerked his head toward the back of the café, and she stood, not even shifting the baby away from her lunch. Without hesitation, she followed Phil through the back of the restaurant and to the rental car he'd parked in the back alley.

He opened the back door. "Get in. Secure her back there."

He ran to the other side, put Mathias into a booster seat, quickly buckled the harness, and hopped into the driver's seat. The second he heard the click of the buckle on the baby's seat, he drove down the alley to a street opposite the café.

Keeping an eye on his mirrors, he made a left, then a sudden right. "Do you have a cell phone?"

"No."

That gave him pause. Couldn't be too careful. "Is there anything that can't be replaced in your diaper bag?"

She looked at the seat next to him where he'd set the bag and then at him. "My wallet."

While he drove, he opened the bag and pulled out her wallet, then handed it back to her. "Get out your ID and any cash, photos, et cetera. Then give it back to me." As she took it from him, he said, "No credit cards or bank cards, though."

Within seconds, she'd handed him back her wallet. He turned onto a causeway and pulled over about halfway across the bridge. Keeping two diapers and a pack of wipes, he opened the passenger window and tossed the bag off the bridge. Then he got back into the flow of traffic.

"Why did you do that?"

He glanced in the mirror, but she was looking out the window and not at him. "I know he has you tagged, but I don't have time to look for it. If you were going to run, you'd probably grab the diaper bag without thinking about it. If I wanted to know where you were, I'd track the bag. Right now, if it was tagged, they know we went this direction."

He took the next exit and turned around to go back over the causeway. As they crossed the long bridge, he kept an eye out on the other side of the road, looking for any suspicious movement by any of the vehicles.

"Where are we going?" Lola asked.

"I promised your sister I'd take you to her."

When he looked in the mirror again, she looked so much like Melissa that it took his breath away. She kept her eyes fixed outside. She'd stretched her arm across the baby's seat to hold Mathias's hand. He'd fallen asleep. Even the excitement of a new car and person hadn't kept him awake.

"After you left the other day, I thought about her. I had a shadowed memory of someone named Missy."

"Yes. Melissa."

She climbed into the front seat, startling him. He hadn't expected any bold movements from her. She buckled herself in and then turned to face him. "He will find me."

"We were careful."

"It doesn't matter." She brushed her black hair off her forehead. "He'll find me. He's probably already on the way home from Colombia. This is a matter he'll take very seriously."

Her stoic tone surprised him. He checked the mirrors again for anyone following him before looking in her direction. "How do you feel about that?"

She turned and looked at her children. "My feelings haven't mattered in a long time."

"Maybe it's time for that to change."

They drove in circles for another twenty minutes. Phil pulled into the parking lot of a large mall and grabbed the device that Daniel had given him. It felt like a clunky smartphone and had a series of buttons along the bottom of the screen. He held it up to Lola and said, "This will pick up any wireless signals. I'm going to scan the kids, make sure there's nothing in their clothes, and then we'll check you."

She nodded and got out of the car, then opened the back door. Phil got out and waved the device over the kids, picking up no RF signals. Then he checked Lola, starting at the top of her head and moving down to her feet. Again, he didn't pick up any signals, but he went ahead and checked her from behind as well. "All clear," he said, turning the device off.

They got back in the car, and Lola asked, "Do you really think he'd put a tracker on us?"

Phil pulled out of the parking lot and checked his rearview mirror. "Do you?"

She looked back at the sleeping children. "I'm surprised he didn't."

When Phil stopped at the security gate at Melissa's building, a uniformed guard with a Sig Sauer on his hip stepped out of a guard shack. "Help you?" he asked, his gaze scanning the back seat.

"I'm Phil Osbourne. Ms. Braxton is expecting us."

He unclipped a phone from his belt and swiped and scanned it, then tapped the roof of the car. "Go ahead."

"Thanks."

He drove into the parking garage. As he turned the car off, Lola said, "What if I don't want to stay here?"

"Then don't." He picked up his phone and quickly shot a text to Bill and Daniel to let them know he'd arrived safely, then texted Melissa. "But besides the fact that she's your long-lost sister, Melissa runs a shelter for people in your situation. No one knows this address. It's completely safe."

After a few seconds, she asked, "What's the catch?"

"There's no catch. The state police do want to speak to you about testifying against your husband about his"—he paused—"*business* dealings. But whether you talk to them or not has no bearing on whether you're welcome here."

CHAPTER

★

EIGHT

Melissa paused at the doorway and looked at the room she'd assigned Lola, making sure everything was in place, then closed her eyes. "God, whatever is going on with them right now, put Your hand on them, protect them. Please let Lola feel happy and free here, and let me show her my love for her in a way she will accept. Guide me and keep me wise and strong."

As she raised her head, her phone chirped. With trembling fingers, she swiped up and saw a text from Phil, letting her know they were in the parking garage.

She raced downstairs and out to the garage. She rushed through the door and got to Phil's rental car just as he got out. Her footsteps faltered when the woman with him got out of the passenger's seat. The breath left her body as she whispered, "Lola."

Phil opened the back door and lifted out a sleeping boy

of about five. Melissa shifted her attention back to Lola, who held a little girl.

Lola stopped and stared at her. "Missy?"

With a sob, Melissa rushed forward. She put her arms around her sister, hugging her and the baby at the same time. "I didn't think you'd remember me."

As they separated, she saw tears in Lola's eyes. "I didn't until I saw your name. Then I remembered." She pressed a kiss to the baby's head. "This is Gabriele. That is Mathias."

Overwhelmed with emotion, Melissa ran a shaky hand over the black curls on Gabriele's head. "Sweet girl," she said. She looked over at Mathias, who had snuggled into Phil's neck, sound asleep. "How old?"

"Five, almost six." Lola put a hand on the baby's cheek. "Fourteen months."

Phil held up the diapers in his hand. "These are what we have," he said. "If you don't have some stock, I'll run up to the store."

"No, we keep stock." She gestured toward the door. "Let's get you out of the heat." She led the way into the building and stopped at the elevator. "This used to be a college dorm." The silence on the ride up was broken only by a small snore from Mathias.

Melissa led the way to room 36. The hallway was as silent as the elevator. She punched a code into the door and opened it, letting Lola precede her inside.

Two single beds sat on either side of the window. A short divider separated the bed space from the couch that faced a television. At the foot of one of the beds sat a crib with a butterfly mobile.

Phil laid Mathias on one of the beds and slipped his shoes

off. The boy put his thumb in his mouth and rolled over. Lola laid the baby in the crib, then wrapped her arms around herself.

A little kitchenette with a range and a small fridge filled the corner behind the door. A table in the shape of a half-moon was pushed up against the wall in the kitchenette and could be pulled out and opened up if needed. Melissa had added a booster seat to one of the chairs and brought in a high chair.

She tapped the paper pinned to the bulletin board above the table. "Here is our meal schedule and menu. We serve breakfast and dinner. You're welcome to stay in your room and cook, or each floor has a full kitchen at the end of the hall by the stairs. I brought in some of the snacks and put them in your fridge and cupboards: little cheese crackers, juice boxes, that sort of thing. There's a pantry in each kitchen. If you see something running low, please let us know." She ran a finger down the receiver of the phone hanging next to the bulletin board. "Dialing zero will get you security, and 911 will automatically go to an outside line. Otherwise, to get an outside line, hit eight and wait for a dial tone."

She realized she had slipped into business mode and was giving her sister—her *sister*—an emotionless rundown of the way the house operated when all she wanted to do was grab her and cry and tell her she loved her. "You are safe here. But please don't call anyone associated with your husband from this phone. It will put everyone at risk." She glanced at Phil, who stood patiently, his face giving nothing away. Suddenly, tears flooded her eyes, and she reached for Lola. "I'm so happy you're here."

Her sister started to step back, then stepped forward and hugged her. "Me too." As they separated, she said, "I don't remember before. But I'm starting to remember you."

"You were three. It was a long time ago."

"What do you know of your family?" Phil asked.

Lola frowned. "It's strange, but it's not really something I thought much about. I knew my father. He was in prison. His sister raised me. Her husband worked for my father-in-law." She spun her wedding ring on her finger, obviously a nervous habit. "When I'd ask about my mom, they just said she died giving birth to my brother. They never told me about you." She shook her head and looked at Melissa. "Why were we separated?"

"There wasn't a will. They just divided us between the two families. I lived with our mother's sister, then her brother."

Mathias shifted and mumbled in his sleep. Phil opened the door. "Why don't you two go downstairs. I'll stay up here with them."

Melissa could read the hesitation in Lola's eyes. "I'd trust Phil with any kids I had. He's great. I promise."

Lola's mistrust clearly extended to her. "I'd rather stay in here." She walked over to the couch. "He'll mumble and turn in his sleep the whole time. He just does that. We're not bothering him."

She sat on the couch, and Melissa glanced at Phil. He put his hands on her shoulders. "I need to go get rid of the car. Call me later, okay?"

On impulse, she stepped closer to him and slipped her arms around him. He hesitated only a fraction before hugging her back. It felt so good when his arms came around her. She relished the feel and smell of him for just a moment.

"Thank you." The words carried so much more meaning than she could ever convey.

As if he understood, he squeezed tight before he let go and stepped away. "You're welcome."

Once the door shut behind him, Melissa sat on the couch, facing Lola. Her sister smiled at her. "How long have you two been seeing each other?"

Her cheeks heated up. "We, uh, we're just friends."

Lola raised an eyebrow. "No, you're not."

"Well, I mean, I hope one day . . ." Her voice trailed off.

"I never had a choice." Lola spun her wedding ring, then paused and slipped it off. "When I turned eighteen, I was told what day I was to be married."

Melissa frowned. "How?"

"We were in Colombia. We moved there when I was four. We lived on the compound for the Vibora syndicate."

Melissa gasped. She knew the name.

"I only came to Miami when Hector was promoted to te-niente." When Melissa simply stared at her, her mind whirling, Lola said, "You look properly shocked."

"Well, it's rather shocking." Melissa didn't know what else to say. "I don't understand how two families could be so different. I wish . . ."

It surprised her when Lola reached out and took her hand. "You wish I'd come with you? I don't. You want to know why?" She looked behind her. "Because I have Gabriele and Mathias. And every single thing I've endured my entire life is worth it when I look at them." She shrugged and released Melissa's hand. "It's not like I was totally isolated. I had friends. We had a social group. I just had no freedom. And I had to endure Hector." She rubbed her arms in an absent

103

way. "Endure. That's the word for it too. Thankfully, he's been very busy since we moved here, and I don't see him too often anymore."

Melissa's heart wept desperate tears, but she kept her face stoic. "You shouldn't have to endure your husband, Lola."

"I know that. But what choice did I have?" She looked around the room. "What made you start this?"

Melissa hesitated. There was a lot of change happening in Lola's life. She could easily cave in and go back to her life just to stay in what was normal for her. Melissa wondered how much more she could handle right now.

But she had never been one to ignore the truth. She operated better in full light and exposure than in darkness.

"Because of what happened to our mother."

With a frown, Lola said, "I thought she died in childbirth."

Images popped up in Melissa's mind. She could still hear the sound of her father's boot striking her mother's flesh. "No. She bled to death, miscarrying after our father beat her."

Lola's eyes widened. "You mean . . ."

With a nod, Melissa reached forward and took her sister's hand. "Yes. While she was pregnant. You and I were hiding, and she managed to get me the phone. Even though the police came quickly, they weren't fast enough. She died before they even got through the door."

Lola put a hand over her mouth and surged to her feet. Melissa stood with her. "I never knew." Lola looked at Mathias. "When Hector found out we were having a baby, he was so happy. He never touched me the entire time. When we found out Mathias was a boy, you'd have thought I'd done something extra special, the way he spoiled me. It was almost like the time before was a dream." A tear slipped out of her eye. "The first time he hit me after, I was so surprised. I think I'd almost convinced myself it hadn't happened before." She turned and looked at Melissa, shame and sadness engulfing her brown eyes. "I couldn't let Mathias turn into his father. When your man offered me a way out, I was desperate."

Melissa put her hands on Lola's arms. "You did the right thing."

Lola closed her eyes and shook her head slightly. "He'll find us. But for now, the babies are safe." Before Melissa could react, Lola gripped her arms, squeezing until it almost hurt. She had a ferocious look in her eyes. "If something happens to me, promise me you'll keep them away from him. Protect them."

Melissa nodded and hugged her. "I will do everything in my power to keep all of you safe. You have my word."

Phil found a spot in front of the appropriate airline and parked his truck. He got out and walked around the front, where Bill grabbed him and hugged him. Then Phil hugged Daniel, slapping him on the back. "Thank you both for everything. Especially for your help today." As much as he wished his friends could stay longer, they had already done so much and needed to get back to their homes and their work. "I wish you would let me pay you."

"Don't even insult us like that," Bill said. "It was good to see you, to work with you." He grabbed his suitcase out of the truck bed. "If you're looking for work, we have more than we can handle."

Phil had enjoyed the planning and execution of the mission,

but that kind of life wasn't for him anymore. "Yeah, thanks, man. I'm good here."

Daniel slipped his backpack on. "Listen to me, brother. Don't let Melissa get away from you." As Phil frowned, Daniel held up a hand. "I know, she needs a whole man, blah, blah, whatever. That girl loves you. And you know, why not? You're a pretty lovable dude."

Bill added, "And quite the catch."

Phil laughed and blushed at the same time. "Goodbye. Godspeed."

When the airport doors slid shut behind them, he got back into his truck and headed to his brother's office. After finding a partially shaded spot, he shot his brother a text and went inside.

Before he'd even finished filling out the visitors' log, Winston appeared at his side. Phil clipped the visitor's pass to his T-shirt and followed Winston toward the inner sanctum of his office.

Winston opened the metal door with his name and gestured for Phil to proceed inside. "I'm assuming it went well," Winston said, walking around the desk to his chair.

Phil sat in the chair opposite him. "Yep. Dropped her off two hours ago."

"Where?"

"You know I can't tell you that." He kicked his prosthetic foot out and rubbed his thigh.

"But she'll testify?"

Instead of replying to his question, Phil asked, "Did you know she lived in the Vibora Colombian compound most of her childhood and into adulthood?"

Winston raised an eyebrow. "I did not." He sat forward

and laced his hands together. "That could prove to be rather valuable information."

"I thought so."

"Is she willing to talk to me?"

"Seems like it." After a second of internal debate, Phil decided to appeal to Winston's sense of chivalry. "I need you to hear me, Brother. That dude, he's a bad dude. And if you can't give her honest-to-God protection, then you need to leave her alone."

Winston's eyebrows came together as a frown darkened his face. "As opposed to what?"

"As opposed to just taking testimony and leaving her to make her own way." He pointed a finger at Winston. "He'll kill her. He'll probably kill her just for leaving him, but if she testifies against him, he'd definitely kill her and make it hurt the entire time."

"Why do you say that?"

Phil shrugged. "I've seen the inside of the compound, looked into the eyes of the people who work there. He's a bad guy, Winston. E-v-i-l. Trust me."

"I do." Winston sighed and rubbed the back of his neck. "You need to trust me."

He didn't even hesitate. "I do."

"When are you going to bring her to me?"

"What works?"

Winston pursed his lips. "How about Mom and Dad's tomorrow night? She's been wanting you to bring Melissa over ever since Easter."

It was Phil's turn to frown. "Every time I bring Melissa there, Mom is convinced we're about to announce our engagement. It hardly seems fair to go there with her."

"And yet, you enjoy her company so much that she'll likely be at your side anyway. Might as well bring her sister too. It will give Mom some kids to play with."

"Yeah, and turn on the dormant grandmother gene that I bet is just raring to rise up and consume her."

Winston laughed. "You can't possibly be afraid of that woman. She's five feet two inches and a hundred pounds soaking wet."

Thinking of their mother and the fierceness of her personality, Phil said, "Dude, she's much more than that."

"True." Winston leaned back in his chair. "I think us all meeting up at the house will be best. Mom can see Melissa, I can talk to Lola, and she'll be safe there."

"I can just bring her here."

"No way. I already told you that this is a very segregated, secure project. We have a leak somewhere inside our organization. Unfortunately, until we discover just who keeps tipping Vibora off, it's not safe here." He paused. "I've even started checking my office for bugs. Sometimes I wonder if I'm just being paranoid, but that's where I am right now."

"I assume you've checked today, or we wouldn't be having this conversation."

"Correct."

"Right." Phil sighed, trying to wrap his mind around one of his brother's coworkers resorting to bugging another office. "Tomorrow's family dinner it is, then."

"You don't need to sound like it's your own execution." Winston grinned. "You snatched Lola from a café?"

He knew Winston had a way to hear what was happening inside the compound. He must have overheard the discussion about Lola's escape. "Yeah. Driver was distracted by his car being towed."

"Risky," Winston said. "Well done."

"If they'd known there was a threat, they would have had a closer eye on her. As it was, he had no reason to think she'd dart." Phil gave his brother a small smile. "But it was a clever ploy, and in the end it worked."

"Hopefully, she'll testify."

"You need to protect her."

"You've said that already."

"Yes, but you haven't confirmed." Phil slowly got to his feet. "Tell you what. You pursue that vigorously, and I'll consider bringing her to dinner."

Winston sighed. "Phil." He didn't say anything else. Phil understood it to mean that he needed to step aside and let his brother do his job.

"Winston." Phil had no intention of budging and hoped that his brother managed to get a witness protection order in place for Lola and her children. He walked to the door and turned around. "I'll see you at dinner tomorrow."

"Yeah."

Phil drove straight to the hospital and walked into the emergency department, carrying the tote bag with his uniform and kit bag. As he passed curtain area three, a familiar voice stopped him.

"Doctor Osbourne," Addison Carmichael said.

He turned to the blond doctor who had been his lab partner their third year in medical school. She approached and slipped a pen into her jacket pocket.

"Addy. You know how I feel about that title. By the way, happy birthday."

"It would have been happier if you'd come to my party. My husband told me he invited you."

"Sorry. I had company in town. I just dropped them off at the airport."

Addy gestured behind her. "You can still practice here, can't you?"

He shrugged. "I don't know why not."

"I have a teenager with a broken jaw and a couple of missing teeth. I've called for a consult, but they're overloaded with patients today and I could use an extra hand. The sooner we get her set, the sooner the pain is relieved."

He hesitated. He didn't like to practice medicine beyond his duties as a paramedic. It was like a reminder of every bad decision he'd ever made. But if it helped someone in pain, he would do it. "Lead the way."

As he walked into the curtained area, he grabbed a pair of gloves out of the dispenser on the wall. A young woman lay on the bed, tears sliding out of her closed eyes. An older woman with the same color of red hair and porcelain skin stood by her bed, gently brushing the hair from her forehead. She looked up expectantly.

He smiled, thankful he hadn't changed into his EMT uniform yet. "I'm Doctor Osbourne."

"This is Izzy."

"Hi, Izzy," he said gently. He paused at the computer to read the notes, hoping to save the mother from having to answer too many repeated questions. "Hit the diving board, huh?"

"Knocked her out. Lifeguard had to save her. The longest stretch of time in my life."

He skimmed over the images from radiology, then said, "I can't imagine." He pulled up a stool and sat at the head of the bed. "Izzy, this is going to hurt. I'm not going to pretend otherwise. But I need to feel and see as much as I can."

Izzy opened her eyes. He could see the fear on her face, but she nodded. She whimpered only once—when he set the bone—which impressed him. When he finished, he tossed the gloves into the wastebasket and made some notations in the computer. "She's going to need her jaw wired shut. The surgeon on call should be able to talk to you beforehand." After he finished typing, he said, "I've ordered some pain meds that won't counter anything the anesthesiologist will do. Your teeth can be fixed after your jaw heals."

The mom resumed running her fingers through Izzy's hair. "How long will that take?"

"I'm not the one who will do it, but if I was, I'd say four to six weeks." He'd personally say four weeks, but he didn't want to get their hopes up.

Outside, he caught Addy as she walked past. "Can I see you?"

She followed him to the nurses' station. When she leaned against the counter, he said, "Don't do that."

She had the gall to look innocent. "I beg your pardon?"

"I'm not coming back to work as a surgeon. I don't appreciate being ambushed this way."

She raised an eyebrow. "You think I broke her jaw so you could help her?"

"No. I think you had a broken jaw and saw me coming and decided to interfere with my life. Again."

"I can't help it if I think you're the best oral surgeon Miami has seen this generation."

"I cannot possibly be the best. I haven't actually practiced for seven full years."

"And yet you maintain your privileges here, and your

malpractice insurance, and all of your CEUs. You intend on coming back."

He sighed. "Addy."

"No, I hear you." She lifted her chin. "Apparently, Mr. Special Forces soldier finds being an EMT more exhilarating than anything else. Still in the medical field, yes, but none of the responsibilities. I get it." She stepped closer and waved a finger under his nose. "You keep a straight face and tell me that the problems you had eight years ago are still problems you face today. Tell me in all honesty that you haven't developed the maturity and fortitude to withstand the temptation."

He just stared down at her, unwilling and unable to argue her point.

She stepped back. "Exactly. I have patients to see, and I'm sure you have an ambulance to get to."

As she turned away, he said, "Hey, Addy?"

When she turned back around expectantly, he said in a soft voice, "The next time you wave a finger in my face, you might not get it back."

A nurse behind him snickered. Addy pressed her lips together and glared at him as she spun on her heel.

Hector Molina walked across the terra-cotta tiles, his canvas shoes making no sound. He didn't understand why his father had called him out of the meeting with the tenientes. The closed-door meetings allowed for no interruptions.

When he tapped on the door with the heavy gold ring on his middle finger, his father's booming voice bade him to enter. His father stood at the side table next to a potted palm tree, pouring very expensive rum over diamond-clear ice.

"Father," Hector said.

Juan Molina glanced at his son with his black eyes. His thick gray mustache did little to hide the hard lines of his mouth. "Is there a reason you came here without your wife?"

Hector opened and closed his mouth before he said, "She doesn't like taking the children on such a long journey for the short visits."

His father took a sip of the rum, then set the glass down and approached him. His backhanded slap snapped Hector's head back. He knew better than to react or stagger or even hit back. He just held his ground, his face stinging in an all-too-familiar way.

"She's gone," his father said.

"Gone?" Hector searched his father's face for any clue as to what he meant. "What do you mean?"

"I mean, you fool, that she was at a café after taking your children to the zoo. One minute she was there, and the next she was gone. With your children."

Anger bubbled up in his chest. "How?"

"How?" His father went back to his drink. "How is because you are a weak man who employs weak men. She had a driver who was supposed to be her guard. I suggest that you get back to Miami and remove parts of him until you have a satisfactory answer as to how."

When Hector started from the room, his father added, "She has been in this compound her entire life. She knows everyone and everything. We thought she'd be an asset like her father but instead gave her to you as a bride. You'd better pray that you find her before she realizes she could bring this entire organization down."

CHAPTER

★

NINE

OCTOBER 27

Melissa shifted the drink carrier, then hesitated slightly before knocking on the door. Just when she was about to give up and leave, it swung open. Phil stood on the other side, leaning into crutches, his eyes wide with surprise. "Melissa."

"Hi. Is it okay that I just stopped by?"

He looked down at the empty spot his prosthetic usually filled. "Uh, sure. Come in." He moved to the side, surprisingly agile with the crutches.

She could smell fresh soap, noticed his damp hair. "I hope I'm not disturbing you."

"I just got off an overnight shift. The last case required a change of clothes and a shower." He pointedly looked at the clock hanging on the wall above his table. "Are we not meeting at seven?"

She held up the paper bag she carried. "Bagels and lox."

She lifted the drink carrier. "Mango and pineapple smoothies."

He gestured toward the table. She set the bag and carrier next to his open Bible and noticed his prosthetic leaning against the couch. Her eyes skimmed over his legs, but his shorts fell past the edge of his stump.

He waited until she sat down to take a seat himself, leaning the crutches against the kitchen bar. He put a pen in his Bible before he shut it, then stacked it and a leather journal off to the side.

"What are you studying?" she asked as she unpacked the bagels and cream cheese containers. She dug through the bag and pulled out the smoked salmon and capers.

"Gifts and talents." He rubbed his smooth jaw. "I seem to have some."

She couldn't help but chuckle. "You do. What prompted this?"

"A friend I went to medical school with keeps insisting I need to be back at the hospital instead of driving an ambulance." He gestured toward the kitchen. "Do you mind getting plates?"

"Of course not." She walked into the kitchen and paused.

"Above the bar," he said. "Knives are in the drawer in front of you. Coffee should be done brewing."

She gathered plates, paper towels, and knives and carried them to the table, then found cups and poured coffee. She set his in front of him before taking her seat. When he held his hand out, she took it, bowing her head as he asked God's blessing on the food.

As soon as they said, "Amen," Phil asked, "Why the impromptu visit?"

"I wanted to have a conversation with you that wasn't in public." Phil could get grouchy. She'd observed that over the months she'd known him. This appeared to be one of those mornings. "Would you like me to leave while you get yourself together?"

His cheeks turned red, and he glanced at his prosthetic. "Not necessary."

She picked up her coffee and sat back in the chair, staring at his face. He held her gaze for several seconds before looking down at his plate. "Thank you for helping my sister," she said.

He spread a bagel with cream cheese, then piled it with smoked salmon, red onion, and capers. He met her gaze again. "It was important to you. I did it for you."

"Thank you." She pursed her lips as she contemplated what to say next. "And the invite to your parents' home tonight?"

He shrugged. "Winston wants to meet with her in a safe place. He thinks there's a leak in his division."

"Will it be safe for Lola to be there?"

"It will be as safe as I'm capable of making it." He took a bite.

She understood that Phil had some specialized training and that his statement did not come lightly, nor did she take it lightly.

She waited until he swallowed before speaking again. She'd made a decision and planned to follow through, but her stomach had tied itself into painful knots. "I want us to be more than just breakfast buddies."

In the middle of ripping a piece off his bagel, his hands stopped moving, he kept his stare fixed on his plate, and for a count of five, it seemed he didn't even breathe. Then he set everything down and pushed himself up, grabbing his crutches in one movement. Without a word, he disappeared into the bedroom.

Melissa sat frozen. What should she do? Should she leave? Eat? Clean up?

Before she could make up her mind, Phil came back out and sat down, letting the crutches fall to the floor. He put his hand flat on the table, and she could hear a metal object under his palm. He slid it across the table to her.

When he removed his hand, she picked up a large coin. It had a gold "II" in the center of a black diamond, which sat inside a silver diamond with the words "freedom" and "goodwill" in gold. She ran her thumb over the coin. When she looked up, her breath caught in her throat at the intensity in his eyes.

"What's this?"

"One year, eight months, twenty-three days."

She turned it over and saw "NA." "One year, eight months sober? From what?"

He shrugged, and his right knee started bouncing. "Morphine at first. A couple of us thought it would be fun. I was young—I entered medical school at twenty. By the time I realized there was a problem, there was a problem."

She couldn't reconcile the person she knew with the person who'd needed this coin. "It's been a long time since medical school."

"It has. As a resident in a public hospital, I had easy access to narcotics. I wasn't using all the time, but I wanted to be, and that was what I realized. I could go days, weeks, but I thought about it all the time."

Suddenly, the way he kept her at arm's length made sense. It wasn't about his combat injury that had led to the loss of his leg. He clearly wanted to protect her from his struggles with addiction.

Without thinking about it, she reached out and took his hand. He looked at their joined hands as he continued. "I woke up one morning, plotting a way to manipulate records so I could get a high, and it occurred to me that I had a serious problem. I went straight to a recruiting center and volunteered. Thankfully, it had been enough time since my last dose that I passed the drug test, but just barely, I'm sure."

"Did you suffer from withdrawal when you entered the Army?"

"No. Never." After a long pause, he said, "A chaplain in officers' training worked with me, taught me how to pray in a way I'd never known how to before. Once I left training, I didn't even think about it. I had the best job with the best team. The things we did . . ." He pulled his hand away. "And then one day in the jungle of Katangela, everything shifted and changed."

She looked down at the space where his leg belonged. "You lost your leg."

"I was shot. Femoral artery. It ended up getting infected and going septic. Regular IV antibiotics kept me alive, but the pain was something I can't explain. We had to cross the jungle just two days after my surgery. I let them convince me to take morphine." He cleared his throat. "By the time I got to civilization, there was no saving it. Post-surgery was rough, and I fought against getting more medication but gave in a few times."

Tears burned the backs of her eyes. She'd had no idea what he'd gone through, how he'd struggled. "And now?"

A dark look fell across his face. "Now?"

"Do you think every day that you want to do drugs?"

His shoulders barely moved in a shrug, and he gave a small shake of his head. "No. I haven't had an issue since officers' training."

She filled in the gap for him. "When you started praying?"

"Yes. Pretty much."

She'd seen addiction too much in her career. The strength of character he had to see a problem embroiled inside himself, to recognize it and put a stop to it before it manifested into something much more, took fortitude that she admired. It made her love him all the more.

She picked up a knife and spread a bagel with cream cheese. "Okay. Any other skeletons?"

Eventually, his intense gaze fell, and he picked up his bagel again. "I can't think of any I'm willing to let out right now."

"Good."

They ate in uncomfortable silence. Melissa washed her last bite down with a cup of cooled coffee and brushed the crumbs off her fingers. After she took her empty plate and cup to the kitchen, she went back to where he sat, pulling her chair around so that she faced him. He stopped eating and shifted to look at her.

She took a deep breath and reiterated, "I would like us to be more than breakfast buddies. I am very attracted to you. I'd like to date you and consider a future with you. I think you've kept me out of reach long enough." She stood and put a hand on his shoulder. "I'm going to leave. You need to process this, and I don't need to be here for that. If you want to continue to see me, then be there tonight. If not, please don't come. I'll just introduce Winston and Lola and let them have their incognito meeting away from us. I won't bother you with it again." She walked to the door.

"Melissa," he said, the word coated with an emotion she couldn't identify.

Despite wanting to walk away, she turned and looked at him. "Yes?"

Several long heartbeats passed before he said, "I'll see you tonight."

She knew her smile didn't reach her eyes. "I really hope so, Phil."

Long after Melissa left, Phil sat there, the remains of breakfast still in front of him. How could she still want . . . ? He shook his head. She clearly hadn't heard what he had to say, or she wouldn't still want him.

At some point, his phone chimed a text from Winston.

It's me.

Two seconds later, his door swung open.

Winston walked in and paused at the table. His eyes roamed over the takeout bag and the extra cup and plate in the sink. "You and Melissa met here for breakfast this morning?"

"Yes," Phil said. "If you thought I was at breakfast, why are you here?"

"I just came to get the boat keys." He went into the kitchen and slid open a drawer, pulling his keys out. "I have a date tomorrow night and want to go by the boat on my lunch hour and stock it with dinner fixings. I won't get a chance tomorrow."

"A date? I can't think of the last time you did something like that."

"Same, Brother. Same."

Phil grabbed his crutches, then pushed himself up and went to the couch. When he sat down, he started the process of donning his prosthetic.

Winston came out of the kitchen, carrying a cup of coffee. "Oh, by the way, I secured protection for Lola Molina and her two children pending the quality of information she has for me."

Phil analyzed that statement while slipping the silicone casing over his stump. "No deal, basically."

"There is definitely a deal, assuming she has actual information. Has anyone tried to glean that yet?"

"She's only been there for twenty hours, Winston. There's hardly been time for interrogations." He stood so that the prosthetic could vacuum seal to his body. As he put weight on it, he listened for the air escaping. When he heard no more air, he could consider the limb fully sealed.

"It isn't about interrogation, Phil," Winston said. "It's about prosecution. Of course she'll get protection if she has something for which she can testify."

Phil loaded the plates into the dishwasher and refilled his cup with fresh coffee. He added cinnamon to it, then went back into the living room and sat in his recliner. "I look forward to hearing what she has to say tonight."

"As do I." Winston sipped his coffee. "Did you tell Mom they're coming?"

"Yeah. They're doing grouper on the grill." Phil set his

121

coffee on the table next to him and blurted out, "I told Melissa everything."

Winston stared at him for several seconds. "Everything as in why you left the hospital and your residency, et cetera?"

"Yeah."

"What did she say?"

He leaned his head back and looked at the ceiling fan. "She said she wants more from me. If I'm not willing or ready to give it, she wants me not to come tonight. Otherwise, she'll take my presence as a yes."

For a second, neither spoke. Then the room filled with Winston's laughter. Phil glared at his brother.

"I'm sorry," Winston said. "It's just that I love her so much. She's more than perfect for you and your moody self."

Phil scowled. "I'm not moody."

"Dude, you're the epitome thereof." Winston settled more comfortably into the corner of the couch. "She even knows about NA and seven years?"

"Yes. One year, nine months." He took a deep breath. "I even told her about the chaplain in officers' basic. The one who taught me to pray."

"You mean the one who saved your life."

He didn't need to reply. Winston knew he knew.

"By the way, the clock is ticking for the residency application at the hospital. Isn't the deadline mid-November?"

"Yes."

Winston raised an eyebrow. "Are you still thinking about it?"

Phil frowned and shrugged. He looked at the clock. "I need to sleep."

"Yes, you do. You need to get up and make it to Mom and Dad's for dinner. Don't leave your girlfriend waiting."

The heavy air had absolutely no breeze, and the stagnant water of the swamp carried the smell of a millennia of rotting leaves, brush, and trees. Insects hummed all around them. The lightweight airboat tilted this way and that whenever someone moved.

Hector looked out over the swamp and listened to the labored breathing of Sebastian, his wife's driver. He nodded, and one of the two other men he'd brought with him began tossing chicken carcasses into the water. Hector heard the splashing of the alligators as they picked up the scent and came into the water to investigate.

Hector turned toward Sebastian, who sat on his knees with his hands tied behind his back, his head bowed, blood pooling around his body. He had long since given up begging for his life and had just resigned himself to die.

He'd not given Hector anything to help him. When he'd run out of the café to keep the SUV from being towed, Lola and the children had disappeared out the back of the restaurant.

Obviously, she'd had help. Sebastian had been the one in charge of her security. Someone must have been in contact with her.

Who? How?

Hector gestured with his head, and two of his men lifted Sebastian by the arms.

"Wait!" Sebastian said. His one remaining eye was swollen shut, but his mouth still worked. "I remember."

Hector walked up to him. The man stank of urine and

vomit. He held a handkerchief up to his nose to block the stench. "You remember what?"

"The ambulance!"

"What ambulance?"

Sebastian started hyperventilating, and Hector slapped him across the face. "What ambulance?"

"Right after you left for your meeting, an ambulance came. We never found out who called it. They were never alone with her, though."

Right after he'd left. Who would have dared to call anyone but his personal doctor? He nodded and turned his back as the men threw Sebastian into the center of the circling alligators. The frenzied attack lasted only seconds.

Now to find out about this ambulance.

Melissa helped Mathias fit the last piece into the puzzle, revealing a farm scene. "Good job," she said, running her fingers through his black curls. "You like puzzles, don't you, Matty?"

He beamed up at her. "Another one!"

"Well, go get it," she said, grinning. Her nephew jumped up and ran across the recreation room to the shelf that contained the puzzles.

Melissa pushed herself to her feet and wiped off the back of her shorts. Gabriele tottered up to Lola and held out her hand. Lola gave her a red block from the stack in her lap. The toddler smiled and carried it across the room to the tower she was constructing.

"You have great kids," Melissa said.

"They are my whole life."

The ding of the front door opening made Lola's eyes widen.

"Listen to me. We have armed security. Nothing is going to sneak up on you." Melissa walked to the door and lifted her hand in greeting to the tenant, then joined Lola on the couch. "It was just Mr. Kline."

Lola cocked her head to one side. "It's odd that you allow men here."

"Studies show that forty percent of domestic abuse victims are men."

"Hmm." Lola narrowed her eyes. "How do you protect the women from the men here?"

"I've never had an issue."

Mathias picked out a Superman puzzle. He dumped out the pieces, then started carefully assembling them.

Melissa took the moment of peace to ask, "Do you go to church?"

Lola stole a glance at Melissa before refocusing on the kids. "I've been to mass a few times, for weddings and funerals, but not regularly." She paused. "I'm married to an immoral man. God does not want me in His house."

Training kept Melissa from reaching out and grabbing her sister's hand. She wouldn't do anything to startle her like that. But she wanted to impress upon her the sincerity of what she was about to say. "Lola, God loves everyone and wishes for no one to be without Him." She gently and carefully put a hand on her shoulder. "If you'd like to go to church with me, I'd love to talk to you more about it."

Lola looked around, her eyes wide. "I don't know how safe it is."

"You're right. But Phil and I would be with you the whole

time." She bent and helped Mathias with a red piece for Superman's cape. "Just like tonight."

"His brother is a cop?"

"No. State prosecutor. He's been investigating your husband."

"And he can't come here?"

"No, honey, he can't. The fewer people who know where we are, the better."

Lola nodded as she handed Gabriele a blue triangle block. "Okay. I'll meet with him in the safety of a private home. But I don't think I want to risk church."

"Fair enough."

Lola smiled. "Tell me about the paramedic. About Phil."

An unexpected smile came to Melissa's face. She thought about their conversation that morning. "I met him at our church's soup kitchen. He'd just come home from being in the Army."

"How long was he in?"

"Five years. After he lost his leg, he came back home."

Lola's eyes widened. "Lost his leg?"

Melissa was reminded how well Phil moved with his prosthetic and how careful he was to never make it obvious that he wore one. "Yeah. He lost his left leg in combat."

"Wow. I never realized." Lola handed Gabriele a yellow block. "Yellow," she said, tapping it. The little girl giggled as she ran off.

"We started meeting for breakfast a while ago, but it's never really progressed." *Until now*, Melissa thought. She believed he'd be there tonight because she believed God intended for them to be together, and even Phil's grumpiness couldn't outmatch God's design.

"So, how do you define your relationship with him?"

Amazing. Wonderful. Strong and steady. "A friend. Friendship."

Lola stared at her with dark brown eyes that looked much wiser than her age. "But you wish there was more."

"Oh yes. Every moment of every day." Melissa smiled. "I believe one day he'll want that too."

"He's a good man."

"Yes." She bent to the floor and turned a puzzle piece that was frustrating Mathias. "So is his brother. You can trust him."

"But he thinks his department isn't safe."

"And because he believes that, he's one step ahead of them, right?"

"True."

Melissa looked at Mathias and then moved back to the couch. "Is there a reason Winston would want to talk with you?"

"You mean, would I be able to give him information to prosecute my husband?"

"Yes."

Lola looked at her lap, fidgeted with the blocks there. "Yes."

Melissa reached out and laid a hand on her shoulder. "Will you?"

A tear dropped onto Lola's hand. She brushed it away, then wiped her eyes. She still didn't meet Melissa's gaze. "I don't know if I'm strong enough." She took a shaky breath. "But I want to be."

Melissa slipped closer and put her arms around Lola. "I'll be right here."

CHAPTER

TEN

Phil's parents lived in a two-story white stucco house with a red Spanish-style tile roof in a gated community in Coconut Grove. Their backyard had a decorative concrete patio surrounding a kidney-bean-shaped pool with turquoise blue water. Palm trees danced in the breeze. At the end of the patio sat a covered area with a gas grill built into the stone fence and a round table that sat six.

Phil's father had worked as a prosecuting attorney for twenty years before his election to the office of county judge then circuit court judge. Their mother had been a defense attorney but left the practice when they had Winston. She'd homeschooled Winston and Phil, making their education rich with travel and experiences. Both boys began taking college classes during their freshman year in high school and graduated with two-year college degrees under their belts. Now Phil's mom worked as a freelance journalist writing pieces about legal decisions and politics. She'd also been a panelist several times on national news stations as an expert in different legal matters.

Winston and Phil had a standing invitation for Thursday dinner. Often during a shift, Phil would show up with Leslie and grab food to go. He had never invited Melissa to the Thursday dinner, though he had brought her to two holiday meals.

Today, as Phil's eyes adjusted to the dimmer, cooler interior of the house, he wondered if coming tonight was the wisest thing. Maybe Melissa needed more time. Maybe she shouldn't make a decision so rashly after having everything dumped on her.

"Philip," his mom said, coming toward him from the arched doorway to the kitchen. She had her frosted hair pulled up into a ponytail and wore a pink dress that looked like a long golf shirt. Her skin glowed with a healthy tan. "I'm so happy you were off tonight. Winston wasn't positive about you being able to come. I told him you'd be here because you invited guests."

"Hi, Mom." He bent and kissed her cheek. "Thanks for the hospitality."

"Pshaw. You should have had Melissa here again months ago." She patted his cheek. "Does this mean that you're actually official now?"

"I, uh—"

"Candace, I hardly think that's your business." Phil's dad, Benjamin, stood a head taller than his wife. He had blond hair streaked with gray and wore metal-framed glasses, khaki shorts, and a red collared shirt. "Besides, you should let him come all the way into the house before you interrogate him.

That way it's harder for him to escape." He shifted a spatula to his left hand and held out his right. "Hi, Son."

"Dad." Phil shook his dad's hand, then followed him out into the backyard. "Smells amazing."

"Your uncle Harvey went fishing Tuesday. Caught a beautiful grouper."

"Is he coming tonight?"

"No. He dropped the fish off yesterday. He had to work tonight."

Phil's uncle was a fire company captain in Fort Lauderdale. He had helped Phil navigate into his work as an EMT.

"Is the pool good for swimming?" Phil asked. "Melissa's sister has a five-year-old."

"It is," his dad said. "Your mom cleaned it today."

Winston sat at the table with a glass of lemonade at his elbow. "Hey, Bro." He grabbed the pitcher from a bucket of ice and held it up. "Want one?"

"Definitely." He sat and shifted his leg out in front of him. "How's things?"

"Good. I was thinking about getting a tee time for Saturday. You interested?"

Phil shook his head. "No. I have to run a 5K. I promised Leslie I'd run with her."

"I'll go," their mom said. "And Delilah. She's off Saturday."

Phil heard a car door shut and stood. "I got it."

In the driveway, Lola was holding Gabriele. Melissa held Mathias's hand and carried a tote bag.

He smiled. "Back here, guys."

He held the gate open as Lola walked by. Melissa paused next to him with a bright smile on her face that made her brown eyes shine. "I'm glad to see you."

She'd had an entire day to consider what he'd told her, and yet she smiled up at him with warmth. Hope bloomed in his chest. He wanted to pull her to the side and talk to her in ways he'd never felt safe to before, but he had her sister to think about right now.

He smiled and put his hand on her shoulder, then ran it down to her wrist. "I'm glad to see you too."

On the patio, he introduced Lola and the kids to his parents. Winston stood and shook her hand. "Mrs. Molina. Thank you for agreeing to see me."

Her eyes widened—in fear or nervousness, Phil couldn't tell. He gestured toward the house. "Why don't you two get the initial interview over before dinner, then it's not weighing you down. Melissa and I have the kids."

Lola looked at Melissa. "Are you sure?"

"Of course." Melissa scooped Gabriele out of Lola's arms. She walked with Mathias to the edge of the pool as Winston and Lola went into the house. "Do you want to swim, Matty?" she asked.

"Yes!" he said.

As Mathias whipped his shirt over his head, Phil tossed the alligator into the water. Before anyone could react, Mathias jumped into the water.

"Wait!" Melissa yelled too late.

As Phil contemplated jumping in with his prosthetic on, Mathias dog-paddled over to the float and grabbed it.

"Apparently, he can swim," Phil's mom said at his elbow.

Melissa unbuttoned her dress, revealing a dark blue swimsuit with a skirt that brushed the tops of her thighs. "I'll go ahead and get in with him."

Phil's mom offered to take Gabriele, then gestured with her head to the pool. "You should join her."

Phil glared at her. "I don't think so."

From the water, Melissa said, "Can you blow up the ring that's in the tote bag?"

He found the ring with the dolphin pattern and blew it up. When he tossed it into the water, Mathias swam to it and slipped it over his head, hooking it under his arms.

"That's why Lola wanted to stop and buy one," Melissa said. "Do you swim at home, Matty?"

"Yes. In Papa's pool."

Phil sat in the shade while his mom followed Melissa's instructions and found the swim diaper for Gabriele. While she changed the baby, she said to him, "There's no reason not to get into the water."

"Mom."

"No, don't 'Mom' me. If we were alone, you'd have been in the entire time you were here. It's not going to shock her to see you swim."

Embarrassment welled up inside him. It was less Melissa seeing him and more her reaction to Mathias seeing him.

Once Gabriele was ready to go, his mom said, "I'll hand her off to you once you're in the water." She looked at his father. "Benjamin, please go get his crutches."

Phil scowled at her. "I don't need crutches."

"I already got them." His dad grabbed the crutches propped against the shed, then leaned them against the table.

Phil pushed the button on the side of his prosthetic and waited for the release of pressure. He shifted it off and rolled down the silicone cover and the cotton sock, then slipped his shirt over his head. Using the crutches, he made his way to the pool's deep end, then dove in and swam up to where Melissa played with Mathias.

When he surfaced, she grinned at him. "Glad you could join us."

For the next half hour, he played with Mathias, tossing him up into the air and listening to him giggle and squeal. Melissa played with Gabriele on the stairs.

When Winston and Lola came out of the house, Phil studied Lola's face. She had been crying but looked less stressed than when she'd arrived. She went to the stairs of the pool and said to Melissa, "I've got her."

Melissa asked her a question that Phil couldn't make out because Mathias took that moment to squeal and laugh. Lola nodded and smiled, then reached out and hugged her sister. Phil glanced at Winston, who gave him a thumbs-up as he poured fresh lemonade.

When Melissa swam over to Phil, he hooked an arm over the alligator and let his body float. She did the same.

"Everything good?" he asked.

"Seems like. He's going to request witness protection."

"Good." He watched his mom come out of the house, carrying a platter. "Looks like food's about ready."

She looked over her shoulder toward the grill just as his dad lifted the lid. "Mmm, I'm starving." She looked back at him and grinned. "Race you."

Before he could react, she'd kicked off and swam to the side of the pool. She gracefully pushed herself out of the pool, then turned and sat on the side. She hadn't even gotten her hair wet.

"Cheater," he yelled as he scooped Mathias up by the middle and swam him to Lola. He tried to ignore the way she stared at his missing leg under the water and turned back around, swimming to where he'd left his crutches.

When he got out of the water, his mom brought over towels. Melissa took one and wrapped it around herself as she crouched next to him, the towel enveloping her entire body. She was silent for several moments, then stood. "Ready?"

It was as if she knew he wanted her not to watch him as he maneuvered himself up. He was glad she didn't offer help. Instead, she waited patiently until he had the crutches secure under him and the towel around his neck.

His mother sat at the table, chatting with Lola, who used a small patch of grass to change the baby.

From the house, Winston carried a wooden high chair that would scoot up to the table. "Mom keeps this as a physical manifestation of her greatest wish," he said with a teasing tone.

"Bah. I keep it because my nieces and nephews keep having babies. Unlike some sons I know." She handed a plate to Lola. "Go ahead and dish up for Matty. I'll help the baby."

While everyone worked out seating arrangements and food, Phil grabbed his prosthetic leg and took it over to a chair near the pool. He glared at Melissa when she joined him.

"You can't scowl me away," she said.

"Can I have some privacy?"

"Nope. This is a part of you that you've hidden away for too long."

Panic tried to close his throat in. "Melissa."

She waited, eyebrows raised. When he didn't say anything more, she said, "You don't scare me with your grouchy tone and mean face."

"Fine," he huffed. He dried his stump, then slipped the

cotton sock over it, trying not to feel so self-conscious. Once he could walk safely, he ripped the towel from around his neck and tossed it on the chair. "Satisfied?"

"To be part of your life? Absolutely." She smiled up at him, then spun on her heel and joined the rest of his family.

He realized how much of his tension had been released simply at her presence just now. She'd seen him, watched him, and never even blinked. Maybe she could handle something more than just breakfast buddies. Maybe they could have a future together.

Even though he pressed his lips together, he couldn't stop the smile that came at the thought. When he reached the table, it felt right to put his arm around Melissa and hug her close while his father asked God's blessing on their food.

While they dined on grouper, rice, and mango salad, a sense of contentment fell over Phil that he hadn't felt in a long time. He looked at his parents as his dad casually squeezed his mom's shoulder in a movement he had witnessed his entire life. Winston smiled and laughed, relaxed and happy. Melissa's joy at having her sister and nephew and niece with her radiated off her. She kept looking over at him, a glow on her face and in her eyes that made his breath catch.

After dinner, while he and Winston did the dishes, Winston dried his hands and reached into his pocket. "Will you do something for me?"

Phil put the last pan away. "Anything."

His brother held out a thin plastic sleeve containing a micro SD card. "Every step I've ever made toward prosecuting the Vibora cartel has met an unexpected end. Evidence goes missing, logs get changed in the computer, witnesses disappear. Whatever."

Phil took the card from him. "What's this?"

"That is the interview I just did with Lola. It's the original, so it's time-stamped properly."

Phil pulled his wallet out of his shorts pocket and put the SD card into it. "I understand. Consider it safe."

"Thanks. I would love to find out who we have working for Hector Molina."

Phil studied his brother. If anyone could flush out the mole, it was Winston. "Bring him down and you might be able to."

"That is my prayer."

OCTOBER 29

Melissa shifted against the metal picnic table seat and looked around the park. That morning, hundreds of runners had flooded the park for the 5K that benefited the children's hospital. She'd watched a different Phil than the one she knew so well. He stretched, relaxed, and interacted with his partner Leslie in a familiar way that implied a close friendship. They'd crossed the finish line together in the middle of the pack, and Leslie had gone off with her husband to get lunch from a vendor in the park.

When Phil suggested he and Melissa do the same, she'd surprised him with a picnic she'd packed for them. They'd feasted on fried chicken and potato salad, chatting about work and the weather and his brother.

They reached into the bag at the same time for the last piece of chicken. She snagged it before Phil could get to it. She laughed and said, "Eat a pickle," then started to take a bite of the leg.

"Eat a pickle?" Moving faster than she could comprehend, he reached out and tickled her. She bent forward, laughing, twisting to get away. "Eat a pickle?"

Finally, he relented, and she put a hand over her chest and held out the chicken. "I'm happy to share."

He picked up a pickle spear and bit into it. "Thank you," he said with his mouth full, then snatched the chicken out of her hand.

With a shrug, she smiled. She looked around the park, her gaze catching a man tossing a disc to his dalmatian.

"What's the plan with your sister?" he asked.

She thought about Lola's upcoming meeting Monday with the federal marshals. "She's hoping to stay at the shelter as long as she can. It's as secure as a safe house. Even the marshals don't know where it is."

"It's not as secure as a safe house, Melissa. It's just in an unknown location."

"With armed guards."

"True."

She gestured at his steel running prosthetic with the rocker for a foot. "How did it feel?"

He shrugged. "I run all the time. Just not in public with a number on my chest."

She hesitated. "I'd like to go running with you."

"Could you keep up?"

She lifted her chin. "I guess we'll have to see."

"I guess we will." He winked, then lifted his hand to beckon Leslie and her husband over. He shook hands with Darius and pointed at Melissa. "Have you met Melissa?"

"We were together during the race." Darius sat down. "Well done. Leslie's time was better on this one than the last three."

"I always run faster with Phil." Leslie looked in the picnic basket and asked Melissa, "Can I have a cookie?"

"Sure." While Leslie opened the bag, Melissa said, "I was just telling Phil that I'd like to run with him."

"We run twice a week before our shifts. I'll let you know next time."

"Thanks." She looked at her watch. "I have to go. I have a counseling session at two."

After she packed the last of the items into the picnic basket, Phil stood with her. "I'll walk with you."

Melissa waved goodbye to Leslie and Darius and walked to the parking lot with Phil, who carried the picnic basket. After he set it inside her trunk, she opened the driver's door, letting some of the heat out. "Thanks for inviting me to come today."

"Thanks for coming." He leaned against the car. "I guess I'll see you at church tomorrow."

"Yeah." She looked up at him, unsure about the intensity that had darkened his eyes. "You okay?"

He reached out and brushed a strand of hair off her face. "Are you still sure about this? About us?"

She stepped closer to him. "You mean because you're increasingly grouchy and fighting against anything that could possibly be construed as intimate?"

He scowled and she chuckled. "There was a time when I knew exactly how to do this," he said. "I'm not sure I have it in me anymore. You deserve . . ."

Without thinking about it, she reached up and cupped his cheeks. The movement clearly surprised him. "I deserve?"

He closed his eyes and whispered, "A whole man."

"Phil, I wish you could see yourself through my eyes."

She stood on her toes and pressed a soft kiss against his lips. He didn't move. She stepped back and said, "I'll see you tomorrow."

"You will."

He moved back and let her shut the door. As she drove away, she looked in the rearview mirror and saw him still standing where she'd left him. "Please help me, God," she whispered. "Help me reach him."

OCTOBER 30

At the shipping yard, Hector stood next to a tower of containers waiting for transport on the rail line. He stared at the three people who had come to meet with him.

"Explain to me how an ambulance driven by the brother of a state attorney ended up at my house," he said.

One of the men shook his head. "There were no emergency calls made that day."

"And you know this because of the bugs you have placed in my residence?"

"Yes, sir." He slipped his hands into his jeans pockets and leaned his shoulder against the container. "And the directional mics."

Hector put his hands behind his back and stared at the men's feet. "Is it safe to assume someone heard my activities with my wife and called an ambulance from your end?"

"It's possible," another of them said.

Hector shook his head. "Wouldn't you have known?"

With a shrug, he said, "We're not always in the same room, Mr. Molina."

He sighed. "What about the call to the Marshals Service? What can you tell me about that?"

"Winston Osbourne made a call to check on seeking protective custody in exchange for testimony."

Hector's stomach turned to ice. "And?"

"And I think he's supposed to bring them his witness tomorrow."

Hector paced back and forth, his mind whirling with this new information. He wanted to break a bone in the man's face. The man should have started the entire conversation off with that news instead of waiting until now.

Finally, Hector turned around. "Tell me how to find this Osbourne. Can you clean up the trail?"

"I can get into his computer and adjust his notes and clear his logs. What do you want me to do about the Marshals Service?"

He had no insider there. Letting out a deep breath, he said, "Cancel the appointment. Maybe he didn't give them enough information for them to follow up."

"He wouldn't have. He tends to play things close to his vest."

"That will work to our advantage."

The man pulled out a phone. Seconds later, the one in Hector's pocket vibrated. "Osbourne's address," the man said.

CHAPTER

ELEVEN

OCTOBER 31

Leslie drove the ambulance with professional precision, weaving through traffic, dodging cars that didn't pull over fast enough, pausing at intersections to make sure that all traffic stopped. With lights flashing and siren running, they pulled up to the park on the water. Phil ran to the back, opened the door, and grabbed the gurney. By the time he unlocked the wheels and pulled it back, Leslie was there to help him lift it down to the ground.

They threw their gear onto the gurney, then dashed to where the crowd had gathered.

"Excuse us," Leslie said. "Coming through."

Phil wondered what could have attracted so many people. They worked their way through the conglomeration and saw a man sitting on a park bench. From behind, Phil could see the unnatural way his head was cocked. When they got around the bench, he froze.

His eyes took in the sight, but his brain refused to process it. Sitting there, blood staining his blue dress shirt and dripping down his pants to plop onto his patent leather shoes, was Winston. On the bench next to him, his hand rested on a severed hog's head.

"Winston?" Leslie breathed, then rushed forward.

Phil beat her to him. He didn't bother with gloves. He pressed his fingers against his brother's neck and almost cried out when he felt a weak pulse. A surge of fear tried to get in the way of what he knew to do next. His mouth went dry and blood rushed in his ears.

For a tiny stretch of time, he closed his eyes and tried to dig into his training, to steady himself so that he could work efficiently and save his brother. Adrenaline flooded through him, making him shake, his thoughts racing far faster than his physical body could respond to mental commands.

"Can you hear me, Winston?" he asked, lifting his brother's suit jacket. He felt as if he swam deep under water, as if his shaky fingers and arms were weighted down.

Leslie was holding a stethoscope to Winston's chest. "Tension pneumo," she said. "Weak heart." It took hours for her to speak those words, for Phil's racing brain to frame them into the proper context.

He ripped open Winston's shirt. Buttons flew all around them. Using the scissors he carried in his cargo pocket, he cut off Winston's tie and cut open the blood-stained T-shirt. He found two stab wounds—one in the left abdomen, one in the right chest. He looked at his brother's back. One more there, terrifyingly near the spine.

"Live. You have to live," he breathed.

Moving with efficiency born in combat, he laid Winston down on the bench, then opened the chest tube kit. In the back of his mind, he knew the crowd observed, snapping pictures with their phones and gasping, but he didn't let their presence prevent him from doing his job. As soon as he had the chest tube inserted, he and Leslie prepared to shift Winston onto the gurney. Out of his peripheral vision, he saw the police arrive.

He's going to die.

The thought came out of nowhere, and Phil felt like he might freeze again. His brain battled with itself in a running internal argument. *He's not going to die!*

"Live, Winston. Hang on!"

His brain has been deprived of oxygen too long. Might get him on a respirator, but what kind of life will he have?

Stop it! We got here fast. He can make it!

While the police worked to get the crowd back and secure what they could of the scene, Phil strapped Winston to the gurney as Leslie started an IV. As soon as she taped it down and they hung the bag, they pushed Winston to the ambulance. Nothing happened as quickly as Phil would have liked.

"I'll drive," Leslie said, stating the obvious.

Phil was already in the back, opening gauze pads and a package of hemostatic gel that would help stop the bleeding. A red haze filled his peripheral vision as anger and fear pumped through his body with every beat of his heart. Who would do this to Winston? How had this happened in broad daylight?

As he worked on each wound, he prayed out loud. "God, this is going to take You."

143

The wounds are mortal. You know that. This ambulance may as well be a hearse.

Stop that! Not now!

Before they got to the hospital, Winston opened his eyes.

Thank You, God. Thank You, Father God!

In that heartbeat, a voice spoke directly into his heart. *Peace. Be still.*

In the wake of that command, a sense of calm overtook him. His hands stopped trembling, and his heartbeat began to slow.

Winston looked at him right in the eye. He looked lucid. He tried to take the oxygen mask off with blood-soaked fingers.

Phil scooted over to his brother's head and laid his hand over the mask. "Hey, you have to leave this on. I put in a chest tube, and you are really low on red cells right now. I thought about stitching up the wounds, but I'm not technically allowed, and I don't want to make more work for the hospital docs."

The mask fogged up as Winston tried to talk. Phil shifted it to the side and leaned his head closer to his brother's mouth.

"Vibora," Winston said. "Recording?"

Phil's stomach twisted. "Yes. Don't talk."

He still had the SD card in his wallet. He put the mask back over his brother's mouth and braced his body as the ambulance pulled into the bay.

Winston grabbed his wrist. With an urgency in his eyes he said, "Love you, Phil. Tell Mom. Dad. Love them."

"Tell them yourself! You're going to make it. You're going to be just fine!" Phil said.

The ambulance came to a stop. Phil shifted, and his prosthesis caught on the side of Winston's gurney. Letting out a growl of frustration through clenched teeth, he twisted his body so he could be at the doors and ready to jump out the second they opened.

Vibora.

At least he knew who. Right now, though, he had to work. Pushing his rage into a box and shutting the lid with the promise of opening it as soon as possible, he let out a slow breath.

The ambulance doors opened. As he hit the ground, he said to the attending nurse who met him, "Thirty-eight-year-old, multiple stab wounds. Chest tube administered in the field for tension pneumo. Hemostatic tissue applied en route. BP is 70/40, pulse 120."

They whisked his brother away. Phil stared at the doors after they clunked shut.

Leslie appeared at his side. "Go on in there. I got this."

He looked down at his blood-covered hands, at the bloody finger marks on his forearm that Winston had left behind, and then at her. "I need to call my parents."

She nodded. "You need to wash up first. Come on."

He knew he should pray right now but suddenly couldn't. Leslie put a hand on his arm and led him into the emergency room. At the bathroom door, she handed him a surgical scrub kit. "The brush in there will help."

At first, when he slid his hands under the water, nothing happened. It was like the blood clung to his skin. His eyes burned at the sight, and he was terrified that they'd never wash clean. When he applied the soap and started scrubbing, the water ran off in a pink, foamy whirlpool. His hands started to shake until he gripped his fingers together, struggling to breathe evenly. As he scrubbed his brother's blood from his fingers, a verse came to his mind unbidden.

For I know the thoughts that I think toward you, says the Lord, thoughts of peace and not of evil, to give you a future and a hope. Then you will call upon Me and go and pray to Me, and I will listen to you. And you will seek Me and find Me, when you search for Me with all your heart.

He couldn't focus on a prayer right now. He needed to get through this on his own. There would be time to pray when he knew Winston was out of the woods.

By the time the water ran clean, he felt nauseated, light-headed. He closed his eyes, sweat pouring down his face.

Control. Discipline. React later. Now he needed control.

Eventually, he managed to scrub his nail beds clean. He threw away the brush and dried his hands with paper towels. When he put his hand on the door to the bathroom, he hesitated. He didn't want to think about what waited for him out there. Finally, he pushed through.

Addy stood at the admittance desk, talking to Leslie. She looked up as soon as the door opened, as if she was listening for the sound. "Leslie just told me that it's Winston."

He tried to generate some emotion, but he had shut everything down. That had been his coping mechanism in combat, but it had taken everything to do it today. "What does it have to do with you?"

She slipped her hands into her jacket pockets. "I'll make sure someone knows you're waiting."

After she walked away, Leslie looked at him with a raised eyebrow. "Really?"

He turned his back on her and dialed his father's cell phone. His dad would do better than his mom with this kind of information.

"Son, hello. I thought you were working today."

"Winston was stabbed." No sense playing around with polite exchanges of pleasantries.

After a three-second pause, his father asked, "Which hospital?"

Phil told him where to come and ended the call.

Leslie had her back to him with her phone to her ear. When she turned around, she said, "I called the shop. Red said to tell you to stay put." She stepped forward and put a hand on his arm. He fought the urge to flinch away. "Do you need me to stay?"

"No." When her face fell, he relaxed slightly, trying to generate his appreciation for her friendship without giving his armor a crack that would break him down all the way. "Thanks, though. Go take care of business."

He leaned against the concrete wall next to a fading poster about mask wearing and social distancing and crossed his prosthetic leg over his good one. He slipped his hands into his pockets, watching the door to the back. He knew better than to try to go back there. If Addy even thought for a minute it might be possible, she would have accommodated him. No, he'd have to wait out here while they examined, stitched, and sewed his big brother and likely prepped him for surgery.

Vibora had done this. Winston had confirmed it. It looked like Phil would need to have a word with Mr. Hector Molina and explain the difference between wise decisions and foolish decisions.

Soon, people in police uniforms filled the waiting area. That was interesting. Maybe Vibora had gotten a cop too?

A man in a shirt with the Florida Bureau of Investigation logo on the chest approached him. "Phil, right?"

He nodded but did not offer his hand to shake.

"I'm Drew Burgess. I've been working with your brother."

Phil unclenched his jaw to speak. "Nice to meet you."

"Your brother is a great man. We all have nothing but respect for him and the work he does."

"He does good work." Phil watched the doors open, and his parents rushed in, looking around. "Excuse me."

He walked toward them. His mom looked up at him, her eyes swimming with worry. "Phil!"

"Mom." He hugged her, breathing in the familiar smell of her hair. That was almost enough to crack the shell around his emotions, but he pulled them in. His mother needed strength, assurance. He turned to his dad. "Dad."

"Any information?"

"I took the call. Leslie and I. I did what I could." With a harsh sound, he cleared his throat. His mom put an arm around his waist. "It's bad."

A sound came out of his mom, and her arm tightened. His dad repeated his question. "Do you know anything yet?"

"No, sir. I've just been waiting."

Always the leader, his father looked around. "I'm going to check in at the desk and let them know we're here."

When he walked away, Phil's mom looked up at him. "Do you have any friends back there?"

He pulled her close. "Yes, ma'am. They know I'm here."

In the counseling room, Melissa kept the light moderately low. Quiet stringed music played in the background. Sometimes her residents didn't want to speak, and she never wanted to have the silence overwhelm them. Fresh flowers sat on the little table under a window, and a desk fountain provided a soothing trickling-water sound.

Melissa handed the stoic woman in front of her a tissue. Pam's eyes swam with tears that she refused to let fall.

"It's okay, Pam," Melissa said. "This is a safe place."

Pam cleared her throat. "I don't know how to feel anything anymore. He stripped all of it away from me."

She clutched a rosary so hard that her knuckles turned white. Melissa took that as a safe sign to go forward with faith-based counseling. "I know it feels like that. Emotions probably brought out a darker side to your husband. Better to keep an even keel and not rock the boat." She reached forward and cupped Pam's hand in both of hers. "But God has given us feelings for a reason. And we feel everything so very deeply. They will gradually come back to you the longer you're safe. A bird flying might make you smile. A memory might garner tears. Just let them flow as they come and remember to relax."

Sharon appeared in the doorway. "I'm sorry, Melissa. Excuse me."

Melissa looked at her, confused. Deep counseling sessions did not get interrupted for any reason. "I beg your pardon?"

Sharon made a small gesture with her head, so Melissa got up and went toward her. As soon as she was in hearing distance, Sharon said, "Winston Osbourne is in critical condition. Check your phone."

Melissa looked back at Pam. "Pam, Sharon will finish up our hour. I'm sorry. I have a family emergency."

Even though she hated to waste a second, she went into her office and tossed her notebook on her desk, then grabbed her purse and phone. As she walked toward the exit, she turned her phone on and saw two text messages from Phil's partner, Leslie:

Keeps going to voice mail. Please call.

Winston was stabbed. Phil is at the ER. Sending details.

She scanned the name of the hospital, then shot Leslie a confirmation that she'd seen the messages.

Winston was stabbed? How did that happen? Had someone mugged him downtown?

Traffic was heavier than she would have liked. She had to dart in and out of lanes and go down a couple of back roads before she finally parked in the hospital garage. She grabbed her phone and purse and found the entrance to the emergency room.

As she walked in, she scanned the crowd. Leaning against the wall, his face a stony mask, was Phil. Her eyes roamed the chairs near him where his mother and father sat before she went straight to him.

When he saw her, his shoulders went back slightly, his chin lifted. She stopped in front of him and looked into his eyes, reading the warring emotions that he didn't let out. Without a word, he reached for her and pulled her to him, wrapping both arms tight around her.

As a trained counselor, she thought she would have all the correct words to say in the perfect order, but she had nothing. Instead, she closed her eyes and silently prayed, just letting her heart talk to God.

Finally, Phil spoke. "It's bad."

"I can tell." She pulled back and looked up at him. "Do you know what happened?"

"We were called to the scene."

Her breath caught in the back of her throat. "Oh no!"

"It was good I was there. I can move faster, think faster." He covered his face and rubbed his eyes, then slipped his hands into his pockets. "Combat experience."

"Right."

Emotion swirled in his eyes, and he looked up at the ceiling. "He was just sitting on a park bench, looking at the water. His hand was resting on a pig's head, like he was petting a dog or something."

Her mouth went dry. "What?"

"I guess the Vibora cartel isn't impressed with his investigative skills."

She took a step back from him. "Vibora? Are you sure?"

"It's what he said." His face darkened further. "They must have found out that Lola is testifying."

Thoughts whirled through her mind. "Is Lola safe?"

He shrugged and shook his head. "I don't know. I think he was going to start the witness protection request today."

"That's my understanding." She rubbed her arms, suddenly aware of the air-conditioning. Before she could say anything more, Phil tensed up and focused on something behind her.

A doctor in green scrubs walked their way. He had curly black hair and wire-rimmed glasses. "Mr. and Mrs. Osbourne?"

Phil's parents stood. His dad put an arm over his mom's shoulders. Phil joined them.

"There's a family room this way," the doctor said. "Let's go in there."

Melissa started to step aside to wait for them, but Phil grabbed her hand, so she followed his parents with him. In the family room, the doctor gestured to the couch, and Candace and Benjamin sat. Melissa stood next to Phil by the door, her stomach twisting in a thousand different knots, clutching Phil's hand and trying to read the doctor's face.

"Winston had three stab wounds, a collapsed lung, and a lot of internal bleeding," the doctor said. "We gave him four units of blood and did our best to repair the damage, but it was too extensive. Despite our best efforts, I'm very sorry, but he died."

The silence that descended in the room felt like an actual weight. Finally, Candace sniffled and gasped. "Died?"

Phil stiffened next to Melissa, then pulled his hand away. She looked at him but could get absolutely no reading from him. He turned and rested his shoulder against the wall, putting his back to her. Knowing the intense conflict inside him and not wanting to interfere in his process, she quietly opened the door and slipped out into the hall.

A sob welled up in her chest. Needing to contain it, she put her hand over her mouth, bending forward at the waist. Winston was a good man, a noble man. He'd fought for his community his entire career. In the years that Melissa had known him, she'd always liked him. Phil loved him so much. How was he going to get through this?

NOVEMBER 1

Photos of Winston covered the long dining room table. Melissa picked up the one of Winston and Phil dressed as Batman and Robin and smiled. She couldn't believe she had more tears left in her body, yet they filled her eyes again and slipped down her cheeks.

Candace found one of a teenaged Winston standing next to their pastor. "His baptism day," she said, setting it on the pile to display for the funeral. "He was seventeen. All of his church friends had done it years before, but he was so careful about all of his life decisions."

Phil came into the room and stopped. Melissa's heart twisted at the wrecked look on his face, at the slight droop in his shoulders.

He cleared his throat with a harsh sound. "I came to see if you need help."

Candace walked over to him. She framed his face with her hands in a natural movement, a movement that told Melissa she had touched him like this many times before. Phil closed his eyes as if drawing strength and energy from his mom.

She released him and stepped back. "Can you go get Winston's suit from his apartment? The funeral director called and asked for it."

His face lightened, as if he was happy he had a mission to accomplish. "Sure."

Candace walked to the buffet cabinet and opened the top drawer, removing a small pad and a pencil. She wrote and spoke at the same time. "Navy suit." She glanced at Phil. "Do you know which one? He wore it to your dad's appointment to the circuit court last year."

"Yes, ma'am."

"White shirt, undershirt, blue socks. Black belt and shoes." She looked at him again. "Make sure the shirt has

French cuffs. And I would love it if you could find his ship's anchor cuff links."

He shook his head. "I don't think he kept anything valuable in that apartment."

She sighed. "You're right. They're probably on his boat."

"I can go there too."

After she tore off the sheet of paper, she handed it to him. "Thank you."

He brushed his lips over her cheek. As he started from the room, he stopped at Melissa's chair and put a hand on her shoulder. "Do you want to ride with me?"

She had a feeling he'd rather be alone, and she didn't think Candace did. Despite wanting very much to go with him, she shook her head. "I'll help your mom. There are so many wonderful pictures to sort through."

He gave her shoulder a brief squeeze and left.

Melissa went back to the stack of photos. There were so many good ones. She didn't know how they'd choose what to display. She picked up a picture of Winston in front of a judge on what looked like a stage and placed it on the "keep" stack.

Candace smiled when she looked at it. "Our homeschool co-op did *To Kill a Mockingbird*. Winston played Atticus. He was perfect for the part."

Fresh tears burned in Melissa's eyes. "I can see that."

After a few quiet moments, Candace asked, "How is Lola?"

"Scared." That was a very tame word compared to the reality. "She struggles with feeling like Winston's death is her fault."

Candace gasped. "I didn't realize that."

With a shrug, Melissa said, "It's basic psychology, especially of a battered spouse whose husband is retaliating. It's one of the things we focus on in counseling. I'm not surprised by the emotions, I just need to help her work through them and understand them."

"Would you rather be with her?"

She studied Phil's mother. An inner strength shone through her, even in the midst of such unimaginable grief. "No. I'd rather be here, helping you in any way I can. Lola understands that."

Candace sat and ran her fingertip over Winston's face in a family picture. Melissa's heart broke again.

"What will Lola do?" Candace asked. "Stay at your home?"

"We don't know what will happen next. We're just waiting for the US marshals to contact Lola about witness protection. Winston indicated that was next."

They worked quietly for some time, then Candace said, "I know my son. He had contingencies."

Melissa hoped she was right. She could keep Lola safe for only so long. Lola insisted her husband would find her. After knowing what the Vibora cartel had done to Winston, Melissa believed Hector would hurt anyone who got in the way of him finding his family. They needed more protection than she could give them.

CHAPTER
★
TWELVE

Phil used his key to let himself into Winston's apartment. He'd steeled himself the entire drive over to breach his brother's doorway.

He had not let himself grieve yet. Grieving would involve letting go of the tightly maintained control he kept on his emotions. When the grieving started, it might consume him. He had things to do before he could allow himself that luxury.

The gaping hole in his heart physically hurt. He and Winston had always been so close. He honestly didn't know how he could go forward with life without knowing his brother had his back. How did one even start back up again?

Those thoughts fled when he stepped into the apartment and surveyed the scene.

Winston was a fastidious person. Everything had a place, and many of those places were labeled so there could be no doubt about where something went.

Which was why when he walked into the destruction of the apartment, he paused, not even certain he was in the right place.

Stuffing spilled out of rips in the couch, furniture lay tipped over, plants were unearthed and the dirt strewn about. In the kitchen he found a mound of dried food piled among scattered empty boxes and packages. The refrigerator and freezer doors stood open along with all the cupboards.

His stomach churning, he went into the bedroom. The mattress had slashes all through it, and the clothes lay in heaps, strewn out of the closet. He checked the bathroom, making sure the person who'd done this wasn't still there.

Rage bubbling through his entire system, he found the blue suit among the piles of clothes. He picked a wooden suit hanger up off the floor of the closet. As he bent to get the jacket of Winston's suit, someone tackled him from behind.

Completely caught off guard, he fell to the ground, and the breath escaped his lungs with a loud grunt. He lifted his body enough to bring his elbow up hard, connecting with his attacker's jaw. He gained enough traction to roll out from under the man and get to his hands and knees.

The man had dirty-blond hair and pale gray eyes. Already, his jaw showed the mark from Phil's elbow strike. He rushed forward, and Phil rolled away and got to his feet, still clutching the hanger. He held it in front of him like a knife.

The man stood and drew an automatic pistol from its holster. He leveled the muzzle at Phil, who shook his head and said, "Dude, don't point your gun at me."

"Where is it?" Dirty Blond demanded.

He glanced over the man's shoulder and widened his eyes, then lifted his arms as if in defense. The ruse did exactly what he intended it to do, making the man glance behind him for whatever impending threat Phil saw.

Phil used the opportunity to lash out with the hanger like a baton, hitting his opponent's wrist hard enough to stun him, draw a little blood, and make him drop the gun. Dirty Blond howled in pain and clutched his hand, falling to one knee. As Phil scooped up the pistol, the man charged him, hitting him in the abdomen with his shoulder.

They fell backward, and Phil shifted to roll. He punched without thinking, hitting Dirty Blond in the right eye. The man punched back, clipping Phil in the jaw. As his head flew back and his neck bones cracked like knuckles, he lost his hold on the gun. Dirty Blond pushed and shoved until Phil lay on his side. The man's right hand pressed against his throat, then suddenly relented.

As he took a deep breath, Phil heard a metallic click and reacted to the flash of the blade before his brain fully registered "knife." He kicked up hard with his knee, using his prosthetic like the carbon-fiber club it was. Instead of connecting with Dirty Blond's groin, his prosthetic leg got deflected by the knife blade, which made a sound like someone keying a car as it scraped down the side of his artificial shin.

The man cursed and lifted his arm. Before he could bring the blade down again, Phil brought his arms up like a striking serpent, then gripped the man's wrist like a vise. He moved as fast as his leg would let him, turning his body and throwing his weight to one knee. The man broke free and crouched, switching the knife to his free left hand. He lunged around, and Phil blocked as he came to his feet, punching down on his forearm.

Phil grabbed the man's left wrist and used it for balance.

He spun like a ballet dancer, lashing out with his elbow to his opponent's neck and spine. He twisted hard and threw the man to the ground, releasing him, then struck him in the throat with two fingers. He had just wanted to make Dirty Blond drop the knife. But the Army hadn't trained Phil to pull punches, and his strike hit its mark, collapsing the man's windpipe.

Dirty Blond dropped the knife and clutched his throat with both hands, gasping for air that would never reach his lungs. His eyes widened and he looked suddenly panicked, struggling to breathe, but he made no sound.

Phil groaned. "No!"

He had not wanted to kill this man or remove his ability to speak. He had wanted to squeeze every bit of information out of him that he could until he knew everything about everyone involved in Winston's murder.

He could beat himself up over this later. Letting go of his frustration for the time being, he retrieved the pistol and jogged to the kitchen. He tossed the pistol onto the counter and surveyed the destruction around him. Winston stored stainless steel straws in a Miami Dolphins cup atop the fridge. Among the wreckage, Phil spotted some of the straws and picked one up, then ran back to Dirty Blond. Without hesitating, he used the razor-sharp knife and sliced into the nearly unconscious man's neck. He inserted the straw until he heard the release of air, then ensured he wouldn't need to perform CPR. In a few seconds, he heard normal breaths.

Suddenly, Phil's bloodied hands started shaking. He went into the bathroom and washed the blood off his hands for the second time in two days. He stared at his reflection in the mirror. It glared back at him with dead eyes and stoic contempt. What had just happened?

He opened the little linen storage closet beside the shower. It had not been ransacked, and Phil found the sports tape right where it should be.

He went back into the bedroom. Dirty Blond lay where he'd left him, unconscious now. Phil cut a few six-inch lengths of the tape and secured the straw into place so it wouldn't slip out or, worse, slip in too far and damage something permanently. Then he searched through the man's pockets, looking for more weapons or some identification. The guy had a set of handcuffs and a heavy keychain in one pocket.

Phil pulled out a flip wallet. Special Agent Thomas Simpson of the US Drug Enforcement Agency.

What?

Using Winston's landline, he dialed 911. When the operator answered, he rattled off Winston's address, identified himself, and requested an ambulance. Instead of staying on the line, he pulled his own phone out of his pocket and called his dad.

"Dad," he said, nausea churning his stomach, "I need your help."

CHAPTER

★

THIRTEEN

NOVEMBER 4

The day of Winston's funeral, a storm hit south Florida with thick black skies and heavy wind that drove giant raindrops against Phil's windows. The pelting sound and occasional blast of thunder reminded him of distant small arms fire and artillery.

The darkness and the raw, destructive power of the storm perfectly suited Phil's mood. He stood in his old bedroom and looked out at the pool that churned with the wind and rain, watching palm trees dip and dive in the tumultuous air. Every time lightning struck, the entire world turned to a tableau of silver and shadow. His throat burned with his need to scream and rage. He felt the temptation to get high whispering for his attention. Instead, he clutched his NA coin and prayed for fortitude and the wisdom to know what to do next.

He ignored the knock on the door the first time. When his phone chimed a text, he didn't read it. He knew what it said. Melissa was at his door. If he ignored her, maybe she'd go away.

The second knock pulled him out of his head, and he glared at the door.

"I'm just going to wait out here for you," Melissa said through the wood.

With a sigh he crossed the room and threw the door open. Melissa stood there in a simple black dress and a pearl necklace. "May I come in?"

Without a word, he stepped back, and she came just far enough into the room to allow him to shut the door behind her. She looked around the large space—the four-poster bed with the blue cover, the bookshelf stocked with science fiction adventures, the shelves crowded with martial arts trophies. She crossed over to a wall and examined the box frame containing all of his tae kwon do belts through his second dan.

Melissa walked to the window where he'd spent the last hour. "Do you ever go out on the balcony?"

He scowled at her. "I used to read out there. I haven't been up here since I moved back."

She put her hands behind her and turned to face him. "Leslie came and went. She said not to bother you."

His eyebrow quirked. "And yet here you are."

"Here I am." She lifted her chin in a way that made him want to kiss her. "I've left you alone for three days. I think it's time to bother you."

His lip lifted in a snarl. "Is that what you think?" He collapsed into his reading chair and lay his head back, closing his eyes. "Whatever."

He heard her cross the room and crouch next to the chair. He jumped when she touched his hand. Opening his eyes, he saw tears streaming down her face.

"I'm so sorry, Phil. What can I do?"

Obviously, she couldn't do a thing. Here he sat, hours after burying his only brother, days after nearly killing a DEA agent, waiting to find out if he would be charged with felony assault or if the charge would morph into murder.

At what point had everything led to this moment? Winston Osbourne was a good, moral man who loved his country, loved his city, and served it with a passion that Phil had always admired. To have his possessions reduced to a pile of destruction and his life ended decades too soon filled Phil with a vile, dark feeling.

He didn't even care what he was charged with at this point. He hadn't been arrested on-site. The environment covered with Agent Thomas Simpson's fingerprints, the trace evidence on his hands and clothing, the condition of the area around the fight—it all corroborated Phil's story.

But he'd likely fatally injured a law enforcement officer. Evidence could go missing, reports could change, and the system Winston served could turn on him in a second if the right people took over the investigation.

The kind of people Vibora obviously controlled.

"Nothing," he finally said in response to Melissa's question.

"Nothing?"

He looked down at the hand she held, remembering the way Winston's blood had stained it. "We were in the desert a while back. We'd gone into a village looking for a contact there that had a map of a secret base. It was an ambush.

One of our guys, Travis Fisher, got shot. I was fresh in the unit. A puppy. Cocky. Stupid." He shook his head. "Most men with my job didn't have medical degrees, hadn't done an ER rotation in a Miami trauma center. I thought I could handle anything. Trying to keep Fisher alive while he told me about his son and his plans to be a chef was about the limit of what I could handle." He paused. "Almost quit that day. Hard not to take my weapon and just walk into the wall of enemy fire and take as many out with me as I could."

Melissa sniffled and closed her eyes, resting her forehead against their joined hands. The old Phil, the whole and complete Phil, would have tried to comfort her, would have been touched at her compassion and emotional reaction to his pain.

He was no longer the old, whole Phil. He hadn't known him in a long time.

"I learned a lot that day. I learned how to disengage. How important it was to stay clinical, focused."

She sat back on her heels. Her eyes were red, watery. "Are you trying to say you're unable to feel? Because, quite frankly, that's absurd. I can see the emotion that you try so hard to suppress. It's all just simmering under the surface of your stoicism."

"You see what you want to see. You always have."

She stood. "This is not the day for a conversation like this."

His voice rising, he snapped, "Then why are you here?"

She snapped back, "Because I love you, you fool. You want to sit and brood? Fine. Leave your family downstairs with their funeral guests and make your mother cope with it without your help. Great. But don't lash out at me and try to make me hate you, because that won't work." She walked to the door. "I know men need time because of the way their brains are wired. I thought I'd given you enough time. My mistake. Call me when you're ready to see me again."

The door shut behind her. He leaned his head back again. His heart physically ached. He wanted to go be with his parents, but he couldn't face the crowd, so he just sat.

An hour went by before he heard another tap on his door. He knew it wouldn't be Melissa. "Come in."

Delilah breezed in with a slice of key lime pie on a little white plate. "I snagged you the last piece. I know it's your favorite."

Phil looked at it, and tears burned his eyes. "Did you make it?"

"Honey, I made three." She set it on the table next to him and walked over to the window, then crossed her arms as she stared out into the storm. "Looks like God's as angry as you are."

"Don't know why. He's got Winston now."

She chuckled. "He sure has." She grabbed the desk chair and carried it over to sit across from him. "Your mama is hurting."

"I know." He rubbed his eyes. "I can't deal with the people."

"I know. She's up in her room now. I thought you'd want to know that." Delilah reached for his hands, held them between hers. "I'm awfully proud of you, boy. You've turned out to be an incredible man. It's an honor to have been a part of your entire life."

"It's not been an easy life."

"Sugar, no one has an easy life. Anyone who says they do is lying." She settled back in the chair. "But you and Winston had a good life complete with loving, stable parents who taught you to love Jesus. Good home. Can't ask for a better start."

He didn't disagree. He shifted, rubbing his left thigh.

Delilah continued. "I saw your girl leave."

"She's not my girl."

She snorted. "Yeah, tell that to someone who doesn't know better."

"Dee—"

"Fine." She stood and bent over to kiss the top of his head. "Go sit in there with your mama. She'd rather have you or your dad than me, and he's dealing with guests." On her way out of the room she said, "Eat your pie first, though. It will make you feel better."

The idea of consuming anything made his stomach recoil. He ignored the plate and left his room.

Phil sat in the wingback chair in his father's study and stared at the photo of his father with Vice President Randal Myers. They'd met when Phil received his Bronze Star for Valor after the mission in Katangela.

His father hung up the phone. "No charges."

"Against me or him?"

"They're still waiting to see if he lives. But he's facing breaking and entering, assault with a deadly weapon, and probably a host of other charges." He walked around his desk and sat in the facing chair. "You did the right thing, defending yourself."

Phil snorted. "Is that what you think is wrong? Dad, I promise you, I've been in worse situations. What I'm trying to understand is how deep this goes. Winston was working in a joint operation with the DEA, right?"

"Right. Investigating a Colombian cartel that has a base here in Miami."

"Yes. Vibora. It means viper. He told me that Vibora did this to him, so we know it was them."

His dad's lower lip trembled, and he cleared his throat. "Correct."

"And Winston suspected someone in his office of working for Vibora. I come upon a DEA agent also assigned to that team who tried to kill me. So, who else?"

"We have no way of knowing."

"Exactly. In the meantime, we have Lola Molina, who can testify against her husband and his cartel, and we don't know who we can take her to. We can't trust the state attorney, we can't trust the DEA. What do we do? Where do we go? FBI?"

His dad rubbed his eyes. "How can we know?"

"I have no idea." Phil looked at the photograph again. "We have friends in high enough places that we should be able to protect a young woman and her two children."

"We should, yes." His dad looked up at the ceiling. "My biggest concern is that we'll bring her out of the protection offered by the shelter and make a mistake, trust the wrong person. Clearly, Winston did." His words ended with an abrupt gasp. A tear welled up in his eye and threatened to slip down his cheek.

Phil reached over and put a hand on his dad's knee. "We aren't going to solve this tonight, Dad. Lola's safe with Melissa. We need to mourn right now." He stood. "Thank you for being the point of contact with my attorney."

"Well, Hamilton and I go back to law school. He'd rather talk to me than you."

Phil chuckled. "Let me know what the bill is."

As he started from the room, his dad said, "Are you okay? Have you been to a meeting since the attack?"

He paused at the door and slowly turned around. "I'm good, Dad. I haven't been to a meeting, but I can go if it will ease your mind."

His dad studied him, then said, "I trust you."

Those words meant more to Phil than he could ever express. "Thanks. Good night."

"Good night, Son."

Melissa used a toothpick to poke at the pickle on her plate. Her uncle Alejandro Leon refilled her water, then perched against the edge of the counter. His deli had closed twenty minutes ago. From about an hour before opening to the moment he locked the front door, he had a line out the door six days a week. Melissa had worked through high school and college at the deli. The constant stream of people from all over the world never ceased to amaze her.

"How was the funeral?" her uncle asked.

"Sad." She gestured toward the glass doors. "Weather fit."

"I thought about you on my way in this morning."

A young man in a Leon's Deli T-shirt appeared in the kitchen doorway. "Yo, Alejandro. Rub's all on the brisket. What next?"

"Put the rack in the smoker. Make sure you secure it level." He shook his head as he looked back to Melissa. "You ready to come back to work for me? I could use someone who knows what to do and just does it without seeking constant approval."

Just the thought exhausted her. "I'm too old."

"Yeah, me too." He pointed at the sandwich. "You want to wrap that and take it with you?"

"No. I'll eat out of the order I'm taking." On Fridays, Leon's Deli donated a meal to the shelter, giving Melissa's cook the night off.

"Edmund should be finished loading it." He turned and yelled to the back, "Edmund!"

Seconds later, her cousin walked through the kitchen door. "All done." He handed Melissa her car keys. "Smoked turkey tonight."

"Thank you." She stood, picked up her purse, and looked at her uncle. "I'm going to go. I love you."

Edmund followed her to the back door. "Hey, Missy, you okay?"

"What?" She stopped and looked at him. "Oh, yeah, um, a friend died. Was murdered, actually. It's been a long week."

"Murdered?" He gasped. "Who?"

"Did you hear about the state attorney?"

His eyes widened. "Yes. That was terrible."

"He went to my church."

He put his arms around her. "I'm sorry about your friend."

"Thanks." She felt weary deep inside and just wanted to be home and shut away from the world for a bit.

He rushed out into the rain to open her car door for her. "Be careful. I worry about you."

"Thanks, Eddie." She slid into her car and started the engine. "See you next week."

After he ran back inside, she brushed the rain off her

arms and face, lay her head back against the headrest, and closed her eyes. The hard rain and isolation of the car gave her momentary solace. Finally, she put the car in gear and drove away.

At the shelter, Aaron waited for her at her spot in the garage. She parked and got out of the car.

"Hi, Aaron. Happy Friday."

He smiled. "Leon's Deli day!"

"Yes. Your favorite. Eddie packed you chocolate cookies too."

"Oh, thanks!"

When she opened the trunk, he grabbed the two big boxes of sandwiches, and she gathered the bag with the homemade mayonnaise and mustard.

"I haven't seen you all week. How are things working out with Terry?"

"Oh man, hiring him was the best decision. I love the nights when we're here together. That only happens two or three times, depending on the week, but it's so much fun."

She smiled, so happy that Aaron and Terry were working out. Rowena was planning to leave for Detroit next week. She'd made a lot of positive changes in the last several days, and even she could see her own personal growth.

"That's great," Melissa said. "He's going to need a friend when his sister moves away."

"I know she's leaving. He moved into the little apartment in the back."

She held the door open for him, and he carried the boxes to the dining area. The table for food service was ready and waiting for her. Aaron started setting up while Melissa went into the kitchen and found the individual packs of chips.

When she went back into the dining hall, she saw Sharon. "Hey."

Sharon turned on her pink heels. "There you are. Everything go okay?"

She hesitated. "He's hurting. His family is devastated. I don't know what he needs from me."

"Maybe nothing right now." She put a hand on Melissa's shoulder. "It's hard to think that, isn't it?"

Sharon was right. Phil probably didn't need her right now, and that hurt. If she lost someone close to her, she'd want Phil to be there, supporting her, holding her up. But he needed to be strong on his own, and she might interfere with that. "So what do I do?"

"I don't know. I'd probably do it wrong. Get too clingy or seem that way."

"Yeah. But if I pull away, won't that also be wrong?"

"It's hard to say. I've not spent a lot of time with Phil." Sharon looked at her phone. "I have dinner with ladies' fellowship at church."

"Have a good time."

Melissa left Aaron setting up and went into her apartment. She sat down in a wingback chair, closed her eyes, and let out a long breath, concentrating on relaxing first her shoulders, then her arms, and on down to her toes. As she felt the tension drain away, she said, "God, I need to know the right thing to do, because I'm afraid if I get it wrong, I'll end up losing him."

She sat in silent meditation for about five minutes, then stretched and glanced at the time. After changing out of her black dress and into a loose shirt and a pair of green yoga pants, she went into the dining room. A few families had already gathered, so she took some time to check in on each one. Once she'd made a connection with everyone there, she grabbed a tray and added a couple of sandwiches and chips for Lola and the kids. Lola typically didn't go downstairs for meals unless Melissa wasn't available to bring them to her.

She took the stairs to her sister's room and tapped on the door. Seconds later, Lola answered. In the days since she'd come to stay here, she'd relaxed, healed. Melissa had watched it happen with her the same way it did with countless other abuse victims. Gradually, the light shone from their eyes, their smiles came more readily and easily. It was like a physical oppression got lifted.

"Turkey sandwiches from Uncle Alejandro."

"Yum. Thanks. How was the funeral?"

"Very sad." Melissa went in and bent to greet Mathias. "I hear you like to play Xbox with Aaron."

"He likes to play the memory game with me."

"That's a hard game."

"I usually beat him."

"That's awesome." Melissa grinned at Gabriele. She'd go hug her, but sometimes the little girl was incredibly reserved and didn't want the attention. She turned to her sister. "How was your day?"

Lola paced to the window and stood to the side to look out. "I am so scared. What they did to Winston . . ." Her voice trailed away.

"Hey, we're safe here," Melissa said. "You're safe here. No one knows where this is."

Lola leaned against the wall and looked over at her. "That's not true, though, is it? Lots of people, hundreds of people, know where this is. You just rely on their secrecy. It

172

only takes one person talking, and the people who work for Hector know how to make people talk."

She was echoing Melissa's thoughts from earlier. "What do you want to do?"

"I don't know." Her voice sounded depleted of all energy. "I only wanted to get away from him. I never thought about testifying against him before. Part of me wants to wait for someone to contact me about testifying, the other wants to run far away and hide on my own."

"No part of you wants to stay?" Melissa asked.

Lola shook her head. "It's not safe to stay. It's better if I go. Better for me, better for you."

"Lola, please reconsider."

"No, Missy. He will find me. And he will punish anyone who is helping me. I'd rather that not be you."

CHAPTER

★

FOURTEEN

NOVEMBER 10

Wearing the uniform of a janitor, Hector worked his way through the intensive care unit. He swiped the mop with enough sincerity to fool the overworked nurses who barely glanced in his direction.

Finally, he made it to the room where Special Agent Thomas Simpson lay attached to a respirator.

A man who compromised all of his core beliefs to attain material possessions, then faced such a close call with death, might reassess what he valued most in life. In the end, that could possibly make him a traitorous business partner.

Best to make sure he was never given the opportunity.

This delicate of a job required Hector's personal attention, because if it went wrong, it could go terribly wrong.

He reached around the breathing tube for Simpson's tongue. Using a pair of pliers, he lanced it to give him the forked tongue of the viper. Then he injected Simpson with four times the amount of cocaine that could give him a heart attack.

By the time the alarm sounded, he was already three floors down and exiting into the parking garage.

Phil lay in his bed and stared at the ceiling, wondering what to do now. How did he move forward when he was filled with such rage that he could barely see straight? How did he ignore the fact that the man responsible for his brother's death lived just a few miles away?

What would happen if he called his friends from his former Special Forces A-Team and told them what happened and that he needed help enacting his revenge on Hector Molina and Vibora? Would they come or would they talk him down?

That was what kept him from calling them. One, he didn't know if they'd come or talk him down. Two, he didn't know if he wanted them to come or talk him down.

He rolled over onto his face and cried out to God to help him, to take away the hate and rage, to still his mind and his heart so that he didn't do something disastrous—something that he wouldn't be able to take back.

For the first time since the emergency room doors closed behind Winston, grief cracked through the wall of anger. He remembered the life he'd lived with his older brother instead of the last words he ever spoke to him. Visions of Christmas mornings and summers on the beach replaced the ever-present image of blood on his hands. Sadness welled up in his soul until he thought it would burst out of him.

The thought that he could get high and muffle all these feelings tickled the back of his mind, a constant presence amid the darkness. He fought it back, unwilling to surrender, and added the need for that special kind of strength to his prayer. Only God could help him fight it back.

Finally he surfaced, showered, and shaved for the first time since the day of the funeral. He turned his phone on. Ignoring the stream of text messages and voice mail notifications, he realized it was Thursday and only six thirty, which meant that he could make it to breakfast if he wanted to.

And he did want to.

Would Melissa also come? Would she show up to see if he was there? He hadn't seen her or spoken to her since she'd left his bedroom the day of the funeral. They'd made no arrangements about today specifically, nor had they canceled.

He got to the diner much earlier than required. He stared out the window, willing Melissa's car to pull into the parking lot.

Delilah appeared at his elbow, startling him. How had he let his guard down so completely? She poured coffee into his cup and asked, "Is she going to show?"

He scowled at her. "I don't know."

"You should call her."

"If she wasn't going to come, she'd have called me."

"Fine." She started to walk away, then turned back and slapped a container of cinnamon on the table.

"I," he mumbled, looking back out the window.

He released a pent-up sigh and refused to look at his watch. He knew what time it was. Just like he knew exactly how many people were in the diner, which people he might consider threats, and every order that had been called out to the cooks since he arrived. He was good with all of the little details.

He sprinkled some cinnamon into his coffee before taking a careful sip, contemplating whether he'd be able to eat. Every time he'd tried for the last week, nothing had tasted good, and he'd lost interest just a few bites in.

When he heard a car door shut, he glanced out the window and saw Melissa as she stood by her car, looking in at him. His heart started pounding. She'd come. What did that mean?

After several seconds, he lifted a hand. She hesitated, then lifted hers and headed into the diner.

Moments later, she slid into the booth across from him. "I didn't know if you'd be here. I thought about calling, but at our last conversation I left that to you, so I didn't want to bother you."

He read no condemnation in her tone or her expression. He stared into her eyes and saw only friendship, understanding, love. "I had my phone off."

"Good thing I didn't try, then." She smiled up at Delilah, who appeared next to them. "Good morning. It's good to see you."

"Same, girl. We kinda wondered if you'd be here since grumpy pants has been so shut down."

Melissa's smile faltered, and she looked from Phil to Delilah. "I think it's a little understandable, don't you? I would think if anyone could relate, you could."

Phil saw the hurt cross Delilah's face. "She's just teasing me, Melissa. She's trying to get me to react because she's worried about me."

Melissa's face turned bright red. She put her menu down. "Oh no. I'm so sorry."

Delilah looked between the two of them, then a big grin covered her face. "I'm not. Thank you." She pulled out her pad. "Know what you want to eat?"

Phil ordered toast and Melissa ordered pancakes. When Delilah left, Melissa settled back into her seat and added some cream to her coffee. "I'm going to comfort-eat on your behalf since you're apparently not doing it for yourself."

Man, he loved her. He loved everything about her. He wished he was everything she needed in a life partner.

"Food doesn't sound good still." He sighed. "I was like that after I lost my leg. I was in a clinic bed in the American embassy in Katangela, and my team leader, Norton, kept trying to bring me cake. I don't even like cake."

She smiled. "Did they not have key lime pie?"

For the first time since last Monday, he smiled. "No. But Dee brought me pie Friday. I couldn't even look at it."

"Must be part of your mourning process."

"I'd thought it was because of the trauma." He paused. "And the narcotics, which was physical as well as emotional and spiritual trauma for me. But now I think you're right."

Melissa tilted her head and stared at him. "You have never talked about losing your leg with me before recently. In fact, I think you didn't even make it obvious that you had lost your leg for several months."

"True. That was easier for me."

She took a sip of her coffee and added more cream. "Why do you think that is?"

What a great question. He considered it, going over and rejecting platitudes and easy answers, and finally settled on, "Because it was the worst ending to the best time of my life. And I've never really truly accepted it."

She propped her elbow on the table and put her chin in her hand, looking at him with amused eyes. "I can see that. It's not easy being human, is it?"

Despite everything, he laughed. "Never."

"Doesn't the VA provide counseling and stuff? It seems like that would've been a fundamental part of your healing process."

"They do. I see a psychiatrist, but I don't go to group therapy. I get group therapy vibes from NA."

"Ah. Right."

Delilah arrived with their food. Phil didn't remark on the fact that she'd put scrambled eggs on his plate even though he hadn't ordered them and instead grabbed the pepper to season them.

When she left again, Melissa poured syrup onto her pancakes. "How are you doing? Is there anything I can do for you?"

Phil's hand faltered, and his fork went back to the plate. "I think I am better today. I didn't think I could be."

"When do you go back to work?"

"Three o'clock today."

After several moments, Melissa asked, "How are your parents?"

"When I left Saturday, they were in pretty bad shape. I'm going over to see them after breakfast."

They ate in silence for a few minutes. Phil pushed his plate to the side and drank the rest of his coffee, then asked, "How did Lola's appointment with the marshals go?"

Melissa raised her head with wide eyes. "Phil, the appointment never happened. No one ever got in touch with her. It was supposed to be last Monday."

He clenched his jaw so hard that he was surprised he didn't break a tooth. "No one contacted her?"

"No."

"Why didn't you tell me?"

She sat back. "You've been a little preoccupied."

He sighed and rubbed the back of his neck. What did that mean, the lack of contact? "Winston said he felt like he had to keep the secret because there was a leak in his office going back to the cartel, but it seems strange that the Marshals Service never contacted Lola."

She shrugged. "Maybe he was gonna contact them on Monday with specifics. He also gave Lola a secret phone. It's possible they don't have that number."

Maybe. Phil rubbed his eyes with his thumb and forefinger. "I'll ask my dad what he thinks. He may be able to make some calls."

After Melissa finished eating, Phil walked her out to her car. He had so much he wanted to lay at her feet, but he wasn't quite ready yet. "Thank you for coming. Thank you for tolerating my need for distance."

She brushed her hair back behind her ear. "I didn't know what was right. And in the end, I was only giving you until today." She opened her car door. "Your family stays in my prayers. Please call me if you need me—day or night. And when you feel like it's a good time to ask your dad about it, let me know what he says."

He nodded and stepped back as she drove away. Shifting mental gears, he focused on Winston and what had happened inside his office. If Winston hadn't yet made an appointment with the marshals, he wouldn't have said he and Lola were meeting them. He would have said he was calling them.

Phil went to his truck, picked up his notepad, and wrote:

Marshals Monday?
Leak?
Who killed him?

His phone rang and his dad's face flashed across the screen.

"Dad," he said as he answered. "I was a second away from hitting your number."

Without preamble, his father said, "Thomas Simpson was killed this morning."

He opened and closed his mouth, unable to think of what to say. Finally, he said, "I thought—"

"He died of a cocaine overdose. And his tongue was cut." His dad paused. "Like a snake."

Phil let out a long breath. "Vibora."

"Obviously, they were worried he'd talk."

Rage brought a red haze over his vision. He closed his eyes and took long, deep breaths until he felt it dissipate. "What does this mean for me?"

"Nothing is different for you. No charges."

"Thanks, Dad. I love you."

"I love you too."

Long after he hung up the phone, he looked at the list and added one more line item.

Simpson—Vibora. Who else?

Melissa walked through the doors of the emergency room. Immediately, memories of coming here last week in the wake of Winston's stabbing assaulted her. This time, though, she had another mission.

The nurse at the admitting desk knew her and waved her forward. "You got room?"

"I do," Melissa said. "I have one more after this if you get someone else."

"I'll let them know. This one has been released. She's just afraid to leave yet. She asked for a little more time." The nurse didn't point or even look as she said, "Boyfriend in chairs. Under the television. Not happy to be relegated out here."

"Noted."

She handed Melissa a sticker that read "Visitor" and said, "Curtain three."

"Thanks." Melissa pulled a clipboard out of her bag and made her way to the curtained-off section inside the treatment area. She pulled the curtain aside and saw a young woman with long blond hair and a bright green cast on her left hand.

"Hi, can I come in?"

The woman looked up. A bruise on her right cheek had started to darken. She had a bandage covering the edge of her hairline. "Who are you?"

She smiled. "My name is Melissa. Is it okay if I come in?"

"I guess." She eyed the clipboard. "I already gave the other woman my insurance."

"That's okay. I'm not here for that." Melissa used her toe to pull a stool closer to the head of the bed. "I'm a counselor. I help people who have been hurt by other people in their families, who need a safe place to go so they don't get hurt anymore."

Tears filled her eyes. "There's no safe place."

"We are very careful to make sure no one ever knows where we're located." She looked around the room. "Do you have children?"

The young woman pressed her lips together and shook her head.

"Okay. Can you tell me your name?"

"Anna," she whispered so quietly that Melissa could barely hear her.

"I'm not the police, nor am I affiliated with them," Melissa said. "So as I ask you questions, know that it's just to determine what I can do to help you and not for any other reason, okay?"

Anna stared at her hands. A tear splashed onto her cast.

"Can you tell me if the person who did this to you is in your home?"

After several long seconds, Anna nodded. "Yes. My boyfriend."

Melissa lifted a sheet of paper on the clipboard and made notations. "Would you like to come and spend a few days with me? You can look at your options after your body has had time to heal."

Anna lifted her head. In her eyes, shame and humiliation warred with hope. "I don't have any money."

"We don't require money, hon. Did they give you all of your paperwork?" Anna nodded and Melissa stood. "Then you're free to go. Would you like to go with me?"

"Yes." Anna moved slowly. She must have injuries beyond what Melissa could see.

Melissa observed each careful step. At the edge of the curtain, she asked, "Would you like a wheelchair?"

Anna paused. Her face had paled and sweat beaded on her forehead. Finally, she nodded.

Melissa put a hand on her shoulder. "Sit. I'll be right back." She went to the nurses' station. "She's going to need a wheelchair."

The nurse on duty said, "I bet. I'd need one too." She gestured with her head. "Just around the corner by the water fountain."

Once Melissa had Anna settled into the wheelchair, she took the familiar route through the back corridors of the hospital to the employee section of the parking garage. In most of the hospitals, Melissa had special parking privileges that kept her out of the normal traffic pattern when securing a victim from the emergency rooms.

She stopped at the passenger side of her car and set the brake on the chair before opening the door. "Take it slow," she said as Anna maneuvered her way from chair to car.

A voice came from behind them. "Hey!"

Anna gasped and put her hands up as if to shield her face. Melissa shut the door and turned to face the man barreling toward them. He had on a pair of jeans belted well below his waist, a red T-shirt with the sleeves cut off, and a baseball cap that advertised a popular beer.

"Hey! Where are you taking her?" He approached with both hands fisted.

Melissa shifted the keys in her hand to access her pepper spray and tried to work out how she'd get to her side of the car. Maybe she'd go through the back door and just climb through the car to the driver's seat. That would get her to safety more efficiently.

The man reached them and punched down on the hood,

then pointed at Anna through the windshield. "You get out right now."

Melissa could hear Anna sobbing. She locked the doors and prayed the man didn't get ahold of the keys. Fear made her hands tremble, so she kept a firm grip on the keys and desperately tried to think ahead of the man. "You need to leave us alone right now. Anna is coming with me."

He didn't come any closer, for which she was thankful. But he pointed at her and said, "I don't care who you are. This doesn't concern you."

"It actually does. Right now, you're going to walk away."

Expletives flew out of his mouth. He rounded on her and took a step closer. "I said this doesn't concern you."

Melissa lifted her chin and stood her ground. She couldn't believe that her voice stayed firm and steady. "I said leave."

The most important thing to her was to keep Anna safe. But if this man got her keys, she didn't know what she'd do. When he lunged toward her with his fists raised, her brain kicked into overdrive and everything slowed. She stepped to the side, intending to get out of his direct path, but knew she could never move fast enough to escape him. And when those fists came down on her, it would hurt. A lot.

She lifted the pepper spray and pointed it at him, waiting until he was just a little closer to spray him. Before she could deploy it, though, some force slammed the man into the hood of her car. Anna screamed. It took a few seconds for Melissa to realize that Phil had secured the man's hands behind him, pulling them up toward his shoulder blades, and was pressing his forearm across the man's shoulders.

"Phil?" Melissa tried to make sense of what had just happened.

When he turned and looked at her, the intensity on his face made her gasp. "Call 911."

She fumbled through her purse and got her phone out, hitting the emergency button. As soon as she relayed their situation, Phil said, "Go get hospital security."

She looked around. "Will you be okay?"

He grinned in a way that made her heart flip. "I can hold this guy all day. Go ahead." He bent down and said to the man, "Hey, punk, your pants are falling down. Maybe you should have used that belt that kept them around your thighs for what it's for, eh?"

The man struggled and cursed, but he didn't come close to breaking free. Melissa felt better about leaving Phil alone with him and ran to the pole in the garage that had the emergency button on it. As soon as she hit it, a blue light at the top started flashing. When the voice on the built-in intercom spoke, she jumped and put a hand over her heart. "Can I help you?"

"Please! We've been attacked!"

It didn't take a full minute for two security personnel to come through the doors. Melissa led them to her car and stood back as they relieved Phil of his prisoner. When the police arrived, they each gave their statements, and Melissa encouraged Anna to also press charges against her boyfriend for his abuse of her.

By the time everything had settled and law enforcement left with the man, an hour had gone by. Anna sat in the wheelchair, appearing more relaxed now that her immediate threat was gone. Phil hovered near the car, clearly still energized from the confrontation.

"Thank you for coming to my rescue," Melissa said.

He gave a slow smile. "Anytime." He gestured toward the entrance. "I'm late for work."

"And on your first day back too."

"Yeah." He started to walk away, then turned. "My dad is going to make some phone calls. I'll call you in the morning."

She lifted her hand, then looked at Anna. "Would you still like to come with me?"

"Will he get out?"

Melissa shook her head. "I can't know that. He's innocent until proven guilty. A judge might give him bail."

Anna chewed on her bottom lip. "I think I want to come with you. Can I go home first and pack a bag?"

With a smile intended to comfort and assure, Melissa said, "Of course. Let's get you back into the car."

As Anna carefully climbed in, she said, "Thank you for defending me."

Melissa knelt at the open door. "Anna, no human being has a right to mistreat you. Regardless of what you've encountered in your past, they simply do not. He is wrong and he's not sorry. Remember that."

CHAPTER

FIFTEEN

NOVEMBER 11

Phil shut his Bible and pushed it away, then slid his coffee cup closer. The spicy smell of cinnamon mingled with the aroma of the fresh brew, creating a very soothing atmosphere.

He looked around his apartment. He'd had an okay day back to work yesterday, suffering through the sympathy and platitudes about Winston. He'd known it would be like that going in, so he just coped and hoped it would be way less this afternoon.

When he thought about getting out of his truck and seeing that man attacking Melissa, his neck muscles tightened. It had taken great restraint for him to keep from causing physical harm to the punk. But he'd practiced the needed discipline and just held him until security arrived.

In the meantime, he kept Anna in his prayers. Seeing that man coming at Melissa had been something he never wanted to see again. He felt the same rage he'd felt that day when he saw her in the emergency room, wanting to physically come between her and anyone who would dare harm her.

He decided to go see her instead of calling her. First, though, he wanted to hit an early meeting. The church down the street had one at seven thirty.

He used to get uncomfortable whenever he walked into a meeting and didn't know anyone there. Then the term "anonymous" struck him and he realized that he did in fact rely on a certain level of anonymity. He appreciated the fact that he could keep the meetings a part of his life and not make them a social club. Over the years, he'd seen too many people rely on the organization to be their club of people.

He arrived during the opening prayer. Standing in the back, he noticed a man with straight dark hair and a black goatee staring at him. Phil bowed his head to finish the prayer but kept his eyes open. When he lifted his head, the man wasn't there. For a moment, he considered leaving and finding him. Something about the stare had set off all his internal alarms. Then again, the room was filled with addicts, some of whom resorted to crime to feed the beast. He might just be feeling a little bit paranoid on the heels of Winston's murder.

He listened to the introductions, stories, and testimonies. The speaker was engaging—a former police officer who would search known drug dealers and pocket what he found. Thinking back to the ready supply of narcotics available to him during his tenure as a surgeon, Phil felt nothing but empathy for this guy. He could tell by the way he spoke that he was a believer in Jehovah God and a follower of Christ. He wondered what the man would say if he invited him to coffee one day to talk about shared experiences.

At the end of the meeting, so many attendees converged on the speaker that Phil just wrote his first name on a page in his notebook. He'd like to think he could look him up, but that would hardly be anonymous.

This early on a Friday morning, he had to battle rush-hour traffic to get to Melissa's. The guard at the gate approached his car. Phil rolled down his window and said, "Phil Osbourne."

The guard looked at his tablet, then nodded and took a step back. Phil thought he might need to introduce himself to the head of security and discuss certain protocols, like confirming identification with something other than words. This was the second time he'd given just his name.

He parked next to Melissa's car, then walked into the building and immediately smelled pancakes and buttery syrup. On his way to the apartments, he stopped at the dining room.

When Sharon saw him, she set down the bowl she'd been filling with fruit salad and walked to him. "Phil, I'm so sorry to hear about your brother."

Every time someone spoke those words, he felt them like an actual blow to his torso. "Thanks, Sharon. Melissa around?"

"She had a middle-of-the-night call that went until a few hours ago, so I imagine she's in her room."

"Great." He went down the corridor and tapped on the door, surprised when Melissa opened it without finding out who was on the other side.

She looked up at him with wide eyes, obviously surprised to see him. She had wet hair combed away from her face and wore a pair of denim shorts and a red tank top. "Phil, hi."

"Hey. Is this a good time?"

"Sure." She stepped back and gave him room to enter. The fresh smell of coconut shampoo wafted up from her, and he breathed deeply to drink more in. She ran a hand over her hair as if self-conscious of its appearance. "I'm sorry. I just got in."

"Sharon said."

He slipped his hands into his pants pockets as she shut the door. She gestured at her couch, and he slowly lowered himself down.

"Are you okay from yesterday?" he asked.

"Yeah. I mean, he never touched me. Thanks to you."

"He was a punk." After a moment, he asked, "Do you often get attacked?"

She fingered her cheek, as if feeling the long-healed wound caused by the brick two weeks ago. "Not usually. I mean, there's been the occasional angry spouse. I've endured quite a bit of verbal abuse, but no one has ever come after me physically, Colombian cartels aside." She sat next to him and crossed her legs. "I didn't know what I was going to do. All I could think about was keeping my keys away from him so he couldn't get to Anna."

"I know I was there because God needed me there. I'd finished lunch with my parents and thought I'd go into work a little early to get settled back into it."

She smiled and reached for his hand, gripping it with both of hers. Her skin was cool, her touch strong. "God is very good," she said.

He looked down at their joined hands for several moments.

"Your parents?" she asked.

"Mourning. It was hard to see my dad like that." He cleared his throat. "He said he'd make some calls today. I gave him your number."

"Thanks. I'm so sorry that you have to bother them with this right now. I'm sure they'd rather be alone."

"I think my dad is happy to have something to do." He pulled his hand away to rub his thigh.

Melissa's eyes followed his movements, and she frowned. "You've been doing that a lot lately. Are you hurting?"

"What?" He looked down at his hand and stopped. "No. It's an unconscious movement. I used to hurt all the time, real pain then phantom pain. But now it's just a nervous habit." He cleared his throat. "Are you free today?"

"Yes."

"Would, uh, you like to go out on the water with me today? Dad insisted I take Winston's boat."

Her smile lit up her face. "I would love that. Can you give me just a few minutes to get ready?"

"Of course."

On her way to the bedroom, she turned and said, "Oh, happy Veteran's Day."

Whenever anyone said that to him, it gave him pause. His military service had given him the best days of his life with the worst ending. But he simply nodded and said, "Thanks."

While she changed, he called a local deli and asked for a picnic lunch, then took the time to wander around her apartment, something he had never done. He read the back of a book on the bookshelf, a murder mystery set in New York City in the World War II era by an author named Violet Pearl. He remembered seeing a movie based on one of her books. Another book was a romance novel with a sweet young couple on the cover. An entire shelf held women's help books, psychology books, and counseling helps.

On the table, an open journal begged for him to pause and glance, but he respected Melissa's privacy and moved to the framed photograph on the wall of her mother, Lola, and her. It amazed him how much Melissa and Lola looked like their mother. It was as if their father had contributed nothing to their gene pool.

When Melissa came out of her room, she had on a pair of white cotton shorts and a loose scoop-necked white shirt. Underneath, he could see her red-and-white-striped swimsuit. She wore a red cap on her head and was stuffing a towel into a straw bag.

"I haven't slept since yesterday," she said. "I have a feeling I'm going to get out on the water in the sunshine and be gone. I will be very boring company."

He smiled. "I think I'll be able to handle it."

Hector stepped away from his meeting with a seller to take a phone call. "This better be important."

"Did your wife have a sister?"

He thought back. "I don't know."

"We've been watching Osbourne's boat. A woman got on it with his brother today. Check your phone."

He looked at the picture, and his heart stopped until he realized that he wasn't looking at Lola. He put the phone back to his ear. "We need to secure her."

"Not a good idea. She runs a battered women's shelter. There's no way she'd tell us anything. However, we can follow her. I think if we find the shelter, we find your family."

He thought about his son. He'd cried when Lola gave him a son. He had a chance to love Mathias the way his own father had never loved him. How could Lola have taken him away like that?

"You don't have a way to find it?" he asked.

"We tried. Her business partner has a huge financial backing with the kinds of resources that can hide assets. We keep hitting walls in trying to locate the property."

"Okay. Find a way to follow her."

"We will. What about Osbourne's brother?"

"I have my own people on him."

Even though she fought it, Melissa ended up napping within just minutes of departing. Phil insisted that she sleep down in the small cabin to protect her from the sun. When she woke up, she felt a little groggy and had a slight headache.

She hadn't taken the time to look around when she came down. It was a small living quarters with a tiny galley and reminded her of the interior of a motor home. She grabbed a bottle of water out of the narrow fridge and went up the stairs and through the hatch.

Phil sat in the captain's chair, his eyes focused beyond the boat. She glanced that way and saw a stone lighthouse on the edge of an inlet.

"Hello," she said.

He looked in her direction and smiled. "I thought the engines slowing down would wake you."

"How long was I out?"

"Barely an hour. I took it slow to give you some time."

"That must be why I'm so groggy." She opened the water and sat by him. He pulled up to a harbor that looked like a sidewalk. "Boca Chita?"

"Yep. You've been here?" he asked.

"I had a cousin get married down here. She used the state park."

"I thought it would be a good spot to stretch the boat's legs. I wanted to do Key West, but I've never gone that far alone." He paused. "Winston wouldn't have hesitated."

"Well, I'm sure he didn't go that far his first solo outing." She ran her palm over the glossy wooden dash. "This is a nice boat."

"It was his dream. He lived in a cheap apartment and drove an old car so that he could get the nicest boat and keep it in an expensive harbor with all the fees and dues."

He expertly came to a stop, and she hopped out so he could toss her the rope and tie up. He disappeared into the cabin and came out carrying the bags he'd gotten from the deli. After he locked the door to the cabin, he joined her on the dock. "I love it here. It's pretty much untouched this time of year. Summer's more crowded. Weekends too. But on a Friday in November, it's great."

They walked to a picnic table, and Phil handed Melissa the tablecloth to lay out while he pulled out the deli lunch. There were individual containers of potato salad and coleslaw and wrapped sandwiches.

"I know it's not your uncle's, but he was too out of the way," Phil said. "It would have taken us an hour to get there."

"I'll eat his tonight, anyway." She unwrapped the sandwich and found roast beef on sourdough. "It's Friday."

"Right. What does Aaron call it?"

She grinned. "Leon's Deli day."

After all the food was laid out, Phil held his hand out. Melissa took it and bowed her head as he asked God's blessing on the food and their time together.

"What will you do for Thanksgiving?" he asked.

"Feed eighteen families." She smiled. "Mrs. Horton is incredible. She'll have three turkeys going in the morning and recruit some of the residents to help her peel and dice and slice." She took a bite of the potato salad, enjoying the creamy dressing. "What about you?"

"It's going to be hard. I don't know what it will look like. Usually, Delilah and her husband spend the day, and she and Mom cook."

His face darkened, and she reached out and covered his hand, which fisted in response. "It's going to be hard as each holiday comes and goes and your family discovers your new normal."

He didn't reply. A muscle ticked in his jaw, and he sat in stony silence for several seconds before pulling his hand away and picking up his sandwich. "It's hard not to go to Hector Molina's house and have a conversation about it."

Melissa gasped. How could he even think that? "Did you tell the police what Winston told you, about it being Vibora?"

"Of course, but the police can't touch Vibora. Hence the pig's head next to my brother. You think any of them are going to try now?"

She set her sandwich down and wiped her fingers on a napkin. "I know you feel like you need to do something. But don't you think that if you did and something happened to you, your parents would be absolutely devastated? To have lost two of their sons to that cartel?"

His features hardened and his eyes darkened. "You don't think that's the one thing that keeps me from doing it?" He sighed and rubbed his eyes. When he lowered his hand, he looked normal again. "It's just my impulse, and I have to fight it. I was praying this morning, and God spoke into my soul, encouraging me to get away, to go into His creation, to find a way to relax." He smiled, his eyes warming. "And here we are."

Joy filled her from her soul outward. "Thank you for including me."

They finished eating and packed their garbage in the boat. "Do you want to walk around the hiking trail?" Phil asked. "It goes all around the island."

"Sure." She looked down at her sandals. "Hardly hiking boots."

"It's okay. The path is pretty solid."

They strolled along the path, reading information signs about the Florida habitat. Melissa stopped to examine a black-and-yellow banana spider perched on a web. "I used to love these things when I was a kid. It was all my aunt could do to keep me from making one of them a pet." She grinned up at him. "I thought it was way cooler looking than the spider Charlotte in that cartoon."

He shook his head. "That's borderline crazy, Melissa. Just saying."

"What? They don't bite. Well, mostly." She looped her arm through his and kept walking. They'd seen other boats in the harbor but so far hadn't come across another person. "You don't like spiders?"

"No." He actually shuddered, and she laughed. "They make my skin crawl."

"Well, you protect me from angry boyfriends, and I'll protect you from arachnids."

He grinned down at her in a way that made her heart pitter-patter. "Deal."

They walked slowly back to the boat. As Phil untied it from the dock, he glanced back at her. "You going to sleep all the way home?"

"Not if I can help it."

He gestured at the floor. "There's a coffeepot that makes a single serving."

"Ah, my love language. Do you want some?"

He bent and unlocked the door. "No. Thank you, though."

Down in the galley, she found the coffeepot, the store of pods, and little containers of creamer. As she waited for the water to heat, she wandered around the room, checking out the space that had been so important to Phil's brother. He was very neat and clean. Everything had a place, and many of the places were labeled. She found that very endearing.

When her coffee was ready and in a travel mug, she carefully put everything back in its proper place.

Phil had just coasted out of the harbor and turned toward Miami. Once she sat down next to him, he put the engines on full, and the power of the motor threw her back against her seat.

She watched him, enjoying just sitting next to him. They got back to the harbor much too soon. As he pulled into the slip, she asked, "Are you going to keep it here?"

He shook his head. "No. It's expensive. More than my apartment. Mom and Dad have a harbor affiliated with their neighborhood. I've put in an application there."

They gathered their garbage, and she held up the cup. "Can I keep this for now?"

"Sure."

In deference to heavy commuter traffic, Phil took back streets and side roads to get to Melissa's home. All too soon, he pulled up to the security gate. She waved at Michael, and he lifted his hand in greeting and opened the gate.

"When I came this morning, they didn't check my ID." Phil glanced at her as he pulled into a space. "They really should check IDs."

She knew he only said that from a position of caring, so she didn't let it bristle her nerves. Her guards knew him because he'd already been there. "I'll reiterate it." She grabbed her bag. "Thank you for including me on your maiden boat-ownership voyage."

He chuckled. "Thank you for joining me."

"I really had a good time."

"Me too."

CHAPTER

★

SIXTEEN

NOVEMBER 14

Phil sat across from his dad and watched him frown on the phone. Finally, his dad disconnected the call and looked at him. "They won't tell me anything. I gave them my number. Hopefully, they'll research and call me back."

Phil rubbed the back of his neck. "What happened, do you think?"

"According to the marshal, someone from Winston's office canceled the meeting. Only, they wouldn't tell me who." He fisted his hand and brought it down hard on the desk. "I wish I knew. I'd like to . . ."

Phil nodded. "I know, Dad. Me too."

His dad gave a wry smile. "I was going to say I'd like to bring them to justice and have them tried in my court."

Phil chuckled. "Me too."

As he stood to leave, his dad stopped him. "We missed you at church yesterday."

Phil cleared his throat. "I know. I really couldn't face the people."

"Yeah. That was hard."

"Honestly, if I'd thought you were going to go, I probably would have. Mom wasn't sure when I spoke with her Saturday."

"I convinced her to go ahead and get the first one over with." His dad stood and walked around his desk. "I have to be back in the courtroom in ten minutes. I'm sorry I wasn't more help."

Phil sighed. "It's okay. It isn't our responsibility to investigate crimes, is it? I have an appointment with Doctor Manning this morning, but then I was going to go by the house, maybe swim some laps."

"I think your mom is working today, so you may miss her while you're there." In an unfamiliar move, his dad grabbed him and hugged him. "I love you, Son."

"I love you too, Dad."

As he left, his dad was putting on his black robe, getting ready to go back into the courtroom. Phil walked through the courthouse, down the familiar hallways, and into the atrium. As he rounded a corner, he saw Kim Jones, a colleague of Winston's that he'd met at a Christmas party at his parents'. He'd seen her at the funeral, but he hadn't spoken to her there.

"Kim!"

The tall woman with short red hair and smooth white skin looked around, then spotted him. Her face immediately fell into that sympathetic look, and he braced himself against remembering.

He jogged up to her. "Hi."

"Hi, Phil. It's been a long time."

"Yeah." He gestured behind him. "I was visiting my dad."

"How's he doing?"

"Trying to figure out how to have a new normal, I think. Thanks for asking." He looked over his shoulder. Winston had liked Kim, and Phil didn't know where else to start. He needed to trust her. "Listen, I have a question and we're not finding answers."

"Sure. How can I help?" She glanced at her watch. "I have about ten minutes before I need to be in court."

He gave a brief summation of what he knew, including Winston helping him get Lola out of the clutches of her husband. "So, I need to ask you how you can help me."

Kim looked all around and then pulled him behind a column. "Are you implying that someone in our office is working with Vibora?"

"I don't know what I'm implying. I'm telling you that Winston was working with other agencies to bring charges against Hector Molina and secured his wife to testify. Within a few days, Winston is murdered and propped up with the severed head of a pig, and one of his last words to me is 'Vibora.' A DEA agent searching his house is murdered in the hospital. The marshals say that someone in his office, in your office, canceled the meeting, but they won't say who."

She checked her watch again. "I don't have any more time." She pulled out a business card and wrote on the back of it. "Listen, if Winston felt he had to be careful about what went into the office, he had a reason. He wouldn't just think that." She held the card out and he took it. "I wrote my cell on the back. Can we meet after work tonight?"

"Absolutely."

"Great."

She rushed away, her heels clicking on the tile floor. Phil slipped her card into his pocket and exited the building.

He'd left his truck in the parking lot of the VA Medical Center, so he took a cab back. When he arrived, he checked in and found a seat in the lobby's corner.

He hated this waiting room. He associated it with so much pain in his life. The first time he'd come here, his mom had brought him in a wheelchair. He was so angry, in pain, so lost. In just under two years, he'd come a long way, but there was still the residual mourning for the life he used to have and the one he'd planned to have.

"Lieutenant Osbourne. He'll see you now."

He stood and walked into the office of Doctor Cecil Manning, former British Special Air Service turned double amputee and US VA psychiatrist.

"Doc," Phil said, taking his normal chair.

"Phil."

Some days, the doctor had on his prosthetics, and others, like today, he used a wheelchair. Phil often wondered if it was his mood or physical need that drove the decisions. He had black hair, rich brown skin, and light brown eyes and had grown up in West London. He'd followed in his father's footsteps and become a soldier. The injuries he'd sustained in Afghanistan had forced an abrupt change of his life path.

"Tell me about your month," Manning said.

Phil couldn't help but chuckle. "It's been a month." He cleared his throat. "I did a procedure with my doctor hat on. An old friend from medical school asked me for a consult, and I set the jaw of a teenager."

Manning flipped open his notebook. "That is a big step. Did it help you with your decisions about going back?"

"Some." He sighed. "I think I'm way more disciplined than I was. I'm stronger emotionally and mentally. I consider it. And then I lose the drive."

"Would you consider maybe a different specialty?"

"Yeah, I mean, I've thought about it. After combat medic and EMT, I feel like I could be a good ER doc. I'm almost thirty-four, though. That would set me back some, timewise."

"Setbacks happen, though, don't they?"

He thought of his brother's hand resting on the pig's head. "Yes." He rubbed his left thigh. "My brother was murdered."

"I saw." Manning flattened his hand over the pen on his notebook. He often did that when he wanted to focus solely on Phil and not on writing. "I'm surprised you didn't jump off with that."

"Yeah." Phil looked at the floor. "It's hard. My ambulance got the call to the scene. It felt like I was back in combat. Same kind of urgency of movements, same kind of emotion and flood of adrenaline. And the whole time I was working on him, I knew it was bad. I knew it. But I tried anyway."

"You and I both know you wouldn't have been able to live with yourself if you hadn't tried." Manning picked his pen up again. "I'm sorry about your brother. How are you coping?"

Phil spent the next forty minutes talking about his anger, his sadness, how he felt lost and didn't know which direction to turn. One of the reasons he liked Doctor Manning so much was because he was a man of astounding faith. They'd established early on in their relationship that Phil wanted faith in God brought into his sessions. Manning prayed with him, talked with him, and gave him exercises to do with Bible verses and prayer time.

When their forty-five minutes were up, Phil left, exhaustion coursing through his limbs.

Outside, the sun was too bright and the noise of the city too loud. He wanted to find a dark corner and look through the materials Manning had given him, find something in there to help him hear God's voice in the midst of this pain that had burned a gaping hole in his soul.

Instead, he drove to his parents' house. He parked in the empty driveway and used his key to go in. "Mom?"

Hearing no answer, he checked the garage and saw her car gone. He went into his bedroom and changed into swim trunks.

When he dove into the cool water, he felt like he was shedding some of the old so that he could put on some of the new. New territories with Melissa, new life without Winston, contemplating his future and what his career should look like. While he swam, he prayed for God to cool off the anger that bubbled just under the surface of everything, because he knew he couldn't deal with it alone.

Melissa rang her uncle's doorbell. Within moments, her uncle Alejandro opened the door. His eyes widened. "Missy! What are you doing here?"

"Do you have a minute?"

He stepped onto the porch and gestured at the wicker chairs next to a big pot of ferns. "Your aunt is resting. She had chemo this morning. Our voices will wake her." They sat down.

"How is she doing?"

"The treatment is hard on her. By the time she gets over it, it's time for another one."

Melissa thought about every conversation she'd had with her aunt since treatment started. "She's never said anything about that."

"She wouldn't."

Melissa reached over and put a hand on her uncle's shoulder. "I'll come early Friday. Maybe I'll bring her some of those cookies she likes."

He smiled. "That would make her happy. Now, Niece, what's up?"

She tugged on her bottom lip. "When my mom died, why did the families separate my sister and me?"

He held up his hands and shrugged. "I was not part of any of that conversation. When you were a baby, your mom asked our sister to be the godmother and me the godfather. Not long after, your mom started moving away from us emotionally. Eventually, we quit hearing from her at all. Of course, now we know it was because your father . . ."

"I know," she said. "He beat her and emotionally manipulated her, and probably intentionally kept her away from her family."

He nodded. "I never even met your sister, and the last time I'd seen you was at your baptism when you were a baby."

"So, you don't know why. It just seems strange to let a baby go to the family of the man who beat his wife to death. Don't you think that strange?"

"My understanding was that his sister and a friend of his were Lola's godparents. That was the justification for separating you." He frowned and clearly considered what she said. "You can't blame his entire family for who your father was. We don't know that that's what it was like."

She knew. Of course, she couldn't say anything because Lola was under her protection. "But the entire time I was being raised by everyone, no one even tried to put Lola and me together."

He shook his head. "You don't know what the adults tried to do away from you. It's possible they tried and were not able to."

She studied his face. Everything about him seemed sincere. "Okay. I appreciate you answering my questions."

She stood, and he grabbed her wrist. "Missy, what happened to your mother hurt us deeply as a family. We came together and vowed to raise you the best we could. We all supported your aunt and uncle with everything, and then we took you in. You know we love you."

She bent down, hugged him, and kissed his cheek, inhaling the familiar smell of his wood smoker. "Uncle Alejandro, I know you love me. And I appreciate everything you did as part of raising me."

He patted her on the cheek. "You are a joy, Missy. God did something right in you."

She started off the porch, then turned back to him. "I've been looking for my sister for a long time."

He raised an eyebrow. "You have?"

"Yes. She ended up in Colombia."

He frowned. "Colombia? Was that where your father was from?"

She shook her head. "No, but the people he worked for are from there."

"Do you plan to contact her?"

Melissa hesitated. She had to protect Lola, but she also had to protect her uncle. She never wanted to lie to him, but she might have to if she answered his question. "To tell you the truth, I never really found out how." That wasn't truly a lie. She hadn't figured out how to contact Lola because she hadn't found her. Phil had. "Anyway, thanks."

He lifted his hand. "Wish I could've been more help."

She smiled. "I'm happy I got to talk with you. I'll see you Friday."

Kim Jones was waiting for Phil when he got to the oyster bar. She'd changed out of her suit and heels and wore a pair of denim shorts and a Wonder Woman T-shirt. He hardly recognized her.

"Hi, Kim."

She slipped her phone into her purse and smiled up at him. "Hi." She looked around. "Thanks for meeting here."

"No worries."

She gestured toward the plastic menu. "Do you want anything?"

He shook his head. "I'm good."

The waitress delivered Kim a glass of white wine. She looked at Phil. "Can I get you a drink?"

"No thanks."

Kim slid her glass to the side and folded her arms on the table. "When I went back to my office late today, I looked in Winston's desk. I'm not sure I knew exactly where to look, but I couldn't find anything about this case."

Phil frowned. "His apartment was ripped apart. If he had anything about this case there, it's not there anymore."

She gave a brief shake of her head. "I want to know details so I can go to my boss with it. I know Winston was working with the DEA to investigate Molina. But my understanding is that they never could get anything concrete. It's just a bunch of supposition. The DEA's next move was to try to infiltrate Vibora with an agent, but they had so far been unsuccessful. They're at an impasse. That was my understanding. They had the compound under surveillance."

"Right."

She looked around and leaned forward. "Do you know where Molina's wife is? Did Winston tell you?"

"I can get you his wife. And all I know is that after speaking to Winston privately for some time, she agreed to testify. He was going to secure protection before she made her official statement. He died the morning of that meeting with the Marshals Service."

"If I arrange a meeting with the marshals, can you produce Mrs. Molina?"

"Yes."

She sat back and ran her tongue over her teeth. "I'd have to talk to her first."

He shook his head. "No. I'll arrange to bring her directly to the office of the Marshals Service. From there, their protection will begin, and you can arrange all the testimony you want."

"Can't do that, Phil. You don't know how it works. I have to justify the order. To do that, I need to interview her."

Anger stirred in his chest, and he bit his tongue to keep from lashing out. "Winston already vetted her."

"I'd love to see his notes. Do you have them?"

He pinched the bridge of his nose. He thought about the

SD card but didn't want to bring it out just yet. "If I had them, I would have given them to you."

"Then I'm sorry. There's nothing I can do."

He clenched his teeth and slid out of the booth. "You could if you really wanted to. But what you're doing right now is all about you and not about Winston or Mrs. Molina. And I don't think that's what your office stands for."

Without looking back, he left the restaurant.

CHAPTER

SEVENTEEN

NOVEMBER 15

Mrs. Horton lifted little Tina up onto the stainless-steel counter and handed her a bowl of rainbow cake sprinkles. "Ready?"

Sharon kept her hand on Tina's back as the six-year-old bobbed her head, making the barrettes at the ends of her black braids clink together.

Melissa took their picture as the three of them doused the yellow buttercream icing on the three-tiered cake with handfuls of sprinkles. When they were done, they all cheered.

Sharon helped Tina down, then Melissa and Mrs. Horton lifted the cake onto the cart. The women quickly lit the twenty-two candles.

Melissa smiled down at Tina. "Are you ready?"

She grinned and nodded, then rushed to the dining room door, putting both hands on it.

Mrs. Horton wheeled the cake to the door. "Now!"

Tina pushed the door open and ran into the dining room, screaming, "Happy birthday, Mommy!"

Melissa, Sharon, and Mrs. Horton followed, singing "Happy Birthday" to Tina's mom, Sasha.

The young mother had tears coursing down her face when they finished singing. She threw her arms around Melissa's neck and started sobbing. Melissa hugged her back and shot Sharon a confused look.

Sharon bent down to hear what the woman sitting to Sasha's left said, then transferred the message to Melissa. "No one has ever celebrated her birthday before."

Melissa cupped Sasha's wet face. "You are worthy of being celebrated, Sasha. No matter what your parents told you, no matter what your ex-boyfriend did to you, you are a beautiful child of God, and celebrating your life on earth is my pleasure."

Sasha nodded and sniffed, then hugged Sharon and Mrs. Horton. "Thank you." She bent down and scooped Tina up. "Who do you think we should give the first slice to?"

By the time they distributed the cake to the residents in the dining room, not much of it remained. Melissa thanked Mrs. Horton for making the cake and hugged Tina, thanking her for her help, then pulled Sharon to the side.

"Sasha is making noises about going back to him."

Sharon nodded. "That's what she said in group today. The other members really hit the point home in discouraging her. I think she heard them."

"Good." Melissa glanced at the clock above the kitchen door. "I have a meeting at church."

"Oh, right! Have fun. I'm on call tonight, so no stress."

Melissa stopped in her apartment long enough to freshen her lipstick and grab her purse. As she headed out, she got a call from Phil. She answered with her video on. "Hi there."

"Hey. Is tonight your festival meeting?"

"Yeah. I have to be there at seven." She made sure her apartment door automatically locked, then walked toward the parking garage.

"How late will it be?"

"The festival is just two days away. Lots to go over, so probably over an hour. Why?"

He shrugged. "Nothing. I'm praying about something, thought you could lend an ear. It can wait for Thursday, though."

She frowned. "Is everything okay?"

"As okay as it can be. I mean, I still have super rough moments."

She pursed her lips into a pout. "I wish I could help you."

"No one can." He looked away from the camera for a moment, then focused back on her. "Have fun tonight."

"Thanks."

She drove to the church, her mind swirling through everything going on in her life—Phil, his family, Lola, the different needs and details of her residents. Taking part in the committee that planned the Thanksgiving festival and dinner for church was a welcome reprieve. She could serve as a member of a committee and not be in charge of anything, not make any decisions—just take her marching orders.

She pulled into the church parking lot, and as she got out of the car, the sound of a loud engine came from behind her. She pressed up against her car as a motorcycle moving way too fast passed so close to her that she felt the heat from the engine on her legs. She put a hand over her chest. What in the world?

She hadn't thought to get a license plate number until she couldn't see it anymore. Should she report this somewhere?

Wondering if anyone else had experienced something similar this evening, she went into the fellowship hall and joined the committee at one of the tables. "Someone on a motorcycle nearly ran me down in the parking lot!" she said.

"Our parking lot?" the committee chair, Fran Nelson, asked.

Melissa explained what happened, but no one else had seen or heard anything. She wanted to dismiss it as an unusual occurrence that didn't require much thought or attention, but she couldn't. The entire meeting, her thoughts kept going back to the motorcycle. Why would someone almost run her down like that? Was it intentional?

When she left the meeting, the parking lot was already dark and she was glad to walk out with the group, still a little jittery about the motorcycle. She had a moment of spontaneity on her way home and decided to swing by Phil's apartment.

It took a moment for him to open the door. He had on his running blade and didn't have on a shirt. "Melissa," he said, clearly surprised.

"Hi. I just finished the meeting and came by to see if you still needed a sounding board."

He looked down and then at her. "I just got home a few seconds ago. In fact, I'm surprised you didn't see me."

"I must have just missed you."

He held the door wider, and she came in. He disappeared into the bedroom and returned wearing a T-shirt that had a Special Forces emblem on the back.

"I'd still like to go running with you," she said.

He picked up a glass of water from the table and took a long drink before he said, "Fine. Thursday morning, instead of breakfast."

She pursed her lips. "I can do that."

His smile made her heart flip. "Deal. I'll even buy you a smoothie after." He gestured to the couch and she sat down. He sat in his recliner. "So, I have a friend I went to medical school with. She's an ER doc I see regularly."

"I met her." She didn't add that she'd met the doctor when Winston died.

"Okay. Great. So, last month she told me about some openings in the ER department. Winston was pushing me to apply."

Her head cocked to one side, she waited for him to elaborate. When he didn't, she asked, "What kind of opening?"

His eyes widened as if he realized he'd left out that detail. "Right! Uh, doctor."

"Really?" She couldn't have stopped the smile if she'd tried. "Oh, Phil, how exciting! I didn't know you were thinking of getting back into it."

He cleared his throat. "Well, actually, I wasn't. But Addy pushed, Winston pushed, and then the other morning it was really on my mind, so I've been praying about it."

Silence stretched between them, and she realized he didn't intend to explain anymore. "Would you like me to pray with you?"

He opened and closed his mouth. "Well, uh, sure."

He'd never asked her to pray with him before. Humbled, she took his hand in both of hers and bowed her head. "Father God," she said, "thank You for the gifts You give us, the tools to use for Your glory. Phil has always had a heart for ministering to others, first as a doctor, then as an Army medic, and finally as an EMT. Guide him to make the decision You desire him to make. Influence him, encourage him, provoke him. Remind him that his talents belong to You. We love You, Lord. Amen."

He stayed silent for several moments when she lifted her head. Finally, he said, "Thank you." His voice was raw, rough. "That was nearly identical to a prayer Winston prayed."

She stood and leaned over to hug him. His arms came around her, pulling her tightly to him. When he released her, she straightened and said, "I'm glad." She gestured toward the door with her thumb. "I'll see you Thursday morning."

Phil stared at the logo of the hospital on his laptop screen. They had five residency openings for the emergency department starting in January. He'd filled everything out to apply for one of them. He'd read over every field, prayed over every answer. Now his finger hovered over the submit button.

His stomach twisted into a ball of nerves. Could he do this again?

He needed to do something to move his life forward. The EMT job was never meant to be anything permanent. He only intended to work it until he could think of what he wanted to do with his life.

Did he really want to go back to being a doctor?

Emergency medicine was not the same as oral surgery. He could probably get back into the surgical field without having to start back at the day after medical school graduation. That would certainly be the easier path.

However, he didn't want the easy path. He wanted the correct path. Before he could find another excuse to hesitate, he hit the button.

They probably wouldn't even short-list him. A lot had happened between his surgical residency and now. The hospital didn't know why he'd quit, but he had left at the end of his residency. The effort and resources poured into him had gone away. That would certainly count against him in this application process.

He leaned his head back against the arm of the couch and stared at the ceiling. "Whatever happens, God, I know it's Your will. Everything was correct, so it won't be a clerical error."

He set his laptop on the coffee table just as a knock sounded on his door. "One moment!" he said, then pushed himself up and hopped over to where he'd left his crutches. When he opened the door, he shifted to hide his left side.

An older man with light brown skin, a thick black mustache, and a long, lean frame greeted him with an open badge. Phil recognized the federal marshal star. "Mr. Osbourne?"

"Yes."

"I'm Jorge Alvarado, out of Fort Lauderdale. I know it's late. Could I come in and take a few moments of your time?"

Phil took a step back and held the door open. "Please." He led the way to his table and gestured at a chair. "Have a seat. Can I get you some coffee?"

"No, but I appreciate it."

He gave Alvarado some credit for trying not to stare at his leg. After maneuvering his chair out, he set his crutches against the wall in easy reach. "How can I help you?"

"Mr. Osbourne, I worked with your brother on securing protection for Lola Molina and her children. But it was a brief conversation without any names, just the situation. Two days later, we received a cancellation of the planned meeting and I had nothing else to go on." He reached into his suit jacket and pulled out a manila envelope folded in half. "Then I received this packet. It arrived in our mail sorting facility two weeks ago, but somehow it didn't get delivered to me until yesterday."

Phil took the envelope from him and recognized his brother's handwriting on the address. "What is it?"

"In a letter, your brother explained that he didn't trust the computer system. That he'd used the proper electronic channels to request help for Mrs. Molina and it had disappeared twice. He felt like someone on his end kept sabotaging his efforts to help her. He wanted me to have a hard copy of her file in case something happened to him before we could meet."

Phil's heart twisted. Emotion clogged his throat, burned his eyes. "He knew."

"I don't know if he knew, but he definitely acted just in case. He also mentioned a recording of Mrs. Molina's testimony." Alvarado paused. "What do you know?"

Phil's heart started pounding. His mouth went dry, and he wished he had a glass of water. Should he mention that he had the recording? Could he trust this man? He stared at the envelope, then looked at the marshal. "I know enough. But I don't know you. I'd need to meet you under more official circumstances, preferably in your office, before I'd be able to tell you anything at all."

Alvarado's mustache moved as he smiled. "I appreciate your paranoia."

"I think it's justified."

"Indeed." Alvarado took the envelope and put it back in his pocket, then opened his badge holder. "Take a photo of my identification card. Go ahead and research me. In the meantime, if the state attorney's office will reinstate the investigation into Hector Molina, then I will be happy to help with Mrs. Molina."

Phil reached for his phone and snapped a picture. "What do you mean, 'reinstate'? I thought there was a joint operation with the DEA."

"I contacted their office and was told that there is no longer a current investigation."

He frowned. Winston had worked for over a year on that case and actually named Vibora when he died. How could there possibly be no investigation? "What about Simpson, the man who was searching Winston's apartment? Wasn't his death linked to Hector Molina?"

"Miami homicide linked fingerprint evidence to a known drug addict that Simpson had used as an informant. He was found dead from a cocaine overdose. They closed the case."

Phil shook his head. "No. I don't buy that."

"Neither do I. I did some digging and discovered that his tongue was spliced like a snake."

"Vibora—viper," Phil said.

"Exactly. The record was changed and there was no investigation. I don't believe some drug addict shot him up. I'd like very much to know how that happened, but I don't know who to trust here in Miami."

Anger bubbled in Phil's chest. "I appreciate the information, Marshal. However, I also don't know who to trust, and that includes you."

"I understand. There's a reason I'm here in person." Alvarado pulled a business card from his pocket and set it on the table, then stood. "It was nice to meet you. I'll see myself out."

After the marshal left, Phil called his father and explained about his visitor. "How could there not be an investigation?"

His dad let out a breath. "I don't know. Maybe the year of monitoring didn't reveal enough evidence to go forward."

"Dad, Lola Molina was willing to testify. She has names, dates, she knows the system."

"We already knew that Winston suspected someone in his office. Perhaps the person there sabotaged the data from the investigation. There's nothing we can do on the outside."

He thought about his meeting with Kim Jones. "Remember the woman Winston brought to the Christmas party two years ago?"

"Yeah. The redhead from his office."

"I met with her last night. She said that she couldn't find anything on the investigation. But if Alvarado has Winston's notes and I give him the interview with Lola, then she might have enough. Maybe I'll call her."

"That's probably a good idea."

"Thanks, Dad."

His dad chuckled. "I wish I wasn't so bound by the law that my hands are tied in helping you."

Letting out a deep breath, Phil said, "Me too."

CHAPTER
★
EIGHTEEN

NOVEMBER 17

After running three miles with Phil and stopping at six exercise stations in between, Melissa lay on a bench and covered her eyes with her arm. When Phil squeezed water on her, she didn't even move.

"Don't even care that you just did that," she said. She lifted her arm and glanced over at him. "Are you even tired?"

He shrugged. "I do this course all the time. My muscles are used to it."

She slapped her belly and sat up. "Ohh, yeah. I'm feeling that."

He grinned. "You'll feel it more tomorrow."

"Don't worry. I'll be back here tomorrow doing it."

He laughed. "You think?" He sat next to her. "I'd give it a day. Take it easy tomorrow."

She looked at him out of the corner of her eye. "I'll see how I feel and decide."

"Fair enough."

She pushed herself to her feet. "Come on. I'll buy you a smoothie."

They walked over to the smoothie truck. Melissa ordered strawberry banana and Phil ordered acai and peach. He took a sip and the cold, sweet drink filled his mouth.

Melissa started toward the beach, then stopped and looked at him. "Can you walk on the sand in your running blade?"

He looked down at the swishing silver blade that replaced the foot. "Yes, but it's hard."

Instead, they sat on a bench and looked out at the water. He took another sip of his drink. "This would be a good day to take the boat out."

She glanced up at the bright blue sky. "Yeah, if you didn't have to go to work in two hours."

His stomach twisted as he decided to go ahead and say it out loud. "That reminds me. I applied for that residency position."

She gasped. "Really?" She reached over and took his hand. "Oh, Phil, that is so exciting."

He shrugged. "It's late. It starts in January. I don't know if they've already filled all the slots, but I felt like this was a decision I needed to make. Even if they don't let me in this year, I've started my mental path."

She screwed her nose up. "Quit being a pessimist. It's entirely possible that they were looking for one more amazing candidate and they'll see your application and put you in the slot. There's a deadline for a reason, and it hasn't passed yet."

"That's true," he said with a grin. He had made a concentrated effort in the last week to not be so grouchy, but this was that old him coming out. "I'm not trying to be a pessimist. I just think I don't want to get my hopes up too much in case it doesn't happen."

"Of course it will happen. And just remember, God's timing is always perfect." She moved her straw up and down in her cup. "When will you know?"

"I'm hoping before Thanksgiving. But I'm not sure."

"Well, I am ridiculously excited. Even if you don't get accepted, this was a huge decision for you to make. Your path to recovery has certainly taken you on some interesting journeys, hasn't it?"

He looked down at his leg. He hadn't thought of that before. "You know, you're right. The decisions that led me to becoming an addict led me down the path to losing my leg. It's a rather profound thought. I may have to consider that for a while."

"I didn't mean to spark profound reflection."

He studied her. "It doesn't matter if you meant to. You did. Thanks."

They looked out at the water in silence for a while, and then Melissa asked, "How are you?"

He pursed his lips and considered his answer. "I miss him. I keep thinking that I'll wake up and it will all have been this terrible dream. So far, that hasn't happened." He sighed. "My parents are doing so much better than I am with it, which is strange to me. I should be the strong one for them, but I'm hurting too much." He didn't add that he'd gone to a few extra meetings to help battle the trickle of a thought of how easy it would be to emotionally escape with chemicals.

In a move that surprised him, she put her head on his shoulder. "Is there anything I can do to help you?"

Emotion clogged his throat. How had he ended up with her in his life? God had truly blessed him by giving him Melissa. "I don't think anybody can do anything for me. I just need to take the time to go through the grieving process. It will happen. I think the timing was just bad on my end."

She took a sip of her drink. "That's rather insightful, Mr. Osbourne."

He raised an eyebrow. "That's Doctor Osbourne to you."

With a laugh that rang out over the entire area, she said, "You are absolutely correct. Please forgive the oversight."

He stood and held out his hand. "The longer you sit here, the harder it's going to be to walk away. You need to go shower and get some heat on those muscles."

She stood and groaned, clutching her abdomen. "Oh my. Looks like tomorrow's going to be a lot of fun. Maybe I will take it easy."

He shook his head and smiled. "I kept telling you." He held her hand as they walked back to her car. "Are you going to see if Lola wants to take the kids to the Thanksgiving festival at church?"

She nodded. "Yes. I think that will be a great way to get her foot in the door at church. She has no experience with it at all. I wish I knew what to say to reach her."

He leaned against the car and crossed his arms over his chest. "It's not necessarily up to you, Melissa. Just love her. If God has something for you to say to her, He'll give it to you."

"True." She looked up at the sky, then at him. Emotions swirled in her brown eyes. "I wish they had never separated us. I don't understand what my aunts and uncles were thinking when they did it."

He put a hand on her shoulder, gently squeezing. "It's possible that the relatives on your father's side pressed matters. If Vibora truly backed them, they would have had the money to fight for custody. Did you ever ask your uncle or aunt about it?"

She shook her head. "I never really thought to ask them when they were alive. My uncle Alejandro said he thinks it was because my father's sister was Lola's godmother, so she went to her. He told me he wasn't part of that conversation. When I mentioned Colombia, he didn't even bat an eye. I think he truly didn't know."

"I'm sorry. I know you're hurting because of it. But at least you have Lola now."

She leaned forward and rested her forehead on his chest. "True. I just wish that we could bring her some closure with her husband. But because of who he is and what he is, there's no room for closure. We can only hide her."

He put his arms around her, wishing he had a way to fix all of the wrongs going on around them right now. "You're probably right. I'm still working on the Marshals Service, and I've communicated with a coworker of Winston's, a woman he saw outside of work sometimes. My prayer is that God will open those doors when they need to be opened." He rubbed his hands up and down her back, then cupped her cheek. "You keep doing what you're doing."

She nodded. "I will." She bit her lip. "I have always known my dad was a bad man. But to know my family is connected to such evil . . ." Her breath hitched and she closed her eyes. When she opened them, the shadows in the corners of her eyes faded. "I have to get to the church to help set up for tonight."

He wanted to keep holding her, keep touching her. With great reluctance, he let her go.

"I'll see you later," she said. "Thanks for the workout."

As she opened her car door, he said, "I get off at seven. I'll come straight to the church."

She grinned. "I'll save you a slice of pie."

Melissa and Fran carried a table to the place marked in sidewalk chalk on the parking lot. Melissa looked up at the sky. "It's not supposed to even want to rain."

"I'm so thankful," Fran said. "Remember that year we had to bring this inside? So many people, so little room." She pulled a tablecloth out of the basket at her feet, and she and Melissa each took an end. "It was that year the tropical storm came through. Imagine, so late in November."

"I guess that's why the hurricane season goes through November thirtieth," Melissa said. She straightened the maroon-and-orange-checkered cloth, then clipped it to the table.

Their Thanksgiving festival had become a community event. Several hundred people would attend tonight.

While Melissa and Fran set up the tables, Phil's mom helped one of the deacons set out metal folding chairs. By the time they finished, they'd set up forty tables with ten chairs at each. Then they set up the potluck stations. Because they had so much food coming, they created sections with main courses and meats, sides, veggies and salads, desserts, and drinks. That should help with the flow of people.

Melissa looked at her phone, fielded a text from Sharon about an appointment for a family counseling session, and then said to Fran, "I have to run, friend. I'll see you tonight."

"You were a lifesaver. Thanks for your help."

Melissa walked over to Candace. "I have to go to work."

The older woman was inserting a sign into its stand but stopped to hug her. "I'll see you tonight," she said.

"Yep. I'm hoping to bring my sister."

"You should. Those kids would love to get out."

She waved as she went back to her car. On her drive home, she listened to a podcast on trauma in the lives of young children. As the speaker remarked on the lasting damage that can happen in the psyche of children who suffer trauma, she couldn't help but think about her own experience at such a young age. How much of who she was now was tied to that five-year-old hiding beside the bed? How many times during those five years had she witnessed her father beat her mother and then coped in the aftermath?

What kind of person would she be today if she'd never had that trauma, if she'd enjoyed a normal childhood with two loving parents and a younger sister? Would she still have been interested in the makeup of men's and women's brains? Would the psychology of sociopaths even interest her? Would God have led her to open the center that had helped hundreds of people over the years?

The revving of a motor broke through her reflection. It sounded very similar to the one in the church parking lot on Tuesday night. She looked in her rearview mirror and saw a motorcycle. Was it the same one?

Heart pounding, mouth suddenly dry, she quickly moved into the turn lane and made a left instead of going straight.

Two blocks later, the motorcycle crossed her path in front of her.

What to do?

She couldn't risk going to the shelter, so she drove to the nearest police station and parked in front of it. She rolled her window down and listened but didn't hear the familiar motor. After five minutes, she got back on the road and took a zigzag approach to her building.

The guard waved her through, and she parked in her space. When she got out of the car, she listened some more but still heard nothing. She must just be paranoid after the close encounter Tuesday night.

Shaking her head to bring herself back to reality, she bent to get her purse out of the car and groaned. She pressed her hands to her abdomen. "So sore," she said to herself. "Silly to try to keep up with the indomitable Phil Osbourne."

She made it to the counseling room with less than a minute to spare. "Hi, Anna," she said, shutting the door. "How are you?"

Anna's green cast on her arm matched the green stripes on her white skirt. She frowned. "Why do we have to meet with you if we want to live here?"

"Because I'm a trained therapist and a licensed counselor. By the time people reach the point where they have to seek shelter from domestic abuse, there's a level of injury done to their emotions, their psychology, their souls. I'm trained to help heal that damage the same way your orthopedic doctor is trained to help heal that broken wrist your boyfriend gave you." She gestured around her. "You've done your first group session, you've met with Sharon. Now it's my turn."

Anna looked at her cast. "You guys keep trying to get me to talk about it."

"Talking helps."

"I don't like to."

"I know. That's not uncommon either." She pulled out the purple notebook she'd labeled "Anna." She had a separate notebook for every resident. "Before you started dating him, did you live at home?"

"Yeah. I was in high school."

"How long has it been since you saw your parents?"

Anna looked at her lap. In a shaky voice she said, "I can't remember."

"Did you have a fight with them?"

A tear slid down her cheek. "Not really. My mom wanted me to wait to move in with him. He yelled at her and my dad yelled at him and everything was terrible." She covered her eyes with her free hand and sniffled. Melissa put a tissue on her lap and she grabbed it. "I never felt safe calling them after that."

"One of the things people like him do is separate you from your friends and family," Melissa said. "They work that psychological angle until you don't even want to see those people anymore. Would you like to call your parents?"

Anna's eyes widened. "He was so terrible to them. I don't know if they would want me to call them."

"How about writing them a letter? You can explain that he's in jail now, that you're safe in a shelter, and that you miss them."

Anna held up her hand. "I couldn't write. Do you think I could just call?"

"Of course."

"Right now?"

Melissa's stomach twisted. "If you feel like you need to do that, then yes. Where do they live?"

"Tallahassee."

She stood and walked across the room, praying that the parents' hearts and minds would be open and receptive to their daughter's phone call. Anna was incredibly weak and so very scared. She needed to not feel alone in the world.

Melissa picked up a phone and carried it over to her. "Here you go, hon. Would you like me to leave?"

Anna dialed the number rapidly, then held the phone up to her ear and nodded. As Melissa picked up her notebook and pen, Anna said, "Mama?"

Through the phone, Melissa heard, "Anna?"

Anna started sobbing. "Oh, Mama. I was so wrong. Please, I was so wrong."

The raw emotion emanating off her overwhelmed Melissa, and she had to ward off tears as she left the room. She went into the group therapy room next door to make notes about Anna's session.

About ten minutes later, Anna came out, smiling. For the first time since Melissa had met her, she had color in her cheeks. "My daddy is going to have a ticket waiting for me at the airline counter. There's a two o'clock flight."

Joy flooded Melissa's heart, and she stood and hugged her. "Oh, that's wonderful."

"Can you give me a ride?"

She looked at the clock. "No, but I'll get you one." She picked up the phone and dialed the guardhouse. "This is Melissa. Can you ask Terry to come to my office, please?"

She led the way to her office and made a notation in the

logbook about Anna's call. Then she opened the petty cash box and handed Anna fifty dollars.

"What's this for?" Anna asked.

"Lunch. And money for your pocket in case you need it."

Terry came into the office. "Yes, ma'am?"

Melissa pulled her spare car key out of her desk drawer. "Will you drive Anna to the airport? She'll give you the airline information."

"Yes, ma'am." He took the key and looked at Anna. "I'll meet you in the parking garage."

Anna raced from the room to go pack her bag, and Melissa said, "I appreciate you doing this."

Terry straightened his uniform belt. "Anything for you, Miss Melissa. I'm happy to help."

CHAPTER

★

NINETEEN

Melissa walked into Lola's room and crouched down to say hi to Mathias. "Whatcha doing?"

He looked up from his tablet. "Matching." He showed her the game. "I pick one, then find the one that matches." He hit a blue square and it revealed a bright red-and-blue ball. Then he chose another square in the grid, generating a match. "I knew it was there because I saw it before."

"Good job."

Gabriele laughed and ran in her direction. Sometimes the toddler went straight to her and loved it when Melissa picked her up and loved on her. Other times, she completely stiffened up and didn't want anything to do with anyone but Lola. Today, she ran straight into Melissa and fell against her shoulder.

"Well, hi there," Melissa said, kissing the top of her curly black head. "I'm happy to see you too."

"She's happier every day," Lola said. "I really think that our home was emotionally oppressive to her. I mean, I know I was so hurt and sad. I'm sure she fed off that energy."

"You're probably right. It's been a few weeks. She's had time to forget." Melissa stood. "How are you?"

"I'm okay. I'd like to decide what I'm going to do next." Lola went into the kitchen area, where a peeled and sliced apple sat on the cutting board. She put half of the slices in a bowl, then started cutting the others into chunks. "I mean, do I just pick a new city? What happens if Hector finds me?"

Melissa snatched an apple chunk. "I don't know that you need to decide now. Besides, Phil is working on getting the Marshals Service back in play. You're safe here."

"I know. But I feel like I'm a burden." Lola scooped the chunks of apples into a bowl and put a silicone lid on it.

"Not to me you're not."

Lola handed the kids their snacks, then pulled out a chair at the table. Melissa joined her. "I appreciate that. But—"

Melissa shook her head. "No 'but.' That's what this place is for. Sometimes residents take a few months before they're able to make the next move, and that's okay. And all of that aside, you're my sister. You're welcome to stay here indefinitely. I love having you here and will be sad when you go."

Lola stared at the tabletop, then looked up at Melissa. Tears swam in her eyes. "I'm so happy you found me," she whispered.

Putting her hand on top of Lola's, Melissa said, "I didn't find you. Phil did it without my knowledge." She smiled. "He knew how long I'd been looking, though."

A smile pushed the tears away. "Does he even know how much he loves you?"

Melissa giggled. "No." She glanced over at Mathias, who stood next to the window, looking out onto the courtyard while he slowly ate an apple slice. "I came to see if you wanted to come to my church with me tonight." She could tell Lola was about to decline, so she added, "It's just a big celebration of Thanksgiving. We'll have a potluck dinner, and they have all sorts of fun for the kids. Bounce houses, face painting, balloon animals." She looked back at the kids. "It will be fun in a safe environment. Hundreds of people will be there, so there will be a little anonymity in the crowd."

Lola pursed her lips. "Okay. Sure. Yeah. That will be fun."

Gabriele ran up to her and held out the bowl. Lola held it while the toddler stuck her hand in the hole and pulled out a piece of apple. She held it up to Melissa, then popped it into her own mouth and ran across the room.

"Perfect. We'll leave at four." Melissa looked at her watch. "I have to run. I have a counseling session in five minutes." She stood. "Bye, Matty, Gabby. See you in a little while."

Phil put his slice of pumpkin pie and coffee on the table next to Lola. She had her back turned and held Gabriele in her lap, watching Melissa and Mathias at a dart-throwing station. When he pulled out his chair, she visibly jumped and spun around.

She put her hand over her heart. "Oh! You startled me."

He looked around at his church family. His father, the judge, was sitting on the seat in the dunking booth, mocking one of the deacons for his lack of aim. He glanced at his mother painting a purple butterfly on a little girl's face.

Then he rested his gaze on Melissa, who held Mathias's hand while chatting with two of her girlfriends.

"You're safe here."

Lola looked down and nodded, then put her shoulders back a little and turned her body toward him. "Did you always go to this church?"

"Yeah. When I was little, it was much smaller. Now we have hundreds of members."

"Did you know Missy all this time, then?"

He took a sip of coffee. "No. We've talked about when she started coming. It was right before I joined the military. At the time, I was working insane hours at the hospital, and I was going through some personal stuff that kept me from gracing the doorway." He smiled. "But she knew Winston. They'd worked on some committees together."

She propped her chin in her hands and smiled at him. Even though he'd gotten used to it by now, he still found the similarities between the two sisters remarkable. "But when you came back from the Army?"

He thought back to the first time he'd returned to church. It had taken his mom weeks to convince him to go. "When I came home from the Army, I started going again. I volunteered one day to work at the church's soup kitchen. Melissa and I worked together. She invited me to dinner, but I had a three p.m. shift that day so I made it breakfast the next day."

Lola smiled in a way that made her eyes sparkle. "And the rest is history."

He couldn't help the smile that appeared. "So far."

Lola looked all around and then refocused on Melissa. "I've never seen anything like this before."

He raised an eyebrow. "The festival?"

She shook her head. "No. This kind of community. I've watched Missy talk to seventeen different people. Every one of them seemed happy to see her, to talk with her. She's hugged necks and kissed cheeks and talked to babies. I've just never seen anything like it before."

He looked over at Melissa, and his heart rate sped up. "Your sister is an incredibly dynamic individual. People tend to want to be around her." He took a big bite of pie, enjoying the burst of spices on his tongue. "She can talk to anyone."

Lola shook her head. "I'm not like that. I don't even know what to say to people in this kind of situation." She toyed with the napkin next to her half-empty plate. "But it's more than just talking to people. It's like they love her." She looked at him with her big brown eyes. "I don't think I've ever truly been loved by people."

"Does she know how you grew up?"

Emotion flared in her eyes, then disappeared. "Not the nitty-gritty. She knows Colombia, but not the compound." She absently rubbed her arms and stared at Phil. "How do you know?"

"My military career took me places, gave me some pretty rich insight into the world." He took another sip of coffee while he contemplated how he wanted to respond. "You have an opportunity here to give your children what you didn't have."

She looked around. "Yes. I don't know how to embrace this, though. My family is Catholic, but they're not good people. To them, the rituals of the religion are just like family traditions instead of something meaningful."

He carefully worded what he wanted to say about what

made his church so special. "It's less about religion and more about community. This is a community of people who come together under a shared love of God. There is a religious ceremony and a 'religion' associated with it, but it's love that generates this environment. Not religion."

She sat silent for several moments. "I'd like to understand that kind of love."

Before he could respond, Melissa walked up with Mathias. "We have a dart master here!"

Lola turned toward him. "Oh yeah?"

He held up a sticker of a dove flying in front of a rainbow. "I picked a sticker."

Lola nodded. "I would have too."

Melissa sat across from Phil, and he turned his attention to her. "You made it," she said.

He gestured to his uniform. "Eleven to seven today. Thanks for saving me the pie."

She glanced at his empty plate and smiled. "You're welcome. Sorry it wasn't key lime. That was gone before I could get to it."

Key lime pie suddenly made him think of Winston's funeral, and a dark cloud tried to insert itself into his mood. With effort, he pushed it back. "I'm surprised my mom didn't have a whole one set aside for me." He reached his hand across the table, and she put hers in it. Giving her fingers a light squeeze, he asked, "Having fun?"

With a grin, she said, "Absolutely. I'm so glad we changed this from October. Having it right before Thanksgiving just adds that extra element of wonderfulness to it."

His mom walked up. "Phil! I didn't know you would be here." She hugged his shoulders from behind and took the chair next to Melissa. "If I had known you were coming, I would've put a key lime pie aside for you."

Phil laughed. "I just told Melissa that I'm surprised you didn't."

"Clearly, you know me well."

His soaking-wet dad joined them and flicked water toward his mom, making her laugh. "Looks like someone finally dunked ya," she said.

He wrapped a towel around his waist. "George Gifford. Gets me every year."

Phil drained the last of his coffee. "That's because he never could beat you in the courtroom."

His dad nodded. "You speak the truth, Son."

Lola stood. "I'm going to take the kids over to that bounce house. Gabby should do okay in the little princess one."

Melissa gestured in that direction. "That one has an age limit of three, so she should be safe."

Phil leaned forward after Lola walked away. "I had a good conversation with her while you were throwing darts. She's seeking what she sees here but can't define it. You might want to get her alone and away from distractions and spend some time talking with her about it."

The smile that covered her face filled him with joy. He wondered how he could actually feel the joy radiating off her. "That is phenomenal. Thank you."

He shrugged. "Hey, I just had pie. She did all the talking."

They chatted with his parents for about twenty minutes. The entire time, he watched Melissa in her happy place, surrounded by her church family, her biological family, and his family. A lump burned in his throat when he thought about the piece missing from his family. Winston would have taken his turn in the dunking booth. He did every year.

He leaned toward Melissa. "Want to walk?"

"Sure."

For the first time in front of the church body, he took her hand. At first, he felt very conspicuous, like everyone noticed. But no one even looked at them twice.

They strolled through the crowds, stopping to chat with friends. One couple asked if they could make dinner plans, maybe double date.

Was he ready for this kind of relationship?

As he glanced down at Melissa, he realized that he was. He wanted her by his side officially. They made plans and continued on.

She grinned up at him. "Nothing like making it official."

He glanced around. "I expected more people to notice."

She waved her hand dismissively. "Everyone already thought so. We're a couple in their minds." She nudged him. "Just took you a little longer than the rest to figure it out."

He laughed and let go of her hand to pull her closer. He waved at a friend over her head, and they strolled across the parking lot to the side of the church. Melissa leaned her shoulder against the brick building. Phil rested his forearm above her head.

"Phil," Melissa said, but he cupped her cheek and put his thumb over her lips to silence her. He studied her face in the moonlight, running his gaze over every feature as if needing to memorize it. Her beauty made his heart beat furiously.

He'd fought his desire for her for so long. He just wanted to quit fighting, to quit resenting how the failures in his life, the decisions he'd made, and the loss of his leg made him feel.

239

Before he could talk himself out of it, he lowered his mouth to kiss her. Just before their lips touched, he paused, giving her a chance to back away, to give it more time, to be certain. She grabbed his shirt and pulled him the rest of the way to her.

To say that she felt perfect against him would be the understatement of the year. As soon as their lips touched, it was as if everything fell into place. She slid her arm around his neck and pulled him closer.

She tasted like coffee and pumpkin pie. Her hair tickled the back of his hand, and her skin felt warm and soft. He thought he could just drown in the feel and smell of her.

He kissed her and kissed her, then finally pulled his mouth away and rested his forehead against hers, his eyes closed as he panted to catch a breath. She slowly slid her hands from around his shoulders and down his chest until they hung limply at her sides.

"Well," she said in a hoarse voice, "that certainly was a long time coming."

He chuckled and leaned back enough to kiss the tip of her nose. "Worth the wait."

While the kids slept the exhausted sleep brought on by excitement, bounce houses, and lots of good food, Melissa and Lola sat at Lola's table with a pot of raspberry herbal tea between them.

"Phil told me that you were asking about the thing that makes our church body so special," Melissa said.

Lola propped her chin in her hands. "It was so beautiful, watching you tonight. You're part of this huge family and everyone just loves you."

Melissa smiled. "It's not exclusive to me, Lola. It's just how our church is. We love God, we love each other. We're a family."

"I think I would like something like that."

Melissa had counseled countless people about the peace that a relationship with God could bring them. She fervently prayed for God to help her with the words that would inspire Lola to seek Him. "It starts with wanting to draw closer to God, wanting to be part of that, for the community could never be enough."

Lola took a sip of her tea and stared at the table. "I have this longing inside of me. I'd like to know more."

Melissa reached across the table and rubbed her upper arm. "I'm happy to help you discover it."

Lola stood and stretched. "For now, though, I have to go to bed. It's almost one."

"How is that possible?"

She chuckled. "It starts with getting home at eleven."

Melissa stood and they hugged. "You can talk to God on your own too, Sister. But I'm happy to discuss it more tomorrow."

"Thank you."

On the way to her room, Melissa spied the light under Sharon's door. She paused and tapped on it.

Seconds later, Sharon answered. She had on a pair of cotton shorts and a blue T-shirt. "Everything okay?"

"Yeah. Just headed to my room and saw your light."

Sharon leaned against the doorframe. "Finishing up some correspondence with a group in Australia. I'm headed down there early in the year to speak. I was hoping you'd help me with some case studies I've done."

"Absolutely. What are you looking at?"

"The people who go back. I want to see if time of year affects it. Like, you know, next week is Thanksgiving. How many will start missing family and friends and decide it wasn't as bad as they thought it was? Et cetera."

"Gotcha." Melissa thought of the reports she'd made. "I could compile data. It's all there. It's just a matter of telling the computer what report to run."

Sharon put a hand on her chest. "Not I," she said with a smile. "I know how to read the data. It's generating it that goes way above my head."

"Right?" Melissa leaned forward, and they kissed each other on the cheek. "Good night, friend. See you in the morning." She crossed the hall and looked back. "Lola is asking questions, seeking God."

Sharon silently clapped her hands together. "I will be praying!"

In her room, Melissa contemplated showering but was just too exhausted to give it more than a passing thought. Instead, she crawled on top of the covers and wrapped up in the soft blanket she kept at the foot of the bed.

As she started to drift off, she thought of Phil and the way he'd kissed her tonight. Oh, and kissed her and kissed her.

"Thank You, Lord," she whispered. "It's so nice to see him happy."

She drifted off to sleep with a smile on her face.

CHAPTER

TWENTY

Phil pushed himself up to the side of the bathtub and reached for his towel. Somehow, his hip slid out from under him and he went tumbling. He landed hard on his shoulder on the tile floor and whacked his head against the side of the toilet.

For several minutes, he lay there, staring at the ceiling, trying to understand what had just happened. Unbidden, his mind went back to that February almost two years ago and the jungle of Katangela.

He'd never even felt the bullet go into his thigh. Not really. But one moment later he felt super dizzy and had to sit down. That was when he saw the blood seeping out of his uniform trousers. He cut them open, using the scissors in his kit. It didn't take long to discover that the bullet had ripped through his femoral artery.

He immediately took his scalpel and tried to get to the

ends of the arteries to clamp them down. But he started going into shock. Before he could finish the procedure, his team leader, Rick Norton, appeared at his side. He clamped off the ends, and then his team carried him on a makeshift stretcher to an American missionary doctor.

She tried to save his leg. Perhaps if he'd been able to stay in her clinic on consistent IV antibiotics and fluids, he would still have his leg. But the local warlord had taken exception to his son dying in the firefight and came after them. Consequently, they'd had to traverse the jungle through rivers and valleys to reach the US embassy.

Phil finally sat up and grabbed his towel, though he'd been lying there long enough that his skin had completely dried. Unwilling to fall again in such a tight space, he crawled on his elbows into his room and pulled himself up onto his bed.

He should put his running prosthetic on and go for a nice jog. Instead, he pulled the covers up over his head and rolled over.

It had been months since he'd felt phantom pain in his left leg, and he knew what he felt right now was entirely psychosomatic. He was angry and depressed about the loss of his brother, stressed about the career decision he'd made, and embarking on a relationship with a woman he'd loved for over a year, and now he'd fallen. His leg didn't hurt. His heart and soul hurt.

What would make him feel better was exercise. And prayer. Maybe both at the same time.

Having felt sorry for himself long enough, he pushed the covers away and got himself standing on one leg. With practiced dexterity, he hopped over to his dresser, pulled out running clothes, and picked up the blade runner he'd left leaning against the dresser.

As he stretched, his phone rang, but he ignored it. On his way out the door, it rang again. Not wanting to speak to anyone, he left his phone on his kitchen counter, then left.

As he walked down the breezeway, a neighbor came toward him with her two kids. He nodded good morning and tried to ignore the kids loudly talking about his leg, or lack thereof. He clenched his jaw so hard that his teeth ached. As soon as they went into their apartment, he leaned against the wall and pressed his knuckles to his eyes.

"Why, God? Why?" he asked through clenched teeth. "Why?"

Pushing away from the wall, he bounded down the stairs and out onto the street. He put his sunglasses on and ran toward the park on the water.

His mind went back to the application he'd submitted for the emergency room residency. Why did he think he could compete with kids much younger than his thirty-three years? Kids who probably had both legs and who hadn't just suffered a tragic loss.

What made him think he could do this?

Oh, right. Winston had. And Melissa did. She had encouraged him until he believed her. To what end? Did he truly want this, or was he just doing it for her? He really needed to analyze that before he took such a big step.

He ran his normal route, trying to pretend that people didn't stare. He rarely chose Saturday to run because so many more tourists were down by the water. He should have paid attention to the day.

By the time he got home, his mood had only darkened,

245

made worse by the fact that he needed another shower. This time, though, he padded the edge of the bathtub with towels so he wouldn't slip and flounder around like a fish out of water.

After he showered, he grabbed an apple and decided he could face whoever had called before. He had two missed calls from Melissa and one from Rick Norton, his old captain. How odd. He'd just thought of him while lying on the bathroom floor. He dialed him back immediately.

"Daddy," he said, using the nickname the team had called their leader. "Sorry I missed your call. I was on a run."

"Bill said you had a blade runner," Norton said in his thick Kentucky accent. "That's very cool." Norton had been an incredible leader, and the entire team had flourished under his command. Phil wondered if he knew that.

He sat on the couch and stretched his leg out in front of him. "What's up?"

"You just came to my mind. God was impressing upon me to pray for you, so I did. I wanted to check and see if there was something more specific you needed."

The fact that he'd felt impressed to pray for Phil soon after his fall made the sweat bead on his forehead. "I fell today."

After a pause, Norton asked, "Is that normal?"

"Not at all." Sighing, he added, "But it's weak. I mean, it makes me feel weak."

"You've never been one to accept weakness in yourself."

"How is DC?" Phil asked.

With a chuckle Norton said, "Not team command, but it's a good assignment." His father-in-law was the vice president of the United States. Because of that, Norton had to accept a noncombat position. "The food is better here than anywhere else."

"I bet it has to be, considering all of the brass there."

"You redirected this conversation to me. I'll accept that, but I'm going to check in on you in a couple of days."

Phil closed his eyes and leaned his head back on the couch. "Thanks for the pass."

"Do you want to pray right now?"

His heart started pounding. What did he need to bring to God that he was ignoring? "I'd like that."

Norton's rich voice flowed through the phone as he prayed for God's hand on Phil's heart. He asked God to ease the emotional pain that made him struggle, to comfort him in his time of loss, and to continue to strengthen his body. After he said, "Amen," he added, "Two years isn't a huge amount of time. You've coped with a lot, and your brother's murder piled it on. Give yourself a break here and there. You're not a superhero."

Phil smiled. "You sound like my psychiatrist."

"Happy to hear you're still seeing one, brother." Norton paused. "I have to go. Are you good?"

"Better than. Thanks for calling."

He hung up and closed his eyes, trying to figure out what he was supposed to do. Why had God sent Rick Norton as a messenger to him?

NOVEMBER 20

Sunday morning brought blue skies like Melissa had hardly ever seen. The sun shone bright, the birds sang, her three favorite worship songs played on the radio on her way to church. It was as if God had hit the happy button for her that morning.

She wore a lilac sundress, and her skin shone rich and tanned against the color. She'd even put on some lilac eye shadow and a purple-tinted lipstick to complete the outfit. As she got out of the car, she grabbed her Bible and a light sweater that she'd use to combat the air-conditioning. Phil pulled up right next to her, and she grinned at him.

"We should be careful about our timing. People will think we're coming in at the same time for a reason," she teased.

He scowled, and she realized it was going to be a grumpy-Phil kind of day. Reining back the jokes and sarcasm, she walked next to him silently. Inside, she went to her women's Sunday school class, he to his men's.

During the lesson, she tried to think of what might have made Phil so angry today. No exchange they'd had felt like it might have sparked his anger, so it clearly had nothing to do with her. It wasn't like him to not speak at all, though.

After Sunday school, she made her way to the sanctuary. When she got to her normal seat, Phil wasn't there. She glanced around but didn't see him. If he needed to not be near her for whatever reason, she'd certainly not beg for his attention.

She had a hard time concentrating during the service. The music, the sermon, the special message—all of it felt very bland and dull.

As she walked down the aisle afterward, Candace stopped her. "Hi, Melissa. I didn't see Phil this morning. Have you seen him?"

She blinked at his mom and her smiling face. "He was at Sunday school, but I didn't see him after."

A line appeared between the older woman's eyes. "Hmm. Well, if you see him, can you ask him to call me? I want to firm up plans for Thanksgiving." She snapped her fingers. "Oh! You're coming, aren't you?"

"Uh, no. Sorry. I eat Thanksgiving with my residents."

The line turned into a full-fledged frown. "Oh. I understand. What time do you eat?"

"Twelve."

"Well, phooey. We always eat at two." Candace put a hand on her arm. "We will definitely miss you." She looked at her watch. "Okay! Must scoot. Much to do before then. See you later."

When Melissa stepped outside, she noticed that the sky had darkened with a coming storm. She could barely remember the bright blue sky from a few hours ago.

Phil waited for her by her car. She set her jaw and marched up to him. "What is your problem?"

"I can't see you any longer."

He couldn't even give her so much as a "How do you do?" Her stomach twisted painfully. "You don't mean that. You've bounced around back and forth for eighteen months. I thought we were finally making progress."

"I do mean it."

"What happened since Thursday?"

He leaned against her car, crossing his prosthetic leg over his good one. "I fell."

She gasped and looked at his legs, then back at his face. "How?"

He shrugged. "I was getting out of the tub. I'd moved to the ledge, like I do every day, and somehow I slipped on some water." He rubbed his eyes with his thumb and forefinger. "I lay there completely helpless, naked, in a puddle of water." When he looked at her again, there was a finality in his eyes that she'd never seen before. "I don't want to keep pretending to be the person you deserve."

She sputtered, opening and closing her mouth. "The person I deserve?"

"I will never be whole, Melissa. I will always be this broken man who used to be able to leap tall buildings in a single bound. I'm broken. No, I'm shattered. I can't make you—"

She shot her hand up in a halting gesture. "Hold it right there, buster. Make me? Make me?" She ripped the car door open and threw her bag inside. "I'm done trying, Phil. Seriously. You've kept me on this imaginary leash for well over a year and then suddenly start acting like maybe you're finally over yourself, and then, bam! Not over yourself yet." She stepped closer and put a finger on his chest. "I have been in love with you for ages, and you just trample my feelings under your feet willy-nilly whenever you get a bug in your bonnet." She got into the driver's seat. "And yes, I know I used the plural 'feet' instead of 'foot.' Move out of my way. There's only room for one in your little pity party."

She slammed the car door so hard she was surprised that the window didn't break. She started the car and put it into gear.

". . . has been upgraded to a hurricane. Right now, it's just sitting out there in the Atlantic. We know it's Thanksgiving week and it's late in November, but we'll be watching Gertrude to see what she does next."

Melissa flicked the radio off and shook her head. Blue skies and birds singing had taken her to church, and three hours later, cloudy skies, a breakup, and a late November hurricane took her home.

Maybe she needed to go back to bed.

Once she was home, she walked out to the courtyard. Mr. Horton had set the grill out for her this morning before he left to preach at his small country church out in the Everglades. She lit the long line of coals, then sat back and watched the flames eat at the charcoal. Her mind went back to Phil. Since she'd met him, he had fought what she thought should be "them" the entire time. But the way he'd acted in the last two weeks made her think "they" had finally won. That his silly notion of incompleteness would no longer be an issue.

Silly her.

The door opened behind her, and Sharon came out of the dining room. She wore a black pantsuit with a leopard-print belt and leopard-print heels and had wound her platinum-blond hair into a French twist. Oversized sunglasses dominated her face.

"Hello, love," she said, gliding on those impossible heels.

"Hey."

"Oh, what happened?" Sharon rushed forward and slipped an arm around her. "Why so blue?"

"Phil broke it off."

Sharon gasped and turned her around. "Again?"

"I know. Again." Melissa sighed and covered her face with her hands. "Why did I wait for him for so long?"

Sharon ran her hands up and down Melissa's arms in a soothing manner. "Because he's perfect for you. Not to mention drop-dead gorgeous. And, honestly, even his grouchiness can be endearing."

Melissa laughed. "It is not."

"Well, at least you're not a puddle of tears now." Sharon directed her over to a table. "Do you think you'll be amenable when he changes his mind? Again?"

Would she? Or would she have the strength to tell him in no uncertain terms that she was no longer interested in him? Or his grouchiness.

"I don't think so." Melissa sighed. "But I want to."

"I know you do." Sharon squeezed her tight, then stood. "You just sit here. Mope. Get it out of your system. Then cheer up for our guests. It's a holiday week and they're going to need joy."

"You're right." She looked up at the gray sky and noticed a patch of blue. "Hurricane's in the Atlantic."

"Gertrude. Had an auntie by that name. Favorite auntie of them all." Sharon winked at her, then headed back into the building.

Melissa watched a bird fly past the patch of blue and tried to reclaim the joy she'd felt that morning.

What was she supposed to do about Phil? Did she even want to try anymore?

CHAPTER

★

TWENTY-ONE

NOVEMBER 21

Even though Melissa had promised herself that she wouldn't wallow in her broken heart, she still found herself lying on her couch Monday night, clutching a throw pillow, tears drenching the hair at her temples. She stared up at the ceiling, trying to figure out what was wrong with her that Phil would reject her love so easily.

He'd fallen? That was the profound catalyst that had destroyed their future? How dare he?

When a knock sounded at her door, she looked down at her baggy blue sweatpants and orange sweatshirt. She sighed and pushed herself to her feet, tossing the pillow back onto the couch. Using the sleeve of her shirt to wipe her tears, she opened the door. Sharon stood there holding two bowls of chocolate ice cream topped with whipped cream and chocolate chips. Melissa laughed through her tears and stepped to the side.

They sat on either end of the couch. "You are a good friend," Melissa said around a mouthful of frozen chocolate.

"I'm just happy to have an excuse to eat calories that I don't feel like I need to work off." Sharon picked up her spoon. "Ice cream eaten after a breakup doesn't count toward your daily caloric intake. In case you were wondering."

Melissa swirled her spoon through the whipped cream. "You know that I never count calories. Life is too short."

"You are less inclined toward curves than I," Sharon said.

Melissa looked at her friend's size two frame but didn't argue with her. She just took another bite of ice cream.

"I'm so mad at Phil right now," she said, sniffling. "But I'm also heartbroken. I just don't know which emotion is stronger."

"Have you talked to him?" Sharon asked.

"No. He wasn't at church last night either." She sniffled. "You know, I waited months and months for him to just come to. If he had quit wanting to casually see me, that would be one thing. But to decide to start a relationship, then just a few weeks later, boom. It's like he tried me out and decided I wasn't what he thought he was getting."

Sharon put the barely touched ice cream on the coffee table and turned toward Melissa. "You know that's not true. He can't stay away from you. That's what those weekly breakfasts were all about. Even with the things he was going through, he still needed that communion with you." She reached out and put a hand on Melissa's knee. "Did he say why?"

"He fell." She wiped her eyes with her sleeve. "It reminded him of his lack of wholeness."

"Ah." Sharon picked her ice cream up and took another small bite. "I can see that, even though it's not fair. Phil's a strong guy, Melissa. I imagine he was quite the soldier."

Melissa glared at her. "So?"

Sharon shrugged. "So, nothing. I can just see his psyche. You cannot plan to be with him until he truly accepts who he is. More, until he truly accepts that God can use him like this and can make it good. He hasn't gotten there yet."

Melissa scowled into her ice cream. "It's been almost two years since he lost his leg. You'd think he'd have figured that out by now."

"Maybe. But maybe he's been in a type of denial. Nothing you can do about it. You're not the one in charge of his growth. But at least I now know how to do a focused prayer." She chewed on a chocolate chip, then said, "I'm going to pray that God will bring a way for Phil to see his true worth." She set the bowl down again and clapped her hands. "That's it. That's my prayer."

"Well, that's very kind of you." Melissa moved her spoon through the dessert, making sure this bite had all of the elements. "It doesn't mean I'd take him back."

Sharon waved a well-manicured hand in her direction. "Pshaw. You will so take him back."

As Melissa put the perfect bite in her mouth, tears streamed out of her eyes again, and she had to swallow a sob with the ice cream. Sharon was right. She would take Phil back if she saw true change in him. But she couldn't continue to yo-yo around.

Sharon picked up the remote, then started skimming through the channels. "Aha! Here's the Christmas movies channel," she said as the logo flashed across the screen.

Melissa screwed her nose up. "You want me to sit and watch Christmas romances with you?"

"Uh, yeah, girl. Nothing will make you feel better than everything coming together in a perfect bow under the mistletoe." She settled back. "Plus it's almost time for Christmas shopping. I want to see the ads."

"You're insane." Melissa watched the perky blond on the screen rush down a small-town street, carrying a box of doughnuts. "Why do I like you?"

"Because I'm adorable."

Melissa would never admit it to Sharon, but she did feel so much better after watching two ridiculously campy Christmas movies and eating the rest of Sharon's ice cream on top of her own. By the time Sharon left, she felt less despair and more determination, knowing exactly how she needed to pray for Phil as well. She liked Sharon's idea: that God would bring a way for Phil to see his true worth. Even if that meant she didn't end up with him, she wanted that for him more than anything. She loved him and didn't want him to continue hurting.

Most of the time, Phil didn't mind the overnight shifts. In the military, he'd had to work his fair share of overnight duty, guard duty, and late-night missions. He'd learned early on not to rely on specific mealtimes, bedtimes, or downtimes and just took them as they came.

Tonight, though, he just wasn't in the mood to be at work. Every time he'd closed his eyes last night, the image of Melissa's face filled with pain and anger swam in his vision. He couldn't block it out, so he couldn't sleep. As much as he tried to convince himself he'd done the right thing, he didn't know anymore.

Now he was on an overnight shift and was at hour twenty-eight of wakefulness.

"Category two," Leslie said, strolling into the lounge. "Can you believe it?"

"Cat two's not unprecedented," Phil said.

"If you tell me again that there's a reason the season goes to the end of November, I may have to physically harm you," she said.

"I probably wouldn't stop you." He scowled and sank lower on the sofa.

"You know, I thought I'd seen all of the various grouchy moods of Phil Osbourne. There was frustrated grouchy, pouty grouchy, angry grouchy, hungry grouchy, cantanker-ous grouchy—like an old man, which is one of my personal favorites—and petulant grouchy. But this one, this dismal grouchy, has to go."

He glared at her. "I am not dismal."

"Son, you are the most dismal of them all." She sat next to him on the couch, the last place he wanted her to sit. For the first time in his career, he wanted a call to come in so she'd leave him alone. "Spill it."

He closed his eyes and ignored her.

"Fine," she said, but she didn't leave. Instead, she turned on the television and flipped until she came to the stupid Christmas movies channel.

He scowled at the television while some blond with too-perfect hair and too-white teeth ran down a pretend Main Street, carrying a pretend box of doughnuts.

"I love me some Christmas movies," Leslie said. "I wait

all year for this channel to do their thing. You know, they tried to do it in July, but I wasn't going to play. I was like, 'Give me Christmas at Christmas.'" She scooted down on the couch so she could put her booted feet up on the table in front of them. "Know what I mean, jelly bean?"

"Jesus was most likely born in September."

"I love this song." She started singing, "Hark! the herald angels sing, 'Glory to the newborn king!'"

He looked over at her. "Are you wanting to die tonight?"

She gave a closed-mouth smile and looked back at the television. "Oh, look, the town police chief. I bet that's the love interest. And I bet he's all grouchy and Scrooge-like and the doughnuts are her way of getting his attention."

The blond opened the box of Christmas tree–shaped doughnuts, and a skinny officer rushed forward to grab two. The police chief asked the woman to leave, and she—in all her perky glory—placed the doughnuts on the counter and left the police station.

"So, all it takes is asking her to leave and she just, you know, goes away?" He glanced at Leslie. "That would make a merry Christmas for sure."

"It's fiction, son." She clapped her hands together as the blond went into her flower shop. "See? All the decorations. Yep, and he's Scrooge. This is gonna be good."

Over the loudspeaker, they received a call to a house fire. Phil pointed the remote at the television. "Gee, will they get together or not? Will the ruggedly handsome police chief who desperately needs to shave off yesterday's five o'clock shadow so that he'll actually look professional find the Christmas spirit?" He clicked off the television. "I guess we'll never know."

Leslie stuck her tongue out at him and led the way out of the room. "Hey, can cantankerous grouchy come out to play? I like him better than you."

He rolled his eyes at her back as they left the room. He glanced at the clock—2:02. He had to endure five more hours of her forced cheerfulness. Maybe he could endure it without resorting to violence. He'd just have to pray his way through the rest of the shift.

NOVEMBER 22

From the rooftop of a building a block away from the shelter, Hector watched the two guards at the gate change shifts as the sun peeked above the horizon. They were incredibly organized and very thorough. They were also all well-armed.

They'd finally located the building. The sister, Melissa Braxton, was very careful. He could go in, but it would be a fight and he didn't know if he wanted that kind of fight right now. Especially after Simpson's untimely demise and the rest of the team looking over their shoulders.

They'd watched the church because they couldn't find the shelter. He'd received the report that Lola and the children had attended the festival, but too many people were around to safely extract them. His father did not want the attention of the local authorities right now.

"Let's keep an eye on the storm," he said to his second in command. "The storm will cause an evacuation if it stays on its current path."

"Think she'll keep the guards if she evacuates?"

"All we can do is watch." Hector handed the binoculars

over. "I want someone with eyes on that building 24/7. Let me know if she moves."

"Roger."

Hector stared hard at the building. His wife and children were inside. *His* wife and *his* children. They didn't belong anywhere but with him. He looked forward to explaining that very thoroughly to his wife when he finally brought her home.

He put a cigarillo in his mouth, lit it, and puffed out smoke. "If the storm stalls or shifts, we'll still have Thanksgiving. Americans tend to get lax around the holidays. Security might get thinner."

"We'll watch."

CHAPTER

TWENTY-TWO

NOVEMBER 23

Two cars had had a head-on collision in a grocery store parking lot. One of the drivers had backed up and driven away. Miami-Dade had already located the abandoned car with its smashed-in radiator, but they were still hunting down the driver.

The driver of the other car had hit the steering wheel hard, then gotten blown back by the delayed response of the airbag.

Phil slid the backboard behind the woman. "Meredith, we're going to move slowly, okay?"

She whimpered and put a shaky hand on the neck brace. Leslie reached in. "No, hon. Leave that there."

With steady and efficient movements, they got her onto the gurney. Phil raised it to push it to the ambulance as a woman frantically ran into the grocery store. He made eye contact with Leslie and shook his head. "The time to stock for a hurricane was yesterday."

"I went into my twenty-four-hour store at two this morning. They had no water, no canned meats. The shelves were completely empty. Crazy considering that Thanksgiving is tomorrow, and you know they were overstocked last week."

"Why do people wait?"

"They never really believe it's going to hit until it's imminent." Leslie opened the back doors of the ambulance, and they lifted the gurney in. "I'll ride back here with her. She's super scared."

"Yep." Phil closed the doors behind her and got into the driver's seat. He had no desire to battle the evacuating traffic, but he had no choice. The northbound interstate was at a dead stop. Anyone staying local had taken to the surface streets, which meant that all the shortcuts would be completely clogged.

He radioed the hospital to let them know they were en route with a motor vehicle accident and started fighting forward. The lights and sirens didn't have the same effect they had on a normal day. With what was now a category three hurricane bearing down, threatening to hit in the early hours on Thanksgiving morning, the people in the city had gone into a mode of mass panic. He had to take each intersection with more care, watch for vehicles on either side of him, make sure pedestrians didn't step out into the street.

"It's crazy out there," he said to Leslie.

"They're scared," she replied, putting the blood pressure cuff around their patient's arm. "I've lived here my whole life. I've never seen anything like the day before a storm hits."

Phil had. He'd seen scared masses before. He remembered

the time in the African jungle when warlords were on their way to a village with the intent of killing people until the hiding Americans were located. He'd been out of his mind in pain, fighting the need for pain medicine, but he still remembered the way the village banded together and got each other to safety before the soldiers arrived.

He hit his brakes and blared the horn as a car not only ignored his lights and sirens but ran a red light. As soon as he cleared the intersection, he thought about Miami right now. Out there on the streets it was everyone for themselves. He'd have a worse attitude about it if experience hadn't told him that once the storm hit, the fear would go away and the community would come together to rebuild. Provided, he thought as he watched two cars clip each other, they survived until tomorrow.

Eventually, they made their way to the ambulance bay, and the emergency room team met them. He got out of the driver's seat in time to hear Leslie rattle off the patient's vitals and what treatment she'd received. As they wheeled her away, he said, "I'm going to grab a cup of coffee."

"That sounds perfect," Leslie said. "Just don't put any of that cinnamon in mine."

He grinned. "But it's so good for you." As he walked away, he threw over his shoulder, "Antioxidants, prebiotics, lowers blood pressure."

"No!" Leslie laughed. "Just some vanilla creamer."

He waved at an orderly he knew, then went into the doctors' lounge and poured two cups of coffee. As he started another pot, Addy appeared at his elbow.

"This coffee is for doctors only."

"Good thing I'm a doctor."

She pulled a mug out of the dish drainer. "Speaking of, rumor has it that you applied for a residency in the ER."

"Oh yeah?" He added Leslie's creamer to her cup and stirred with a wooden stick. "Where'd you hear that?"

"Well, actually, from the director who called me for a reference." She punched his shoulder. "Good on you, sir."

"Well, I'm not in yet. And I'm old. We'll see if I can make it through residency."

"Hey now," she said with a smile. "We're the same age."

"Yeah, but you're an attending."

She put a tea bag in her cup, then added hot water. "Well, I'm excited. I put in a good word. With your military service and your medical school grades, I don't see how they can give it to anyone else."

He sprinkled cinnamon into his coffee, then put lids on both cups. "Thanks, Addy."

He went back out into the bay and found Leslie wiping down the gurney. "You are a lifesaver," she said as he handed her the cup.

They leaned against the back of the ambulance. "Are you in the evacuation zone?" he asked.

She shrugged. "No. We're a couple miles in. Darius is on tonight. His unit is working the evac zone, though." She shuddered. "I hate it when that happens. It's so scary. I always worry about looters and crazy people with shotguns."

"That would be scary. He's a good cop, though. He'll be fine." Phil pushed his shoulder against hers. "Besides, it's a category three. Half the people won't even leave."

"Got upgraded to a four, according to the news." She pulled her phone out of her pants pocket and held it up. "Just now."

"We're about to have a much busier shift."

"Yep." She took another sip of coffee and pushed off the ambulance, then slapped the gurney. "This is clean. Supply is good."

Before he could reply, his phone rang. "Just a sec." Glancing at the screen, he answered with, "Hi, Mom."

"Hi. I know Melissa's Thanksgiving is important to you. We're happy to shift to an evening meal instead of a mid-day meal."

Phil tensed. He hadn't told his mom that he had broken up with Melissa. He hadn't had the heart to add one more thing to her plate. So he decided he would just spend the rest of tomorrow figuring out how to tell her that Melissa wouldn't be joining them for Thanksgiving evening. "That works for me, thanks."

"Also, it looks like your apartment is in the evacuation zone. Are you coming here?"

"I haven't even looked." He closed his eyes briefly and thought about the day. "I can, yes. Better than riding it out. I heard it just got upgraded." He took a sip of his coffee and enjoyed the taste of the spice.

"Yes. A four. If Melissa and her sister and the kids also want to come here, we have more than enough room."

Knowing his mom, she wanted to make sure everyone was safe and in her line of vision. "I'll pass the message on." He heard a radio call coming from the cab. "Gotta run. Just got a call."

"Be careful. I love you."

"Love you too." He hung up and said to Leslie, "I have to make a call. Can you drive?"

"Sure thing." Leslie went to the driver's side as Phil shut up the back. "Everything okay?"

"Yeah. Just not used to planning hurricane evacuations on Thanksgiving eve."

"Crazy, isn't it?" She pulled out of the ambulance bay before she hit her lights and sirens. "All I can say is that it better not mess up Black Friday shopping. I already have my eye on some deals."

Melissa checked her rearview mirror again. She thought someone on a motorcycle had turned with her three times, but now she didn't see the bike anymore. Maybe she was being paranoid. But she'd thought the same thing twice last week.

As she pulled up to the guard gate, she rolled her window down instead of going on through. The wind blew a palm frond across her windshield, making her jump.

The guard came out of the shack. "Yes, Miss Braxton?"

She looked behind her again. "I feel like I was followed."

"The motorcycle again?" He scanned the street up and down. "I'll keep an eye out."

"Thanks."

"If I see one, I'll call the police." He looked up at the sky. "What are the plans?"

"I'm going to check evac orders right now. If we have to evacuate, I'll have detailed instructions quickly."

"Yes, ma'am."

Once she parked, she headed straight to her room and turned on the television.

". . . in fact, not unprecedented," the weather reporter said. "It's late in the season, but the season does go until November thirtieth for a reason. Gertrude is expected to make landfall in the downtown area. For now, the governor is calling for a mandatory evacuation in these areas"—he pointed to the map—"and a recommended evacuation here in the blue." He looked at the screen. "Going to put a damper on those Thanksgiving plans. Randy? Back to you."

Melissa sighed and stared at the evacuation map. She was on the edge of suggested and mandatory. She rubbed her eyes. She'd love the chance to just sit and mourn what should have been with Phil, but stupid Gertrude and Thanksgiving and responsibilities . . .

She pushed back the tears, left her apartment, and knocked on Sharon's door. Her friend opened it almost immediately.

"What do you think we should do?" Melissa asked, stepping into Sharon's realm. She crossed the silver carpet and perched on the edge of the pink-and-silver couch. The silver chandelier above them had been turned down to moderate light, and the television mounted on the wall was turned to the same weather station Melissa had been watching.

"We're right on the border." Sharon sat on the couch and crossed her legs. "Two days ago, I booked twenty-two rooms scattered between three airport hotels in case we ended up having to evacuate."

"Bless you for thinking ahead this way. I just kept watching the storm and couldn't believe that it was actually going to come this close to Thanksgiving." Melissa thought about twenty-two hotel rooms and whistled through her teeth. "That's a big bill."

"Oh, please. I spent more each night in Paris last Christmas."

"That's your personal account, not our business account."

She paused. "Well, merry Christmas, then. Now I don't have to think about what to get you."

Melissa smiled. "Okay, so we need a bus or something." She stood. "I'll get going knocking on doors. I'll start with the second floor."

"I know a car service that prides itself on its confidentiality. We should be safe using them. I'll call for some cars and then hit the third floor."

"Have them meet in the cafeteria by two thirty."

They left Sharon's apartment. Melissa headed to her office first and hit the speed-dial for the security company. "Hi, Mr. Racene. Melissa Braxton."

"Yes, I was waiting to hear from you."

"We're going to evacuate. As soon as we have everyone out, you can get your men home. I'm sure they're all worried."

"Great. We'll see you in the morning, then?"

"Absolutely. Assuming we still have a functioning building."

She went into the kitchen and found Mrs. Horton slicing a pan of cornbread. "For my cornbread dressing," Mrs. Horton said.

Mr. Horton came in through the dining room door. "Back patio is cleared of anything loose. Terry helped me put the porch swing and the fire pit in the parking garage."

"Thanks. I'm glad you're both here. We're evacuating. We're just too close to the line for us to feel safe."

Mrs. Horton's hands paused. She looked around. "I have Thanksgiving tomorrow."

"We'll have to have it late in the day or on Friday." Melissa put an arm around her shoulders. "Better safe than sorry, right?"

"Bah!" Mr. Horton said. "This building has stood since

1947. Some storm named Gertrude is not going to knock her over."

"Nevertheless." Melissa squeezed Mrs. Horton's shoulders. "Now, put everything away. I want you guys checking into your hotel in a few hours."

She walked out, chuckling as Mr. Horton complained to his wife about the ridiculous evacuation order. He'd been this loud and against evacuation three years ago and had come back to a completely intact building with lots of "I told you so's."

In the hall, she spotted Aaron. "Hi, Aaron."

He turned around, his bushy red beard catching the fluorescent light. "Hi. I came to make sure Terry knows to not stay here. My mom and I are going."

"Do you know where?"

"Sure, yeah. Gran lives in Miami Lakes. We're going to go camp out on her dining room floor."

"Sounds like an adventure."

"So I'm just going to check on Terry now."

Melissa nodded. "Last I heard, he was helping Mr. Horton get everything out of the courtyard. But Mr. Horton is in the kitchen, so maybe he's gone to pack a bag."

As he started to walk away, she said, "Aaron, don't stay too long. If you can't find Terry, your mission is to help your mom evacuate."

"Roger and wilco, Melissa."

She made her way down the hall and was thankful when she managed to speak to all of the residents on that floor. As she walked up to the third floor, her phone chirped an incoming call. Her heart froze when Phil's face filled her screen. Despite wanting to ignore him, she swiped up.

"Yes?"

He looked tired. "Two things. One, Mom said she'd hold Thanksgiving dinner until evening tomorrow if you wanted to join us. Two, I'm going to stay at Mom and Dad's tonight. They said you're welcome to join us. I have a strong sense that she'd feel better if we were all where she could see us."

Heart pounding, she took a deep breath. "Clearly you haven't told your mother anything."

"No. It's too much right now. Without the hurricane, I had planned to make excuses through the holidays."

His mother had pushed aside the mourning of Winston to celebrate Phil and Melissa finally making everything official. It was like it had given her a new spark in life. Melissa loved Phil's mom, but she didn't appreciate his assumption that she'd keep up a facade so he could avoid explaining reality to the woman. He didn't seem to understand the level of heartbreak he'd caused. Or maybe he did. It was possible he simply did not care.

Did she really believe that?

"I'm hardly responsible for your mother's feelings," she said.

Phil stared hard at the screen. "Nor am I. I'm simply passing on the message."

Melissa closed her eyes briefly and took a deep breath through her nose. "Fine." She pursed her lips. "I'll spend the night with her tonight because I like her a lot and I don't agree with your reasons for breaking up with me and I'm holding out hope that one day you'll wake up and quit being so selfish." She said it all in one breath, then felt heat flood her cheeks.

His mouth thinned. "The invitation extends to your sister as well."

She shifted plans in her mind. Phil's parents' neighborhood had guards and would be much safer than a hotel for Lola. "Fair enough. I can accommodate that."

After several long heartbeats, he said, "Thanks. I'll come pick you up after work. Give me a few hours. Lola and the kids should fit in my back seat."

When Melissa got to the third floor, she spied Sharon walking away from room 310. "Did you talk to everyone?"

"All but Lola. I figured you'd go to her." She pulled her phone from her back pocket. "First van is here." She tapped on the phone, then slipped it back in her pocket. "I told him to give us ten minutes and his tip would be worth it."

Melissa gestured at Lola's door. "Phil's mom wants Lola and me at her place."

Sharon tutted. "She needs to see all her chicks." Then she gasped. "Wait a minute! Did he not tell her you two broke it off?"

"He broke it off. I didn't. And no, he said he was waiting until after the holidays."

"Talk about 'it's complicated.'" Sharon turned to the stairs. "I'm going to grab the first vanful. I'll cancel your rooms in case there's someone else who needs a hotel tonight."

"That works. Thanks, friend." Melissa tapped on Lola's door. Mathias opened it and grinned up at her. "Hi, Matty," she said, bending down to meet him at eye level.

"Mama is changing Gabby."

Lola's voice singsonged from the bed area. "Come in, Missy."

Melissa walked into the room. She could smell Mathias's peanut butter sandwich. "We're evacuating."

Lola nodded. "I heard Sharon in the hall. Matty's already packed his bag. I was just changing the baby."

Melissa smiled and waved at Gabriele. "Phil's mom asked if we'd stay with her. He's going to pick us up when he gets off work."

"Oh." She glanced around. "Okay. That will probably be easier with the kids than a hotel."

"Take your time. He'll be a while. I'm going to help Sharon get everyone into vans and checked into hotels."

"Thanks," Lola said. She put her hand on top of Mathias's head. "Finish your lunch. We're not packing it like we thought."

He went to the little table and climbed into the chair, then picked up the sandwich and took a bite.

On her way out the door, Melissa glanced back at Lola. "Need anything?"

Her smile was warm and reached her eyes. "Not anymore."

CHAPTER

TWENTY-THREE

Melissa rode in the van with Terry and three residents who had four children between them. The wind had seriously picked up. Palm trees bent, and paper and plastic bags swirled in the air. The darkening sky made the hour feel much later. She felt the fringes of a headache that often came when the barometer dropped in pressure.

The van driver pulled up to the airport hotel, and Melissa had to fight against the car door to get it to open. The valet assisted her, and she smiled at him. "Bit windy," she said.

"Ma'am." He opened the side door, and the residents piled out. While they collected their luggage from the back, Melissa went into the hotel and got everyone checked in.

She headed to where everyone waited by the large fountain in the lobby and handed each person their key. "We're expecting the storm to be done and gone by morning. We'll know soon if you have to stay another night."

One of the residents held up the plastic key card. "Should we stay here and wait?"

"Definitely," Melissa said. "I mean, obviously you're free to do whatever you want, but the storm is gonna be big and you're safe here. The shelter is not affiliated with the hotel in any way, so there's no reason for someone to look for you here. Feel free to order room service. Like we outlined before we left, there's a stipend on each room for meals. Breakfast is here in the lobby in the morning."

She hugged each woman, spoke to the children, and then turned to Terry. "Are you okay being left alone?"

He nodded. "I'm good. I've never had my own hotel room before."

With a smile she hugged him. "Have a good time."

When she went back outside, the driver was waiting for her by the van. She sat in the back seat and texted with Sharon, confirming that everyone had rooms and understood how the meal stipends worked.

When she got back to her building, she used the app on her phone to give the driver an extremely generous tip. "Happy Thanksgiving. Stay safe out there tonight."

He lifted his hand. "I can go home now. Met my budget for the day. Happy Thanksgiving to you."

She dismissed the security company, thinking that with the coming storm and Phil returning soon, there would be a curtain of safety. Inside, the building felt different. No noise came from the kitchen area, no movement from the courtyard, no noises of children or the ringing and chirping of cell phones. It was just silence.

She went into her office, sat down in her chair, and closed her eyes. "Thank You, God, for the ease in this evacuation.

Watch over Lola and the kids and me as we head to Phil's parents'. It's only going to get worse out there. Thank You for the magnificence of Your creation, God. Your majesty is extraordinary." She paused. "And . . . Phil." God knew.

After she filed patient notes and resident reports in the weatherproof and fireproof filing cabinet, she added her notebooks and the petty cash box. There was no way to know what damage the hurricane would bring, but she knew at least the contents of that filing cabinet would not be harmed by fire or flood. She checked Sharon's desk and made sure that nothing needed to go in there before she locked the cabinet, turned all the lights out, and headed to her room.

She'd been so busy helping everyone else get ready that she hadn't done so herself. She grabbed an overnight bag and threw in some toiletries and a change of clothes. Once her bag was packed, she texted her sister to let her know she was in her apartment.

Lola

Matty is sleeping. Gabby is refusing to go down.
Time frame?

Melissa looked at the clock. Phil wasn't due to get off work for another hour.

Two hours or more.

Perfect. Let me know if that changes.

Melissa texted Phil to let him know that she was ready to go and to call her on his way. She gave him the code to get into the gate, then she decided to follow Mathias's lead and lie down. She stretched out on the couch and thought about the fact that Phil's mom wanted her there tonight and was willing to adjust her traditional Thanksgiving plans to accommodate Melissa's schedule. That meant so much more to her than Candace could have realized.

Despite the heartbreak he'd caused her, she felt confident in Phil's love for her. But she didn't feel as confident in the possibility of their relationship going forward or in his ability to work through the last two years of his life. Still, to have his parents' blessing on their relationship seemed to give it so much more staying power.

As she dozed off, she thought about their kiss the other night and the way he had started looking forward to his future.

Phil parked in the shelter's garage because he didn't want flying debris to smash into his truck. Just as he was getting out, his phone rang. He recognized a number similar to Winston's office number, and his heart clenched. "Phil Osbourne."

"Phil, Kim Jones. I know tomorrow is Thanksgiving, but I wanted to establish a time to interview Mrs. Molina."

A garbage can went skittering across the sidewalk outside. "Rather a stormy night to be having this conversation, isn't it?"

"If we can get some useful testimony out of her, it's possible we can serve a warrant tomorrow. Catching them on Thanksgiving might give us a surprise advantage."

That made sense. "Fair enough. Mrs. Molina will be with me. I'm picking her up from a women's shelter right now."

"I can come to you."

"No, we don't let this address out. How about I take them to where they're going to shelter and call you from there? In fact, since my father is a judge, he can swear her in and take her testimony and submit it to you."

"That sounds perfect! Thank you for facilitating that. You can email me the sworn testimony." She gave her email address. "I can text that to you too."

"No need. I got it."

"Be safe out there. I'll look forward to that email."

He looked at his watch. It should seem odd that she'd called at six thirty the night before a holiday in the midst of a hurricane evacuation, but he knew the way his brother had worked and made concessions for that.

He went to the side door and turned the handle, but it didn't budge. He ducked back into the cover of the garage and called Melissa. It took three rings for her to answer in an incredibly groggy voice. "Phil. Hi."

He smiled. "Were you sleeping?"

She cleared her throat. "I think so. What time is it?"

"It's time to let me in the door." He laughed. "I'm at the garage side."

By the time he made it back to the door, she had it open. She looked ruffled and sleepy, and he couldn't help but wish he could cup her cheek and kiss her hello. "Sorry to wake you."

She rubbed her face with her hands and pushed her hair back. "I only laid down for a minute. I did not intend to sleep for over two hours."

"Two hours?" he said as they walked to her apartment. "Did you sleep last night?"

"Of course not. All I could think about was men on motorcycles following me and what Mrs. Horton was going to do with four turkeys in a hurricane."

"A man on a motorcycle followed you?"

"I swear someone was following me a couple of times. But by the time I got here, they were gone. I told the guards about it and they were keeping an eye out, but no one ever saw anything."

"Melissa, why didn't you tell me?"

She glared at him out of the corner of her eye. "Are you serious?"

He felt a twinge of guilt. Of course she wouldn't tell him. He'd broken off their relationship.

She went to her kitchen and filled a glass with water. "How bad is it out there?"

"Pretty bad. Streets are finally empty. It was a hard shift. People get crazy when a storm is coming."

"That's because they're scared." She drank half of the water and then climbed on the couch in the living room and pulled her legs under her. He sat next to her. "A primal personality emerges in a lot of people when they're scared."

"Oh, I know."

She chuckled. "I'm sorry you had a rough shift. Bad weather always makes it worse."

"I appreciate that." He laid his head back against the couch and yawned. A three-hour nap sounded like something he could do right now. "Did you get everyone settled?"

"Yes. I really hope the hurricane doesn't do something funky and make the airport area a dangerous place too. Otherwise, I just dumped seventeen families and three staff members into the path of a category four hurricane."

"Five now."

"Five?" She swiped up on her phone and pulled up the news. "How is there a category five hitting us the day before Thanksgiving?"

"It's not unheard of. It's just rare."

"That's crazy." She checked a few texts, then tossed her phone down on the coffee table. "I wondered if we needed to bring food for your mom. She'll suddenly be feeding two more adults and two kids."

"The last thing my mom needs is more food in her kitchen. I promise you, there is more than enough."

He watched her as she gathered her thoughts. She would never know how attractive she was to him right at this moment and how much deeper and further he fell in love with her just like this. He had always admired her strength and fortitude, but he also liked the fact that she could be sleepy and cuddly.

He let out a quiet sigh. He needed to let her go, to have her all the way gone. Clinging to her did neither of them any good. He'd get his mom through the holidays and then do the right thing.

"We need to move before it gets worse out there. Is Lola ready?"

"I don't know. Last we communicated, I told her I'd let her know when you got here." She grabbed her phone again and typed on it. About ten seconds later, it chimed with a reply. "She's on her way down."

"I talked to a US marshal named Alvarado. Finally, I have someone looking into what happened with Lola and her appointment."

Melissa's eyes widened. "That's fantastic. Now all we

need to do is find out who Winston was talking about in his office. Then maybe we can start figuring out what happened."

He nodded. She knew how much finding out who was responsible for Winston's murder was a priority for him. Just as she knew he had only so much he could do about it.

"Before Lola gets here, I wanted to thank you for what you're doing for my mom and dad," he said.

"Honestly, Phil, I'm doing it for you too. But this is it. It's not fair to me to string me along like this. I'd like to get on with my life."

"I know." His chest burned, and it took real willpower not to rub it. "I'm sorry."

"Well, you're the only one who can change that right now."

He shook his head. "I think I made the right decision."

She stood. "You're going to be miserable without me. So you're hurting, you're scared, and now you're going to be miserable. Well played, Doctor Osbourne."

When she went into the kitchen and rinsed out her glass, he closed his eyes and pinched his nose. Maybe this was a bad idea. But now he had to take her to his parents'. She had nowhere else to go.

She came back into the room. "Sorry. I'm always a grouch after I nap." She took a deep breath, let it out, and smiled. "So, you're planning on two Thanksgivings. Have you ever done that before?" After a second, she added, "Assuming we still have buildings and a Thanksgiving meal after the storm."

Her mood shift confused him, but since she'd turned pleasant, he decided to play along. He shrugged. "One is lunch and one is dinner. I eat lunch and dinner every day."

She snorted. "With pies and puddings and sides? I've seen you eat. You have not eaten Thanksgiving twice in a day."

He slapped his stomach with both hands. "Never underestimate me."

"Yeah, okay." She gestured toward the bedroom. "I'm going to grab my bag, freshen up a bit."

As she went into her bedroom, he raised his voice. "You only need enough for one night."

"Yep!" she hollered back.

He heard a tap on the door to her apartment, so he got up and crossed the room. When he opened the door and found Lola holding Gabriele in one arm and Mathias's hand with the other, he smiled. Then he read the terror on her face and spied the man behind her.

His blood froze as the man raised a gun at him.

CHAPTER

★

TWENTY-FOUR

Phil analyzed the situation as he took a step back. He needed to remove Lola and the children from any line of fire. His brain had kicked into overdrive as he considered and rejected several scenarios. He took another step backward, enhancing his limp so he would appear weak.

Lola walked as if her bones would shatter if she moved too quickly. Phil gestured with his head behind him and hoped she would get the message.

The bedroom door opened, and Melissa came out carrying a tote bag. "I did pack for two days, but only because I'm a serial overpacker—" She stopped when she saw Lola, who looked from her to the man at the door. Melissa gasped. "What?"

"Mr. Molina has instructed me to contain you until he arrives," the man said. "He would like to have a word with you about his wife."

Phil faced a choice. Did he eliminate this threat, or did he wait to see if the minion had to contact Hector Molina and let him know he had everyone in one room? Because he really wanted Molina to come.

"So, the plan is that we wait here for him?" Phil asked.

Minion turned and leveled his gun at Phil.

Melissa had rushed forward and scooped up Mathias. She and Lola backed up until they were as far away from Minion as possible.

Phil wanted to assure them that everything would be okay, but he had no idea what kind of firepower Molina would bring with him. He stepped to the side to split Minion's attention between himself and the others.

Minion pulled a flip phone out of his front pocket and hit a button. Seconds later, he said, "I have them all contained." He looked from Melissa and Lola to Phil. "Yes, together. And with the children." He paused. "I can hold them twenty minutes. No problem." He ended the call.

Lola lifted her chin. "I recognize you."

"I recognize you too." He called her a foul name. "You won't be recognizable much longer." He chuckled. "Big mistake leaving Hector. Big."

Everything about Phil had changed—his countenance, his energy. He became hyperfocused, and the stern shift to his face made him almost unrecognizable to Melissa.

"Are they coming?" he asked.

The man with the gun smiled, showing silver teeth. "Yeah. Scared? You should be." He stepped closer to Phil. "Your brother was scared. Yeah, I was there."

In hindsight, Melissa wanted to say that she saw Phil move, but everything was over so quickly she didn't have time to even realize he had. One minute the man was standing there holding a gun on Phil, and the next he was on the floor and Phil had the gun trained on him.

"Do not ever put a gun in my face." Phil lifted his chin toward Melissa. "Got any duct tape? Maybe some zip ties?"

She tried to answer intelligibly but had a hard time grabbing a thought. "Uh, maybe some zip ties."

"That would be great."

She rushed to her kitchen and started opening drawers. She was sure she had zip ties that she had bought to organize her computer cables. In her junk drawer, she found the package. "Like this?"

He gave a nod and pulled one out, then stuck the package in the cargo pocket of his uniform. "You two take the kids up to Lola's room. Do not answer the door. Take your phone."

The power went out with a loud click.

"Go!"

The room was plunged into darkness. Phil closed his eyes so he didn't distract himself with the need to try to see. He heard Minion lunge to his feet and fully anticipated the blow to his torso. He grabbed Minion by the neck to restrain him and took the blow of Minion's shoulder to his gut. His leg gave out from under him and they fell.

Minion managed to grab Phil's wrist and fought him for the gun. Somewhere beyond the immediate struggle, he registered the baby crying.

Minion had his left leg trapped. If he struggled too much,

he might lose the pressurized suction and it would come off. He had to use his upper body strength to dominate.

Fisting his left hand, he brought it up to where Minion's face ought to be. The satisfying slap of flesh on flesh told him he hit point. Minion grunted loudly, and his hold on Phil's wrist loosened. Phil started to pull his hand away when Minion grabbed the muzzle of the gun.

Ugh! His stupid leg. *Please, God.* Using all his available strength, Phil shoved with his left hand and kept hold of the gun with his right. Finally, he knocked Minion back and lunged forward to get the upper hand. When Minion grabbed his wrist with both hands and brought a foot up to kick him away, Phil squeezed the trigger.

He pushed Minion away, then got to his feet and took out his phone, accessing the flashlight. Minion lay unmoving, blood pooling around his head.

"Do you have any flashlights?" Phil asked, panting.

"Yes," Melissa said. While she went into her bedroom, he checked his leg, making sure the struggle hadn't loosened it. Then he bent down and examined his attacker. The bullet had grazed his temple, cutting a deep swath just above his ear.

Phil searched the man's pockets and took his cell phone and a knife. He looked over at Lola, who had two crying kids. "Can you get me a dry washcloth?"

"I can't leave Matty. He's scared of the dark."

Melissa came back with a box. She withdrew three flashlights and handed one to Mathias. "Here you go, buddy. Can you help your mom find a washcloth in my bathroom?"

"Shine one here," Phil said, rolling Minion over and taking one of the zip ties out of his pocket. Once he secured his wrists, he rolled him back over and took his pulse. Strong and steady. "He'll live."

Lola returned with the washcloth. Phil pressed it against Minion's wound while he called 911.

In disgust, he tossed his phone down. "All circuits busy."

Melissa looked up at the ceiling. "The storm."

Phil stood. "I want you guys up in Lola's room. Let's go."

Lola gasped. "What about you?"

"I'm going to greet your husband."

Phil scooped up Mathias, who clutched his flashlight like his life depended on it.

With tears streaming down her face, Lola carried Gabriele to the door. Melissa followed, pausing to look at the man on the floor. "What are you going to do with him?"

Phil glanced down. "Help me move him." He looked at Lola as he set Mathias down. "Go. We'll be up there in a minute."

Melissa handed the box to Mathias. "Can you carry my hurricane box? It has candles and matches in it."

Mathias nodded, and Lola directed him out of the apartment.

"Do you have any rope?" Phil asked Melissa.

She pressed her lips together and shook her head. "Maybe Mr. Horton does somewhere, but I wouldn't know where to look."

"How about a sheet?"

She nodded and took the flashlight into her bedroom, then came out with a white sheet. He used his pocketknife to slash through it, creating strips. They dragged Minion into her bathroom. After cutting off the zip tie, he used a surgeon's knot followed by a locking knot and tied Minion's wrists together, then tied the other end of the cloth to the sink's pipe. He gagged the man with a strip of cloth.

"Give me some light," Phil said. "Let me check his wound."

The bleeding had started to dissipate. Minion's pulse was still strong, his breathing steady.

Phil pulled, tugged, and tightened, then stood. "He should be fine until we can get police here."

Melissa stepped forward and put a hand on his chest. "Can we just go?"

He slipped his phone and knife back into his pocket, then cupped her face with his hands. She didn't resist, and he closed his eyes and briefly savored the feel of her cheeks against his palms. "It's time for this to end. For Lola and for Winston."

Tears filled her eyes. "But Hector won't be alone."

"I know." Still, he'd tackled bigger odds in his time, and he had the element of surprise on his side. He smiled and pressed his lips to her forehead, then hugged her close. "Trust me. That isn't going to matter."

CHAPTER

★

TWENTY-FIVE

Melissa squeezed Phil tight, then stepped back. Fear filled her stomach with ice. She wanted to fight and scream and rail, but that wouldn't do any good. She *had* prayed for God to open Phil's eyes, bring a way for him to see his worth. This might be a bit overboard, but it would likely do the trick.

"What can I do?" she asked.

He put his hands on her shoulders. "I need you out of my way. I can't worry about you and them and do this. Can you do that for me?"

Her breath hitched, clogging her words, so she nodded. "Will you go up there with me?"

"Yes." In the hall, he paused. "Do you have a gun?"

"Uh . . ." It took a moment for the words to register. "I have a shotgun."

"Let's get it."

They ran back to her apartment. She punched in her code,

but it didn't work. "Oh yeah, the power is out." She stood on her toes and ran her fingers along the top of the doorframe until she felt the cool metal of the key.

"That's not a safe place to keep it," Phil said.

"Noted. Hardly a time for a lecture."

"Nevertheless."

She opened the door, then went into her bedroom. In her closet, she grabbed the shotgun from the corner. She turned to give it to Phil, but he held up his hand. "It's for you."

"Phil, I haven't shot this thing in years. My uncle got it for me when I opened the shelter and took me to the range only once."

"It's just like riding a bike. Do you have shells?"

She felt along the top shelf of the closet until she encountered the cardboard box. It was heavier than she remembered. She pulled it down and held it up.

"These are rock salt," he said.

"Okay. What does that mean?"

"It means it will hurt a lot, but it would take a super lucky shot to kill someone."

That didn't bother her. The idea of killing someone, regardless of the circumstances, didn't appeal to her.

He stepped closer and took the flashlight and box of shells. "Hold it with both hands," he said, then guided her left hand farther along the smooth wood of the barrel. "Invert it."

"Oh, I remember." She inverted the gun and moved the slide forward, then Phil held out a round. "Like you said."

"Just like riding a bike."

She loaded eight rounds, then turned it back around. He pointed to the switch on the facing. "Here's your safety. Make sure it's on unless you need it." He paused. "Then make sure it's off."

Her hands trembled on the shotgun, but he needed to know she was safe and protected. She would give him that knowledge so he wouldn't be distracted by her. What would happen if it came down to her having to pull the trigger was a question to which she didn't know the answer.

"Okay." She flipped the switch to turn the safety off then back on again.

He cupped her face with one hand. "You've got this. I promise." He gave her a brief, hard kiss, then stepped back. "Okay. Upstairs with you."

She took a deep, shaky breath. "Let's do this."

Phil led the way, running down the hall to the stairwell. They took the stairs two at a time.

At Lola's door, Melissa knocked. "It's us."

It took a few seconds before Lola opened the door. Phil walked in and checked the apartment from one end to the other. "Since you have a window, you need to not use the flashlights in here or he'll know where you are."

Lola looked over at Mathias, who clutched his flashlight. "He's afraid of the dark."

Melissa stepped forward. "Then let's take him into the bathroom. We can shut the door and the light will be brighter."

Phil nodded. "Use towels to block the light."

They gathered the candles and flashlights and bottles of water, then went into the bathroom. Lola transferred the crib mattress to the bathtub and laid the now-sleeping Gabriele in it. Melissa put the shotgun above the cabinet.

"Only open the door if it's me," Phil said.

"What if it's not you?"

"They shouldn't know where you are." He started to shut the door, then stopped and said, "Keep trying 911."

"I will." She blocked the door with her foot. "I love you, Phil."

He closed his eyes. When he opened them, he smiled. "I love you too."

Then he kicked her foot back and shut them in. Melissa looked over at Lola. "Towels."

They shoved towels at the base of the door, then Melissa sat with her back against the door while Lola lit a candle and put it on the sink. She placed another one on the back edge of the bathtub.

"I'm glad you had a key with you," Melissa said. "I didn't even think about the door codes until I tried to get back into my apartment."

"It's easier for me to use the key holding the baby," Lola said. "I've never used the codes."

Mathias allowed them to take the flashlight from him. Lola pulled the tablet out of the box and handed it to him. "No Wi-Fi, but you can play a game until the battery dies." She ran her hand down his hair. "What an adventure, huh?"

He didn't speak as he took the tablet from her and turned it on. She looked up at Melissa. "This is how he was after . . ." Her voice faded. "It would last the rest of the day. I think it's a coping mechanism."

Melissa smiled at him. "Maybe after tonight there won't be any more stressors." She held out her hand, and Lola took it. "Let's pray. Right now, that's the best thing we can do."

What Phil wouldn't give for a solid pair of infrared night-vision goggles. Instead, he had to settle for adapting to the dark and praying that Vibora lieutenants didn't typically carry night-vision technology. He disabled the emergency exit lights that provided a faint red glow in the hall, opting for total darkness as a cover.

He collected a couple of knives from the kitchen, then went into the dry storage room. He found giant boxes of cornflakes and grabbed them all. After sprinkling a box about five feet from the front door and back into the hall, he did the same thing at the door to the garage area and the dining room door that led to the courtyard.

Through the dining room window, he saw the nearly black sky. He could hear the wind even through the closed door.

While he waited for the sound of someone coming through one of the three doors, he found Marshal Alvarado's number and dialed. The first three tries, he got an all-circuits-busy sound. The fourth time, the call went straight to voice mail.

"Hi, Marshal Alvarado. Phil Osbourne here. I'm at Melissa Braxton's shelter for domestic abuse. I've restrained a member of Vibora but not before he called for reinforcements. I'm alone here, so it would be helpful to maybe have some backup. I'm going to text you the address. I don't think you need to be told how important it is for that information to stay protected." He paused. "I am going to trust you, man, like you asked me to."

He went to the stairwell, sat down on the third step, and closed his eyes. "God, help me."

He couldn't trust that Alvarado would have a way to receive the message or that he could get to him. A category five hurricane would make travel through the city almost impossible. He was on his own.

A lot of the cartel's effectiveness came from instilling fear into the general populace. Hang bodies from overpasses and no one wants to be the next body. Come to targets in groups to overpower them and most enemies become compliant. The idea of this big and powerful entity that couldn't be touched was fed by Hollywood and books. But the truth was that every one of those men coming tonight was a human being with the same circulatory system and brain function Phil had. None of them were invincible. They were just used to their reputation.

He would use that to his advantage. The minions didn't have a lot of experience with shows of force that didn't come from their side. He might teach them a lesson.

He checked the seal on his prosthetic leg. The fight with Minion had worried him, but everything still felt good.

Before he talked himself into taking his leg off and putting it back on again, he heard the crunch of boots on cornflakes. The muscles that had started to relax while he waited tensed back up. His heartbeat quickened, but he kept his breathing regulated.

He silently stood and gripped the gun. With eyes closed, he listened. The dining room. They'd come in through the courtyard. Good. They would come out in the hall about twenty feet from where he stood.

He crossed the hall and put his back against the wall. He could hear muttered Spanish but couldn't fully make the words out. Clearly, someone had figured out the purpose of the cornflakes. They might have guessed Phil had gotten the upper hand with Minion.

As if on cue, Minion's phone vibrated in his pocket. He darted back across the hall and up the stairs. On the second-floor landing, he answered the phone. "Hola?"

He picked out most of the words shot to him in rapid

Spanish. Where was he? Where were the women and children?

He left the phone open and on the landing without replying. In the silence of the building, one of them should hear the phone, see the light. He went up the stairs about halfway to the third floor and waited.

He didn't hear so much as sense the man who came to check out the phone. He knew when the man was in the stairwell with him. It was like the air got displaced, the silence sounded different, the darkness moved differently.

When the lights of the phone rose from the ground as someone picked it up, he lunged, bringing the butt of the pistol down hard where the man's head should be. The metal struck bone with a sick thud, and the body crumpled to the ground.

Wasting no time, Phil grabbed a zip tie and secured the man's hands. He stopped and listened, closing his eyes so the darkness didn't distract him. He heard no other sound. If other men were here, they weren't in this hallway.

Moving as quietly as possible, he dragged the man down the stairs and to Sharon's apartment. He ran his fingers along the top of the doorframe and encountered a key. Shaking his head, he let himself into Sharon's apartment. He briefly lit his phone to get a layout of the furniture, then dragged the man into the kitchen. He rushed into the bedroom and ripped the sheets off the bed, then quickly cut one into strips. He tied the man tightly and secured him to the pipes under the sink. Once he checked that the man couldn't reach any weapons no matter how he contorted his body, he gagged him, then quietly left the apartment.

Between the candles and Melissa, Lola, and the two kids, it didn't take long for the bathroom to get very warm. Lola checked Mathias's tablet. "The battery is at eighty percent," she said. "I'm so glad I charged it this afternoon."

"Me too." Melissa ran her hand down his head, feeling his heat and sweat. "Hey, Matty, I'm going to blow out the candles and you can use the light from the tablet."

He looked up, eyes wide with fear. "No!"

"Hey, I promise it will be light enough. Let's check." She blew out the candle in the bathtub, and the small room became much dimmer. Then she picked up the candle on the sink and said, "Ready?" She blew it out, and the glow from his tablet filled the area around him. "See? Now, when you're done playing, just let me know and I'll light another candle."

Gabriele whimpered and turned over. Lola checked on her, then sat on the edge of the bathtub. "I'm so sorry about all of this."

"I hardly think you're at fault."

"If I hadn't left . . ."

"If you hadn't left, then Matty here would grow up to be just like his father. Or he'd put himself in front of you and his father and face horrible consequences." Melissa put her hand on her sister's knee. "I have been doing this a long time, and I've seen a lot more than people would believe. The fact is nothing was going to change, and it would only get worse. Your only option was to leave, and I'm so thankful that Phil found you and was willing to help you."

"At the cost of his brother! Why is my life worth more than Winston's?"

"Honey, Winston died because he was investigating your husband and his cartel. Your testimony would have given them what they've been investigating for years. No matter what, when he got close, they would have come after him. Your willingness to testify and be part of what stops their crimes isn't what killed him."

She believed that. She prayed Lola wouldn't continue to blame herself, that she would see the bigger picture involved.

"I think I know what you mean," Lola said. "But I just don't know how to live with it."

Melissa looked over at Mathias. "You raise these kids to be the best people they can be. You pursue that relationship with God and pour it into their lives." She sat back on the pillow and leaned against the corner of the room. "I promise you that if Winston had to do it over again, he'd do it all the same." She closed her eyes and silently prayed, straining to listen for any sound coming from beyond the room.

Lola scooted closer and put an arm around her. "I'm scared, but I believe that if Phil didn't think he could protect us, he would have sent us away, storm or no storm."

Melissa believed that too. She leaned over and put her head on Lola's shoulder. "Since I've known him, he's struggled with his identity because of his leg. I pray he doesn't let that get in the way of what he knows to do."

The muffled sound of gunshots reached them. Melissa gasped and Lola started trembling. They wrapped their arms around each other and prayed together.

CHAPTER

★

TWENTY-SIX

Phil dashed from Sharon's apartment to the doorway of Melissa's locked office. There was a tiny bit of light coming from the exterior hall door, and it was enough for him to make out the shadow of someone moving toward him. He strained to listen, hearing only one set of boots on the tile.

He flattened himself against the wall, and as the man walked by, he swung with the butt of the gun, missing his head but hitting him on the shoulder. He heard the crack of bone, and the man cried out and spun toward him. Phil adjusted his range and struck down, this time getting the man right on the temple.

His opponent crumpled to the ground. Phil collected his MPC carbine rifle and slung the strap over his head, then dragged him into Sharon's apartment. He used the rest of the sheet to secure him to the bathroom fixtures and gag him. After searching the man's pockets, Phil found a phone and an extra magazine for the rifle. He took the man's belt off and wrapped it around his own knuckles, putting the buckle on top for maximum damage.

He went back into the hall and crept along the wall. When he reached the dining room, he paused, listening to the men talking. They spoke in Spanish, and he could understand only some of the phrases. He shook his head when he realized that Molina was sending the men out one at a time, leaving several with him—likely for protection.

As he backed away from the door, the sound of the side door slamming shut made him freeze. Down the hall, he saw a light bobbing and heard someone whistling "Victory in Jesus." Heart pounding, he raced toward the light.

"Hey!" Aaron said as he shone his light on Phil. "Hey!"

Phil stopped running and looked behind him. He had mere seconds. "Aaron, I'm Melissa's good friend. You're not supposed to be here."

"I know. But then I thought about looters, so I came." He gestured with his flashlight. "You're not supposed to be here either."

"Let's go together, shall we?"

He hadn't moved fast enough. Before he could turn Aaron around, the sound of boots pounding reached them.

"Por ahí!"

"Come on, Aaron, we have to go," Phil said.

They ran down the hall. "Why are we running?" Aaron asked.

They reached the end and turned the corner to the side door. Phil skidded to a stop when he saw a man standing outside. The man smiled and opened the door, pointing a gun at them.

"Hey!" Aaron said. "You can't come in here! That door should be locked."

Phil moved Aaron against the wall. "Stay very still."

The man raised his gun, and Phil shook his head. "I told your friend," he said as he grabbed the man by the wrist with one hand and the barrel of the gun with the other, "don't point a gun in my face." With a twist and a breaking of bone, he took the gun from the man and pointed it at him.

The man cried out and clutched his broken wrist. Phil slipped the gun in the waistband of his pants, but before he could restrain the man, two more arrived. Phil grabbed the first man and pushed him forward. "Hold him, Aaron. Don't let him go."

Aaron grabbed him by the back of the neck with his big, beefy hands and slammed him up against the wall. "You shouldn't be here," he growled.

The other two men stopped, training their guns on Phil and Aaron. "Give up, man," one of them said. "Hector is not afraid of you, and there are too many of us to win."

"Hector's not afraid of me?" Phil moved before the man could comprehend his intent. He took the gun right out of his hand, then struck him across the temple with his belt-covered fist. The man cried out and clutched his head. "He should be."

Still bent over, the man charged him, hitting him with his shoulder. As he slammed Phil against the wall, Phil brought his elbow down hard on the center of the man's back and raised his left knee up, hearing his nose break from the double force.

The man howled and started bleeding all over Phil's uniform. Phil pushed him back and punched him in the temple with his belted hand. He fell down, stunned, and Phil re-trained the gun on his partner. "You need to drop your gun."

"No comprendo," the man said with a sneer, then raised his gun toward Aaron.

"No!" Phil said, firing two shots.

The man fired at the same time. He fell back, and Phil raced forward and snatched the gun out of his hand, then put it in a cargo pocket in his pants.

The stunned guy started to stagger away, but Phil grabbed him and used the belt and zip ties to tie his hands and feet together. Then he rushed to Aaron, who'd slumped against the first prisoner on the wall. In the light of the flashlight, Phil could see the sheen of sweat on his face.

"He got me," Aaron whispered.

"I'll check it, Aaron." As Aaron slid down the wall, Phil kept his gun trained on the prisoner. He unhooked the man's belt, then worked it off him. "On the ground," he said, pointing with the gun. The man put his hands behind his head and knelt down. Phil pushed him face-first onto the floor and used zip ties and his belt to tie him like his friend.

"We've got to get you out of here," he said to Aaron, bending and inspecting the wound in his abdomen. "They're going to come. We need to move."

"Okay." Aaron grunted and got to his knees. "It hurts."

"Push through the pain, Aaron. I know you know how to. Just like when you'd get hit on the ice." Phil bent and put Aaron's arm across his shoulders. "Up you go, big guy." He helped him out the door, and immediately, the wind tried to knock them over. It took the breath right out of him. "We're going to Terry's room."

"Terry isn't there."

"I know, bud. He won't mind."

They went around the building and stopped at the gate to the courtyard. A padlock secured it. Gone were the days when Phil could kick a gate in. "Do you know the combo?"

"Yes. Twenty-seven, twenty-seven. My number on my jersey. Melissa helped me code it."

"Smart girl." He checked behind him, unable to hear because of the wind. Using one hand, he put in the code, then opened the gate. "We have to stick to the fence all the way around because the bad guys are in the dining room."

He glanced toward the dining room door, but the dark night revealed nothing. They walked as quickly as Aaron would allow along the fence to the little bedroom off the shed. Using the butt of the rifle he had recently acquired, he broke the window on the door, then helped Aaron inside.

The room was shrouded in darkness, but a brief flash of distant lightning gave him enough information to get Aaron to the bed. "It's important that you don't use your flashlight," Phil said. "But I'll leave it with you if you need me to."

"You'll come back?" Aaron's breath came out in shallow wheezes.

"Yes. I promise." He rushed to the bathroom and returned with a thick towel. "Press this against your belly where it hurts." He put a hand on his shoulder. "You did really good, Aaron. I'm proud of you, and Melissa will be proud of you too."

"Okay," Aaron said. "I'll wait here."

Phil could not leave him alone wounded and defenseless, but he had few options left. He held up the MPC. "Ever shoot anything like this?"

Aaron nodded. "Mine was bigger."

Phil grinned. "Like riding a smaller bike." He tossed the spare 30-round magazine onto the bed and unslung it from around his neck. "Just in case."

Aaron nodded again. "Just in case."

Melissa couldn't breathe. "I'll be right back," she whispered.

"Where are you going?" Lola demanded. Her hair was matted with sweat.

"Just wait here." She slipped out of the bathroom and shut the door behind her, breathing in the much cooler and cleaner air of the larger room. Going from memory, she silently moved the nightstand away from the window, then pulled one of the mattresses off the bed. After she propped it up against the window, she put the nightstand back to secure it. Then she took a blanket from the bed and pressed it against the bottom of the door.

She gingerly crossed the floor, afraid that her feet would make sounds below her, and opened the bathroom door. "I put a mattress over the window." She lit a candle and put it on the table, then went into the bathroom to retrieve the shotgun. After leaning it against the doorframe, she scooped Gabriele up. The poor baby was soaked with sweat. Lola took the mattress out of the bathtub and put it back in the crib, and Melissa gently laid the baby down.

Lola took Mathias to his bed and encouraged him to lie down. His hair was wet with sweat too. "You have to stay on the bed and be very quiet," Lola said.

Melissa tugged on his toe. "Wait until morning. It will be so calm and beautiful outside."

She sat at the table. Lola sat across from her. "What do you think is happening?"

"I'm afraid to think." Melissa leaned back and watched the candlelight dance on the ceiling.

"What about the gunfire we heard?"

"I don't know." She rubbed her eyes. "I have no idea." She pulled her phone out of her pocket and saw the universal "no" symbol over the signal. She'd had a signal earlier, but it had come and gone before her call could go through. "Still no service."

"How can there be no service for so long?"

She put the phone on the table. "Maybe they jammed the signal. Is that just something that happens in the movies?"

Lola laughed and put her face in her hands. "I don't know."

"Aren't we a pair, then?" Melissa tried not to give in to the fear that clawed around her heart.

From a distance, she heard banging, then a sound she couldn't quite place. After a few minutes, she heard it again, this time closer. "I think they're kicking in room doors."

Lola's voice hitched. "Missy!" she said in a harsh whisper.

Melissa got up and retrieved the shotgun. When she sat back down, she faced the door, double-checking that she could find the safety switch. Another few minutes passed and another door got kicked in. If they'd started at the end of the hall, they had six more rooms to get to before this one.

"Please, God," she whispered. "Don't let Phil be dead. Or injured. Or gone."

CHAPTER

★

TWENTY-SEVEN

Phil crouched by the door to the dining room, waiting for the next lightning flash. He stared where he saw shadows, ready to assess the situation.

There. A flash that lasted barely a second gave him the information he needed.

Hector Molina sat on one of the tables. Two men flanked him, holding semiautomatic rifles with cut-down barrels. Those rifles would kick like a rodeo bull, but that would not stop the bullet they fired from killing Phil.

Molina apparently didn't have a weapon.

Phil recognized the two men he'd fought in the hall. Someone must have found them and released them. That meant one had a broken wrist and the other a mild concussion at minimum. He felt sure they could not fire those enormous rifles with any accuracy at the moment. He could take all three before they knew what hit them.

He dropped the magazine from the pistol and found only

two rounds remaining. He reinserted it as quietly as he could. Counting the one in the chamber, he had three rounds. The pistol in his pocket held five. He should have left Aaron the pistol and kept the carbine.

Still, when life gives you lemons, squirt lemon juice in your opponent's eyes with it, right?

Just when Phil was about to go through the door, pistol blazing, he heard the unmistakable sound of a shotgun firing.

Melissa!

He ran toward the stairs and took them three at a time. When he got to the top, he turned toward Lola's room. He saw candlelight and heard a man cry out.

He ran down the hall, and before he got to the open door he called out, "It's Phil," so that he didn't get sprayed with rock salt too.

The door hung from its hinges at a precarious angle, and the frame was broken. In the doorway, a man lay clutching his shoulder.

"He kicked open the door," Melissa said. Her eyes were wide, and she still gripped the shotgun, pointing it at the door.

Phil stepped over the injured man. "Good job. I'll take that." He held his hand out, and Melissa gave him the shotgun. He slapped the pistol into her hand. "Hold this for me for a minute."

The sound of booted feet on the stairwell echoed down the hall.

"Grab the kids," Phil said. "This way."

Melissa scooped Mathias off the bed, and Lola took Gabriele out of the crib. Nothing in his immediate surroundings would stop a bullet from the rifles, but Phil didn't think

Molina wanted to risk his children. They needed to be secured until he could eliminate the remaining threats against them.

His mind raced. He went over to the refrigerator, sized it up, and pulled it away from the wall. "Get behind it. It's the only thing here that might block a bullet."

Phil didn't wait to see them comply. He went back to the doorway. The man on the ground had gotten to his knees and pulled his pistol out of his pants. Phil trained the shotgun on him. "Live or die, dude, it doesn't matter to me either way. At this range, I can take your face off."

The man slid the gun to him and held his hands up.

"Best decision you've made all day."

Three lights bobbed down the hall as men ran in Phil's direction. He aimed his shotgun at one of the lights and fired. The light fell and the man howled. Everyone stopped.

"Finally coming to do your own dirty work, Molina?" Phil asked.

He didn't know for sure that Molina had one of the lights, but his men were down to three, so unless he somehow got through the downed cell towers, this should be the last of him and his crew.

"I'm just here to see my wife," Molina said. "It didn't have to turn into this."

"I don't think 'see' is the verb you're looking for," Phil said, aiming toward the light that Molina held. "Your English is obviously failing."

"Listen to me, Philip Osbourne. I will kill your entire family one at a time. Don't think that I—"

Phil fired. Molina screamed and the light fell to the ground. Before the last of the minions could escape, Phil shot him too.

Taking the flashlight out of his pocket, Phil grabbed the uninjured arm of the man nearest him, then walked down the hall, keeping the shotgun ready and dragging the man behind him. When he got to Molina, he could see the dark spread of blood across his chest. He imagined that the rock salt hurt.

Part of him wished he could deliver a fatal shot. No one would blame him. He was protecting the women and children down the hall. Molina was a violent, dangerous man who had killed many. Phil could just put the gun to his chest and fire, sending pellets of salt into his heart. This man who had stabbed his brother and set him on a park bench next to a pig's head, who had wrecked his parents, broken Phil's heart, taken from him the man he loved and respected and looked up to—this man deserved to die. He deserved to die in ways that Phil could make last, in ways that would make this evil man beg to be released from this life long before his heart beat for the last time.

After acknowledging that part of himself, Phil set it aside. Taking this man's life, in whatever form or fashion he imagined, would make him no better than Molina and his crew. It was not up to him to send Molina to meet God and answer for his sins. God's timing was perfect.

Using zip ties, he secured all four men. As he searched them for weapons, removing knives and pistols, he called out, "Melissa!"

Within seconds, her voice came from the dark doorway. "Phil?"

"I need a hand. You can use a light."

She turned her flashlight on, then came down the hall.

"I need either duct tape or rope or telephone line. Anything like that. A clothesline would work too."

"Okay." She went into one of the rooms closest to him. He looked down at Molina. "That shot looks like it hurts." The man glared at him, then started cursing him in Spanish.

"That's okay, buddy." Phil patted Molina on the head. "I understand."

Melissa unhooked the cord from the landline and ran back into the hall, then handed it to Phil. "I'll be right back," she said. She gathered cords from two more rooms before returning to Lola's.

"He got them all," she said, going to Lola's phone. "We're okay. Hector is down the hall with him."

"Did he kill him?" Lola came out from behind the refrigerator.

"No. He's just injured."

Her sister put her hand over her eyes and bent over. Melissa took precious seconds to hug her.

"It's over," she said, then raced down the hall.

Phil used the cords to secure each of the men to the stair railing. Melissa recognized Hector Molina from the photograph she'd seen in Phil's apartment. She'd admit only to herself that she wanted to kick him in the face. Maybe she had some of her father in her.

Phil walked to the end of the hall and looked out the window. Melissa joined him. He glanced over at her, put his arm around her, and pulled her close. "I have men tied up all over this building," he said softly.

"Do you think they can get free?"

He shook his head. "No. But they might wake up and start yelling." He let her go. "I have to go take care of Aaron."

She gasped. "Aaron!"

"He came to protect you from looters. He got shot." He held out the shotgun.

She hesitated only a second before taking it. "Take this," she said, handing him the pistol. "I don't know how to use it."

Phil checked the safety, then tucked the pistol into the back of his waistband. "Thanks. Stay where you can see these guys. Don't turn your back on them. If one of them moves, shoot him."

"Okay," she whispered. As he turned away, she said, "Phil!"

He turned back toward her. He must have known what she needed, because he put his hand on the back of her neck and pressed his forehead against hers. "I'm sorry. I love you and I have to go."

When she closed her eyes, tears slid down her cheeks. He pressed a kiss to her forehead and released her before walking down the stairs. After taking a deep, cleansing breath, she walked back to where the men were tied. She went into the nearest room and grabbed a kitchen chair, then sat down facing the stairs, keeping her eyes on the prisoners.

"You are making a giant mistake, Melissa Braxton," Hector said. "When I get free, I will kill you slowly."

It took a lot for her not to respond. Because he'd killed an officer of the court, he likely wouldn't be free anytime soon. The only thing she worried about was Lola coming out of that room. As long as she and the children stayed put, all would be well.

CHAPTER
★
TWENTY-EIGHT

Phil rushed down the stairs. In the courtyard, a gale-force wind knocked him down, and he rolled up against the building. He got to his feet, bent his head, and walked one step at a time to the room near the shed.

Adrenaline still pumped through his system, giving him strength he wouldn't normally have. He dodged a tree branch that flew past him and finally got to the door. The room was still dark.

"Aaron, it's me—it's Phil."

"Ohhh!" Aaron said, clutching the towel to his stomach. "You came back."

"I said I would." He turned on Aaron's flashlight and put it on a bookshelf facing the bed, then sat on the edge of the bed. "I need to look at the wound."

"Okay," Aaron said, panting.

Phil lifted up his T-shirt. The entry point was just to the

right of the belly button, and the bleeding had slowed. Aaron had done a good job of applying pressure. Phil checked behind him and did not find an exit wound, so the bullet was still inside him.

"Okay, buddy, it's important that you lie very still." He pulled his phone out of his pocket. Still no signal. "I'll be right back. I'm going to go get my truck, okay?"

Aaron moaned. Phil prepared himself for the wind and walked back into the courtyard. He fought for every step and finally made it to the parking garage. "Please, God," he said when he got into his truck. "This is going to take You."

He drove out of the garage and across the courtyard. He parked as close to the door of the room as possible, then raced back inside. Aaron had sat up.

"Let's go, buddy. Time to go to the emergency room."

"They shouldn't be in there," Aaron said. "I have to stop them."

Phil put his hands on his shoulders. "I stopped them. You helped me. Remember?" He helped Aaron to his feet and they staggered to the door. "The wind is strong. Brace against it," he said and opened the door.

The truck battled the weather all the way to the hospital. Phil dodged flying limbs, garbage cans, even a lounge chair. Finally, he pulled into the ambulance bay and lay on his horn. When a nurse hurried out, he said, "Twenty-something male with upper-right abdominal GSW."

The nurse ran inside and came back out with a wheelchair and Addy, who stopped when she saw him. "Phil?"

"Hey, Addy." He helped Aaron into the wheelchair. "This is Melissa's night guard. I have to get back. I left the women with some pretty bad guys."

She shook her head. "What bad guys?"

He faced her fully. "I promise—promise—to tell you about it over coffee tomorrow."

She looked at Aaron and back at him. "I have to call the police."

"Yes!" He ran around to his door, remembering that she would have access to the radio. "We have no signal. Send the police." He rattled off the address. "Tell them we need them as soon as they can come, but I've secured everyone for now."

Without waiting for her to agree, he drove away. Anxiety crept up his neck, tightening his muscles almost painfully. He drove around a car stopped in the middle of the road. Giant drops of rain had started to fall, reducing his visibility to almost nothing. His windshield wipers couldn't keep up with the torrential downpour.

He glanced at the clock. He'd left Melissa thirty-two minutes ago. He had to get back, to relieve her from guard duty while they waited for the police.

Thankful to have the shelter's garage to park in, he left the truck right by the door and raced inside. He checked on his prisoner in Melissa's apartment first. Still out cold. Then he crossed the hall and checked on the two in Sharon's kitchen and bathroom. One had come to and was frantically struggling against his bonds.

Phil shone the flashlight on him, and he immediately stilled. "Hi there," he said. "I'm going to take you to your leader." He would rather keep everyone where he could see them.

Before he cut the sheet, he zip-tied the man's wrists. Then he grabbed him by the upper arm and helped him to his feet. "Let's go, big guy." He turned the flashlight off and slipped it into his pocket.

The man started struggling and cursing. Phil closed his eyes and pictured the kitchen's layout, then slammed the man against the wall to get his attention. He held the muzzle of the pistol against his cheek. "Feel that?"

The man started quaking and finally whispered, "Sí."

"I thought about disposing of you. Still deciding if keeping you alive is more trouble than it's worth. Make a problem for me and you inform that decision. You would not be the first man I shot tonight. Not even the second. Comprende?"

The man nodded. Phil wouldn't kill him for any reason outside of self-defense, of course, but he didn't know that.

Phil kept a firm grip on his arm as they left the apartment and entered the hall. He marched him up the stairs to the third-floor landing. "Sit down," he said.

Melissa was sitting in a chair guarding the four men on the floor in front of her. The man with Phil gasped when he saw his teniente lying on the floor, blood covering the front of his shirt.

Phil used his belt to tie the man to the stair railing. He shook the railing to make sure it would hold, then bent down and put his nose against the man's. He could smell the fear radiating off him. "Don't move," he whispered.

Melissa had her shotgun pointed straight at Molina. When Phil approached, she lowered the weapon. "I thought I was going to have to shoot him to make him shut up."

She stood, and he took the gun from her. "I can do that for you if you want," he teased.

She pressed a hand to his shoulder, and they walked partway down the hall. "Aaron?" she whispered.

He shrugged. "Shot in the abdomen," he said softly. "No

exit wound. That isn't good. But he's a big guy, strong. We'll go to the hospital as soon as we can."

"Lola!" Molina screamed. "I know you can hear me, you sniveling—"

Phil fired a round into the ceiling. Molina cried out.

"I just need an excuse to make you permanently regret your life choices, Hector Molina. Give me one." Phil tucked the pistol into his waistband, gripped the shotgun in both hands, and walked up to Molina, leveling the business end at the man's face. He knew it smelled like gunpowder. "I am not afraid to finish the job. Are you afraid I will?"

Molina glared up at him but didn't say anything else. Phil walked back to Melissa. He wanted to tell her a thousand things—maybe a million things—but the words washed up against the dam he had built in his stream of consciousness. They broke against the dam and dissipated, and then his thoughts crystalized into the immediate priorities.

He took a breath. "Go take care of your sister. I'll wait for the police."

Melissa didn't know what she expected to find when she went back to Lola's room. Hector had screamed for Lola for almost thirty minutes, but she had never even popped her head out of the room. Melissa stopped short when she saw Lola and Mathias sitting on the bed, watching something on his tablet. They each had on headphones connected to a splitter.

Lola gasped when Melissa came into the room, then pulled the headphones off and left Mathias on the bed. She and Melissa met in the kitchen area.

"I was worried you'd hear him," Melissa whispered.

Lola closed the door as best she could on the broken frame. "As soon as I heard his voice, I put the headphones on Mathias. They're noise canceling. He wears them on airplanes because it's so loud."

Melissa pulled her into her arms. "You are very wise, sister mine."

"I can't believe it's over," Lola said on a sob.

"It's over," Melissa said with a confidence in her voice that surprised her. As much as wanted to go to Phil in that moment, to put her arms around him just as she did her sister, instinctively she knew he now wrestled with remorse for the violence he had committed tonight. She understood that he longed for a life of peace. She'd love to comfort him until he could grieve the loss of his brother and process everything that had transpired. Instead, she remained here with her baby sister, who she longed to get to know again and who needed her now perhaps more than ever.

Lola stepped back and looked at her son. "His grandfather will try to come for him."

Melissa glanced at Mathias and imagined what kind of man had raised his father. Her shoulders tensed, and she once more thought of Phil. They had a plan, and she knew he would see it through. "Phil is working with the Marshals Service. You'll get protection. He might come, but he won't be able to find you."

"It's almost more than I can comprehend," Lola said, rubbing her arms. "I've wanted to escape for so long."

Melissa really admired her sister's strength. Lola had held up remarkably well. "Your greatest fear was that Hector would find you. Well, he did, but Phil stopped him." She rubbed Lola's back.

Gabriele started fussing. Lola went over to the crib and scooped her up. "It's so hot in here," she said. "She doesn't sleep well in the heat."

"Do any of us?" Melissa rubbed her temples and walked over to the window. She took down the mattress and put it back on the bed. Without the barrier, the sound of the rain pelting the windows filled the silent room. "It's right on top of us," she murmured. She tried looking outside but could see nothing but water drops on the black window.

She wanted to get to the hospital and check on Aaron. It wouldn't be safe out there right now, but she still fought the impulse to leave and make her way the three blocks to the emergency room.

Lola sat on the couch and nursed Gabriele. Melissa sat with her. "Hurricanes give me a headache," Lola said.

"Me too." Melissa propped her elbow on the couch and leaned her head into her hand. "How involved were you with your husband's business?"

Lola tensed. Gabriele must have felt it, and she fisted her hand and bumped her mother's chest. In an almost absent movement, Lola grabbed her little hand and kissed her knuckles. She looked over at Melissa. "I worked closely with Hector when I was young. His father was grooming me as a teniente. I hated it, though. Then Hector started paying me attention. When I was eighteen, I was told to marry him, and at first I really resented it. But he wooed me and charmed me, and we fell in love. I thought he believed like me, that we needed to go away and do something else. He tricked me with moving here. It wasn't to break free, it was to run this part of the business. I'd packed to leave when I found out. That was the first time he hit me."

Melissa processed what she said. "You were running drugs?"

She shook her head. "No, I was managing people who ran drugs."

"Wow." Melissa couldn't imagine the lifestyle that had raised someone like that.

"I'm not proud of it. His father thought I was still involved in small ways until Gabriele was born. I quit going to Colombia then. A part of me was worried he'd take her from me to punish me. At least here I had a tiny bit of control."

"You have valuable information you can give them. You can testify."

"Oh, yes. I can give them so much. So much." Lola put her hand on Melissa's knee. "I can help right the wrongs I've done."

Melissa covered Lola's hand with her own. "You have a lot of strength of character. To be raised in the environment that produces someone like Hector but to see the wrongs for what they are is just God's love for you, His protection of your heart and soul."

Lola looked down at Gabriele for several moments before she asked, "You think? You think He can overlook who I was before?"

"I absolutely do."

CHAPTER

TWENTY-NINE

NOVEMBER 24
THANKSGIVING DAY

The morning after a storm, the sun always felt like it shone brighter, the air felt more crisp and less humid, and the sounds of human hustle and bustle seemed hushed in comparison to the sounds of nature beginning to recover. Phil stood next to his prisoners, who lay on the wet grass at his feet, and watched a seagull strut back and forth, eyeing him suspiciously. Hector Molina had his hands bound behind him, his ankles zip-tied together, and a bloodied tissue hanging out of his nose to stem the bleeding. Blood crusted the front of his shirt. Phil had set and splinted his counterpart's wrist, tied his elbows behind his back, and zip-tied his ankles. Three other minions lay passively hog-tied at Phil's feet, and the two tied to the sinks inside had not yet regained consciousness.

An unmarked car pulled up seconds before a cruiser with lights flashing. Phil took the pistol out of his belt and hooked it to his thumb, then held both hands up. A uniformed officer approached him with his pistol drawn, took the weapon from him, and cuffed his hands behind his back.

"This man attacked me and kidnapped me!" Molina said. "He is holding me against my will."

Phil closed his eyes for a moment and took a deep breath, then turned to Molina. "We discussed what would happen to you if you didn't shut up, didn't we?" Fear crossed the other man's face, and Phil nodded. "Let's keep that understanding, shall we?" He looked back at the officer. "There is a dead man and two more detained men inside."

"Dead?" The officer looked back at the detectives getting out of the car. "How so?"

"I'll explain it to the detectives. The arsenal of perhaps illegal weaponry is all theirs, by the way."

Another unmarked car arrived, and Marshal Alvarado stepped out. The detectives approached first, but Alvarado was on their heels. He gestured toward Phil. "Why is this man cuffed?"

"He had a gun." The officer crossed his arms over his chest.

"Is he not allowed to have a gun?" Alvarado hooked his thumbs into his jeans pockets. "Last I heard it was a free country, and Lieutenant Osbourne here has as much right to carry a gun as you do. Maybe more."

"He was also just accused of kidnap and assault, and apparently there's a corpse." The officer glanced around. "I felt the situation warranted caution."

Alvarado sighed and made a spinning motion with his finger. Phil turned, giving Alvarado access to unlock the handcuffs. "I only got your message about twenty minutes ago. What happened?"

Phil explained the night in complete detail as one of the detectives and one of the uniformed officers went into the building.

"How many rounds did you fire?" the other detective asked Phil.

"Three. From two different weapons," he said. "I piled their guns on the desk in the office. Collected eight total."

"And the body inside?"

He shrugged. "Don't know how many rounds he fired. I'm sure your crime scene people can figure it out."

"No, I mean, did you shoot him?"

"Yes. No choice." Phil explained the shooting of Molina's other minions, then how he secured Hector Molina and the rest of his team. "It's been a long night." Alvarado bent to lift Hector by the arm, and Phil said, "His buddy there has a broken wrist. He's going to need medical attention." He gestured at the building. "I checked the vitals of the two unconscious men inside not long before you got here. They should be okay, but they probably need to stay in a medical ward overnight."

The detective wrote notes as fast as he could. "Do you have anyone to corroborate your story?"

"Melissa Braxton can. She's the director of this facility, and she was here for the whole thing. His wife"—he pointed at Molina—"is here with her two children seeking shelter from him. That's why he came."

The detective raised an eyebrow. "He brought a team of seven to convince his wife to come home?"

Alvarado answered for him. "No, he brought a team of seven to murder his wife and keep her from testifying against him, and to kill anyone else here as well. He's Víbora's top lieutenant in Florida and under investigation for multiple counts of drug running, extortion, and murder."

The detective looked up from his notebook. "Víbora?"

Phil nodded. "He also had my brother Winston Osbourne, attorney for the state of Florida, killed. Marshal Alvarado was working with the state police on that."

"Is Mrs. Molina here?" Alvarado asked.

"She is. She and Melissa are in the dining room. They're ready to be interviewed about last night."

More marked police cars arrived, along with two ambulances.

"Let's leave the men to the local police," Alvarado said. "Please take me in to see Mrs. Molina."

"Yes, sir." Phil turned and smiled at the detective. "Anything else before I go?"

"Not for now," he said. "Your story sounds credible. Stay available in case we have further questions." He barked orders for the officers to get the prisoners to the hospital.

In the hall, Alvarado said, "You may get arrested in the end."

Phil caught the sarcasm in his voice and looked at him out of the corner of his eye. "If I do, then I'll tell my entire story in court, only I'll name names. Won't it be interesting to see that on the record?"

"No doubt." Alvarado put his hand out. "It's an honor to know you, sir. I assure you, whatever you need from me to help clear you of this, it's yours."

"Thank you."

They shook hands, then Phil opened the door to the dining room. Melissa got up from her chair and rushed to him.

He pulled her to him, wrapping his arms around her, pressing his lips to the top of her head. All the things that had held him back from her disintegrated in the wake of her touch.

"I was so scared," she said against his collarbone.

He smiled. "Me too." Reluctantly, he released her and stepped back to make introductions. "Melissa Braxton, Marshal Alvarado."

"It's nice to meet you," Melissa said. "Thank you for coming this morning."

"Would have been sooner if not for the storm. Didn't get Phil's message until they restored cell service."

Lola set Gabriele down, and she toddled toward Phil. Seeing her happy and healthy helped him start to decompress from the night. He leaned toward her. "Hi, sweet girl. You look a little less worn out from the night."

Gabriele patted Phil on the nose twice, then headed toward Mathias at the other end of the room.

"She slept through everything, including the shotgun," Lola said. "Is everything okay now?"

Alvarado smiled warmly at her. "Mrs. Molina, everything is exactly okay now. I have some paperwork for you, and the Marshals Service has authorized me to take you into protective custody immediately. I'll keep you safe until they need your testimony."

A sob escaped Lola, and Melissa put her arms around her. "How can I leave you now?" Lola asked her. "I just found you."

"You and the kids will be safe," Melissa said. "We're going to arrange to trade letters. And I understand that a few times a year, we can meet in some remote airport. That will be enough because it has to be."

Lola looked from Melissa to Phil. "Won't what Hector did here last night be enough to arrest him?"

"Yes, ma'am." The marshal cleared his throat. "But we want him for everything to put him away and keep him away. Last night was just assault. He was simply trying to come see his wife and everything got out of hand."

Lola gasped. "That's not what happened!"

"Of course not, ma'am. However, it's what he will say happened, and he has the assets and resources to make sure these charges don't stick. With your testimony, we can seize those assets, freeze those resources, get a very detailed and thorough search warrant, and in the end possibly even tie him to Winston Osbourne's murder."

Lola pressed her hand over her mouth. Tears slipped out of her eyes. "Okay. I will testify." She walked over to where Mathias played with a child-sized basketball hoop. "Time to go, Matty."

He dropped the ball and turned to her. "It's time to go? Where are we going?"

Lola smiled. "On an adventure."

Phil didn't feel comfortable letting Lola out of his sight until the marshals had secured her away from Miami. Alvarado seemed to understand how he felt and let him ride along.

In the SUV, he called the hospital and asked for Addy. He waited on hold for five minutes before she came to the phone. "It's Phil," he said.

"Never could get police. Our lines were down."

She could have radioed them, but he didn't press. "No worries. They came first thing."

"Are you okay?"

He glanced over at Melissa next to him. After a moment's hesitation, he reached over and took her hand. "Yes."

"Your friend is in surgery. I'll call your cell when he gets out."

"Thanks." He hung up the phone.

"How is he?" Melissa asked.

Phil shrugged. "No news yet."

Melissa sighed and looked out the window. Lola sat on the bench seat behind them, both kids in car seats next to her. When they arrived at the federal courthouse, Alvarado signed them all in.

"Since it's Thanksgiving and they evacuated a good part of eastern Miami, other than the guards, we should be the only ones here," he said. "We have a state attorney who will take Mrs. Molina's initial statement, and the leader of the task force from the DEA will arrive too."

Melissa put her arm around Lola's shoulders. Phil wished there was a way to keep Lola in Melissa's life permanently, but a cartel like Vibora would put a high price on her head and would never stop hunting her. The protection she needed had to be total and complete to work, and that meant it would take the government and everyone cooperating for her safety.

Inside the conference room, Melissa helped Mathias find a page in his coloring book. Lola shifted a sleeping Gabriele onto her shoulder and sat down in a large conference chair, rhythmically patting her back. Phil could see the shadows under Lola's eyes and the stress lines around her mouth. He prayed that she would have peace from now on.

He walked across the room to Alvarado. "Who pulled the short straw from the state attorney?"

Alvarado slipped his glasses on and looked down at the open file folder. "Kim Jones."

"Ah."

"Know her?"

"I do. She worked with my brother."

Alvarado smiled without any warmth. "That should make this easier."

Phil pulled his wallet out of his pocket and dug out the SD card. "I wanted to give this to you when it was safe."

Alvarado frowned. "What is it?"

"A recording of Winston's conversation with Lola. It will give you an idea of his angle in speaking with her."

Alvarado nodded. "Thank you for trusting me with it."

Phil heard the ding of an elevator. He glanced at Lola, who looked through the glass wall out into the sea of empty cubicles. Her eyes widened, and her hand stilled on the baby's back. She looked all around, then caught Phil's eyes. He walked over and leaned down toward her.

"I know that woman," she whispered.

Phil glanced at the window and caught Kim's profile as she walked toward the door. "Know her?"

"Yes. She used to come to Colombia and meet with Hector's father." Her eyes filled with tears. "Please, Phil, the children!"

Adrenaline surged through his system. He had trusted her. Winston had trusted her. She was the leak!

He turned and intercepted Kim as she came into the room. "Kim," he said, holding his hand out. "What a surprise."

She smiled. "I asked for the assignment. It was the least I could do for Winston."

If she hadn't said his brother's name, he might have just

asked a couple of questions. But looking at her bright smile and coral pantsuit, knowing that she bore at least some responsibility for Winston's murder, he just snapped. When she placed her hand in his, he gripped it, then spun her around, bringing her hand up behind her back and slamming her into the table. She struck it with surprising force and a loud thud. He gripped the back of her hair, holding her still.

"Hey!" she screamed as she struggled. "Have you lost your mind?"

He looked into Alvarado's shocked face. "Lola recognized her. She's with the cartel."

Alvarado moved quickly, pulling handcuffs out of his belt and securing Kim while reciting her Miranda rights to her.

"You've both gone insane." She sneered at Lola. "I've never seen that woman before in my life."

Lola lifted her chin. "I can give you the dates I saw her there."

"Good." Alvarado nodded at her. "We'll be needing those." He looked at Kim. "Winston Osbourne told me that someone in your office was feeding Vibora information. I'm sure it won't be overly difficult to find out if it's you." He picked up the phone and dialed a number. "This is Marshal Alvarado. I have a prisoner I need transported to booking."

The elevator announced another arrival. Phil tensely waited to see who would come around the corner. Alvarado clearly did too, because as soon as he saw the lanky man with the black beard he said, "DEA."

"Roger." Phil relaxed.

Kim started struggling against the cuffs, and Alvarado gripped her upper arm. "Let's go meet your transport at the elevator, shall we?"

As he pulled her away, she screamed obscenities, demanded release, and insulted everyone in the room.

Mathias looked up from his coloring. "Those were ugly words."

Melissa kissed his head. "They were. From an ugly lady."

The DEA agent walked into the room with wide eyes. "That felt a little extreme. I bet there's a story there."

Phil chuckled and held out his hand. "Phil Osbourne."

"Winston's brother. Nice to meet you." The man gave a firm handshake. "Nathan Adams."

Alvarado returned. "Well, I guess we need another representative from the state attorney's office."

Lola's face fell. "Do we need to wait to do this until then?"

Alvarado shook his head. "No, ma'am. You've waited enough. Let's get your initial interview over and start the paperwork." He looked at Phil. "You and Miss Braxton don't have to stay."

"Can we?" Melissa asked.

Nathan nodded. "Sure. It might take a couple of hours."

Phil walked over to Melissa and rubbed her back. "We can wait."

CHAPTER

★

THIRTY

Melissa sat in the vinyl chair next to Aaron's bed and wrote in her journal. She tapped her pen on her lip as she tried to word the things that had happened in the last twenty-four hours. The attack on her house, when she had never felt so scared in her life. Phil's incredible prowess, the way he'd saved them single-handedly. She'd intellectually understood his military experience, but to see him in action had impressed her in a way she didn't have words for. Then having to say goodbye to Lola and the kids. As long as the Vibora cartel still operated, Lola could never come out of hiding. But knowing she was safe, knowing they could still communicate with the aid of the Marshals Service, made the goodbye a little less painful to bear.

Now she watched the heart monitor track Aaron's rhythm, listening to a machine breathe for him. She closed her eyes and prayed for God's intervention on his behalf. He had been so brave and had done his job so well.

The door to the ICU room slid open, and she glanced over to see Aaron's mom come in. She had Aaron's curly red hair and his large frame. She smiled at Melissa. "Thanks for the spell," she said, her voice rich with an Irish accent.

"My pleasure." Melissa stood and stretched. Her body ached with fatigue. "Did your house fare okay in the storm?"

"Aye. Everything is as I left it." She ran her fingers through her son's hair. "He's a brave lad, this one."

"He is. He's so good at his job."

Mrs. McIntyre's red-rimmed eyes met Melissa's. "He loves that job. It keeps him going."

"I hope he comes back."

"I'm sure you can count on it."

Melissa put her pen and journal in her purse, then slipped the strap over her shoulder. "I have to go. Will you call me when there's a change?"

"I will." Mrs. McIntyre sat in the chair Melissa had just vacated and pulled a paperback book out of her bag.

Melissa followed the signs to the emergency department, then paused at the desk. "Doctor Carmichael said you'd know to buzz me back," she said to the nurse on duty.

The nurse glanced at the sticky note next to the phone and nodded, then hit a button, opening the door to the inner sanctum of the ER. Melissa entered and pushed through the door to the doctors' lounge.

Phil didn't even turn to glance in her direction, but Addy stood up from the couch. "How's Aaron doing?"

"He's still out. Mrs. McIntyre will call me when there's a change."

Phil sat in a low chair, his legs out in front of him and his head back against the cushion. He had his eyes closed, a soft, peaceful look to the normally hard lines on his face.

"He crashed about twenty minutes ago. I told him to leave, that I'd get you home, but he insisted on waiting."

Melissa felt a warm glow spread from her chest and down her limbs. "He worked hard last night."

"Yeah." Addy dumped her mug in the sink and rinsed it out. "He gave me the ten-second play-by-play. Even with the total lack of detail, I think I got a clear picture." She gestured at him. "And not a scratch on him."

"He's pretty remarkable." Melissa walked up and brushed at the hair on his forehead. Before she could react, he grabbed her wrist in a viselike grip and his eyes flew open. She gasped. It took a second for him to see her face, for his eyes to clear, before he let her go.

"Never touch a sleeping soldier," he said, pushing up. "Not safe."

"Especially after the night you had," she said with a shaky laugh.

He stood and pulled her close. She went into his arms, burying her face in his chest.

"You two need to go, get out of here, sleep. Worry about buildings and residents and jobs tomorrow," Addy said. Melissa turned her head to see Addy waving her hands as if shooing them away. "Go on now. I need to get back to my shift."

"Thanks for your help," Phil said. He steered Melissa to the door and dropped his arm from her shoulders.

"Yeah. Next time you drop a gunshot victim on my front door, you get to help."

He grinned. "Hopefully I'll be able to."

When they walked out of the hospital, Melissa looked up at the blue sky. "It's always strange how the world is so calm after a storm."

"I thought that this morning. We'll get the tail of it soon. Wind's already picking up." As they got in his truck, he glanced over at her. "I agree with Addy. We've been going for a couple of days. Your people are all still in the hotels. Lola is wherever she's going. My mom has clean, cool bedrooms just waiting for us."

Melissa looked at her phone and saw a text from Sharon encouraging her to take the rest of the day away from every-thing. She wrote back,

I'll see you in the morning.

Seconds later, Sharon replied,

Turn your phone off. Love you.

Melissa glanced over at Phil. "Sounds heavenly." She looked in the back seat and smiled. He'd grabbed her over-night bag that she'd packed—had it only been yesterday? It felt like a lifetime ago.

Phil pulled up in front of his parents' home as banshee sea breezes screeched out the final death knells of last night's hurricane. The clouds lined up in long dark rows that stretched from north to south as far as the eye could see, looking like a recently plowed field behind a fading sun. The fresh feeling of a new start that had followed the storm crept further and further away with the fading light. A thick, humid heaviness replaced it as the shadows lengthened into the darkness of night.

He put his truck into park and killed the engine. Melissa sat quietly. He knew she waited for him to make his way around the truck and open her door.

But he didn't.

More accurately, he couldn't. No matter how many times his exhausted mind commanded his fingers to loosen their grip on the steering wheel, they just grasped it more tightly. For so many hours he had moved forward and onward and had done what needed doing on sheer will alone. Apparently, his will had hit an insurmountable wall and he had consumed every last shred of his resources.

Sitting in the safety of his parents' driveway with Melissa by his side, he felt as if he could not take one more step. His heartbeat roared in his ears. His mouth filled with saliva. He gasped for breath. Clinically, he realized he had started down the path of a full-blown anxiety attack.

He felt Melissa's hand gently touch his forearm and only then realized that he had shut his eyes tight against the world. When they flew open, his headlights were out. The walk to the front door remained illuminated by the porch light, which burned like a lighthouse beacon in his vision.

Melissa's voice floated to his ears. "Are you okay?"

Her touch felt warm, soft, perfect. His spirit wanted to return that touch in kind, to reassure her, to lend her some of his strength and make her feel secure. But every part of him suddenly rejected the idea. He had no strength left to offer. In his quest to save Melissa's sister, Winston had lost his life. Phil had committed unsanctioned violence, and a life had ended as a consequence. He could already feel the ice-cold tendrils of remorse for the hurt he had caused snaking into his mind.

He didn't want to experience that inevitable remorse. He didn't want to feel the overwhelming grief that he had repressed over his brother's death. He didn't want to feel this endless frustration at the loss of his leg. He didn't want to deal with constantly disappointing this woman at his side. But above all else, he did not want to be comforted right now.

Melissa's fingers tightened on his forearm. "Phil?"

Suddenly, he wanted to get high. The temptation of the sweet escape offered by drugs would numb these oncoming emotions. He could put off confronting the raging flood before it overtook and drowned him. That initial sting and burn after the pinprick needle, and then he would feel nothing but a dull vacuum, nothing but drug-induced artificial peace.

No, a voice in his heart insisted with undeniable authority. *You know what you must do.*

He had shut his eyes again, and now he began to silently weep. Knowing who had just spoken directly to his heart, knowing with the certainty of faith, removed the last of his roots, and he surrendered to the flood, to the tide, to the raging current of emotions. The tears pouring out of him might as well have been the ocean of grief in which he found himself drowning. The sob that burst out of him exploded from deep inside.

Melissa must have unbuckled and scooted over toward him. He felt her arms come around him. As much as he didn't want her to touch him—as much as he didn't want any help from anyone—in equal measure he needed her touch, he needed her comfort, and he needed her love.

"Please," he said. It was the only word he could manage, but whether he intended to beg her not to touch him or plead with her to hold him even tighter, he didn't know. Then he wasn't even speaking to her. Instead, he was continuing the conversation, praying from his very soul.

Please, God. Please make all this right. Please make everything right.

"Shh. It's okay," Melissa whispered against his ear. She had shifted until she sat sideways on his lap. She pulled his head down, and he wept against her. "It's okay, Phil."

"I'm sorry," he said. *I'm sorry, God, that I hurt those men. I'm sorry. I'm sorry for anything I've done or said that led to Winston's death.*

Melissa gently kissed his hair, the corner of her mouth grazing the top of his ear. "It's okay. Shh. Shh. Shh."

The voice inside spoke again. *Peace. Be still.*

Melissa rocked him gently, back and forth, just like a child one-tenth his size.

In the cab of that truck, in the darkness of the balmy Miami night, with the glass fogging up all around him, he poured years of anger and sorrow out like water. He opened himself fully to God's voice, and God spoke to him through Scripture.

"My grace is sufficient for you, for My strength is made perfect in weakness." Therefore most gladly I will rather boast in my infirmities, that the power of Christ may rest upon me.

Melissa began to quietly pray. "Dear God, we thank You for Your love. I lift Phil up to You right now, Lord. Though we know that we could never be enough on our own, as we place our faith in Christ's sacrifice on our behalf, You make us righteous. You redeemed us. In our own strength, we remain inadequate, never clean or able enough, and sometimes not willing enough. But when we humbly dedicate our short supply to You, almighty God, You take it and work miracles with it. You use us. You are always enough."

Phil gasped, his entire frame shaking. He mourned. He silently lamented.

"It's too much for us to handle on our own, God," Melissa prayed. "But Your Word tells us, 'Now to Him who is able to do exceedingly abundantly above all that we ask or think, according to the power that works in us, to Him be glory in the church by Christ Jesus to all generations, forever and ever. Amen.'"

When her prayer ended, a new day began in Phil's soul. It felt as if he rose from the depths of the torrential tide and the storm raging in his heart and mind had completely vanished. He had room in his heart now that God had evicted the pride there. Slowly, his sobbing subsided. He grieved for his brother. He grieved for the friendships that he had put on hold, and he vowed to mend fences. He acknowledged his remorse for the violence he had committed in recent days.

At some point he had started speaking aloud, and Melissa quietly prayed along with him. He had surrendered everything. Even in his confusion and pride, God had used him, and for that he felt grateful. Now he knew exactly what he needed to do—love Melissa the way she needed to be loved. He could not imagine living even one more day apart from her.

He swiped at his cheeks almost angrily and grabbed the back of Melissa's neck so suddenly that shock filled her eyes. He gentled his touch and brought her lips slowly but firmly to his own. After a few heartbeats, she moaned against him. Seconds later, he felt the wet tickle of her tears on his lips.

"I love you," they said in near harmony when they parted.

Through tears of joy, Melissa said more quietly, "I love you, Phil."

"I love you too."

CHAPTER

THIRTY-ONE

ONE YEAR LATER

Phil looked down at the turquoise waters from eight hundred feet. In the seat next to him, Melissa grinned. "It's so peaceful. I thought it would be kind of crazy." She looked up at the parachute canopy above them. "But it's quiet."

"You should try jumping out of a plane." He closed his eyes and felt the wind against his face. "It's the most peaceful two minutes of your life."

"We should."

His dad drove Winston's boat below them, cutting a path of white through the water. Phil glanced at Melissa and watched the sheer joy radiate from her.

They stayed up for twenty minutes, then his dad reeled them in. The closer they got to the boat, the louder the world around them became. Eventually, they placed their feet on the deck and detached from their harnesses.

As he and Phil packed up the equipment, Melissa said, "I'm going to go get a drink down below."

Phil nodded and gathered up the parachute.

"How was it?" his dad asked.

Phil smiled. "Incredible. Do you want to go before we get it all put away?"

"Nah. Maybe next time."

"Definitely will be a next time. This is the second time I've rented this equipment. It was perfect."

Melissa came back on deck with three waters and handed them out. "It was more than incredible. No wonder Phil went Special Forces, if he got to parachute all the time."

He laughed and shook his head. "I'm afraid that this is a much different experience."

She snorted. "Well, yeah. I mean, no one was shooting at us, right?"

They took their time making their way back to the dock. They tied up the boat, gathered all the equipment, and loaded it into Phil's truck.

Phil's dad tapped the roof of the truck. "I'll walk home, kids. See you in a while."

When Phil and Melissa got in, they immediately rolled down the windows to let the heat out while he turned on the air-conditioning. He glanced at the clock. "We can get to the shelter in time for Thanksgiving."

"Mrs. Horton will be pleased," she said. She rolled her head on the back of the seat and looked at him. "I can't believe it's been a year."

"I know. It's been a year of firsts, hasn't it?" Good and bad. A year of no Winston, a year of a solid relationship with Melissa, and almost a year of practicing emergency medicine.

338

Every day he'd woken up happier, until one day he realized he hadn't scowled since the day before. His soul had gone through so much healing after the night of the hurricane, the night spent fighting the Vibora gang. The affirmation that he could still defend those he loved took away the sadness and suffering about his leg. It soothed his soul over the mistakes he'd made in his past.

The investigation into the state attorney's office had revealed no other leaks besides Kim. The DEA cooperated with the FBI in an internal investigation, and so far, three total agents had been found compromised by the Vibora cartel. The investigation continued.

As Phil struggled to adjust to a life without his brother, he knew Melissa had a similar challenge with her sister. Knowing Lola was alive somewhere out there but not being able to see her yet had been hard on her. She'd barely let it show, though. She stayed energetic, helpful, and happy, and she did more every day to teach Phil how to see the light in the world than she would ever know.

Melissa snuggled against Phil's side, her head on his shoulder. He smelled like sunshine and cinnamon. "I'm so full, I can barely move," she said.

"Mmm, don't move." He squeezed her against his side and laid his head back against the swing. "You know we have to go to my parents' and do this all over again."

"Why did I not show more self-control? You'd think I would know better."

"You weren't lying when you said Mrs. Horton puts on a mean spread."

"Every year."

Melissa didn't think she'd ever been more content in her life. She rested her hand against Phil's chest, and he picked it up and pressed a kiss to the back of it.

It took a minute for her to register the cool metal sliding over her finger. She gasped and sat up, staring at the diamond ring in the afternoon light. "Phil!"

He turned to face her. "Melissa, I have been in love with you for years. I just never felt like I was enough for you. A year ago, I was reminded that my leg did not define my character or strength and that I could compensate as needed. I was ready to ask you this the next morning, but I wanted to give you time to trust me again." He cupped her cheek with his hand. "Please forgive my arrogance and agree to be my wife."

Sparks of joy burst in her chest. She had hoped and prayed and prayed and hoped that he would take this next step. But since he'd had to go through his year of firsts without Winston and had been working so many extra hours as a resident in the ER, she hadn't pressed or pushed. She'd found contentment in waiting on God's perfect timing.

She stared at the ring, then looked into his eyes. "Of course I'll be your wife. I've just been waiting for you to ask me."

He cupped her cheek and leaned forward, pressing a kiss to her lips. He tasted like pumpkin pie and cinnamon coffee.

When she settled back against him, she held her hand up to let the ring catch the light. "You know what I prayed for you after you broke up with me last year?"

He chuckled. "What?"

"I prayed that God would bring a way to help you see your true worth." She looked up at him. "Of course, I probably should have been a little more specific. What I thought was

340

that God would give me these profound words that I could speak to you and you'd hear them. I never anticipated that a Colombian cartel would attack my shelter and you'd have to face them single-handedly." He grinned and she smiled. "But whatever works."

"Whatever works."

She snuggled back up to him and listened to the sounds of the birds in the trees. "I hope you never have to come to my rescue again, but I'm so thankful that you were here that night."

He kissed her head. "I will always come to your rescue."

She looked at her ring again. "It's a beautiful ring."

"For a beautiful woman."

She raised her face for his kiss, ready for another year of firsts with him solidly by her side.

DISCUSSION QUESTIONS

Phil is very angry with God about his circumstances. When Job appealed to God to express his righteousness, God answered with, "Where were you when I laid the foundations of the earth? Tell Me, if you have understanding" (Job 38:4).

1. Do you think this means that we don't have the wherewithal to be angry with God or to question our circumstances? Or do you think that God created us as emotional beings and will understand our anger? Explain.

Melissa struggles with her feelings for Phil. Even though she asked him out the first time, she has waited a year for him to take the next step.

2. Do you think it's unreasonable for her to have waited without any indication from Phil of his feelings for her?

3. Do you think it's selfish of Phil to take the time he can have with Melissa and not give her what she really needs or wants in return? Why or why not?

Melissa suffered a terrible trauma as a child. She watched her mother get beaten so badly she died as a result, and then she had her baby sister taken from her without knowing where she went.

4. Do you think that Melissa's choice to hold back from pushing Phil is due to her childhood trauma? Explain.
5. How has funneling her resources and energy into helping people like her mother moved Melissa toward healing from her trauma?

On her way to church, Melissa enjoys bright skies and songs that make her happy. After Phil breaks up with her and she heads home from church, the sky is cloudy and dark and the radio annoys her.

6. Have you ever had an experience when the very environment around you seemed to fit your state of mind? Explain.
7. How much do you think our filter of a situation affects our perception of the environment?

Phil is trained in hand-to-hand combat in a way that doesn't leave room for pulling punches or holding back.

8. When he incapacitated the agent in Winston's apartment, do you think he did anything wrong? Should he have been more aware of his training and expertise and found a way to restrain the agent without potentially fatally wounding him? Why or why not?

9. Do you think Phil's killing of a man while defending Melissa and her family is justified, or should he have found a way to restrain the man without killing him? Explain.

Phil feels less than whole, which is why he feels unworthy of pursuing a relationship with Melissa.

10. As Phil is a man who professes a love for Christ and lives a life following God, is his perception of himself selfish and sinful in nature? Why or why not?

11. Phil not only has a missing limb, he also has an addiction problem. Do you think his feelings of inadequacy are justified?

12. Saving Melissa and her family the night of the hurricane snaps Phil out of his attitude about himself. Do you think such an extreme situation would warrant such a change in attitude? Explain.

RECIPES

Phil's mom grills grouper for their family dinner night. This is a beautiful main course that can be prepared outside on the grill or inside under the broiler. Mango salad and seasoned rice go perfectly with this light fish.

———— Grilled Grouper ————

¼ cup extra virgin olive oil
zest and juice from 1 lemon
½ tsp salt (kosher or sea salt is best)
¼ tsp ground black pepper
4 skinless grouper fillets

Whisk together olive oil, lemon zest and juice, salt, and pepper. Add fish and gently toss. Let sit for at least 15 minutes.

On the grill: Preheat the grill and lightly oil the grates. Grill fillets until the bottom of the fish turns opaque and you can see the darker grill marks (3 to 4 minutes). Flip and cook another 3 to 4 minutes. The fish should flake easily with a fork when done.

Under the broiler: Preheat the broiler, and place fillets on a lightly greased broiler pan about 6 inches under the broiler. Broil 5 to 6 minutes, or until fish flakes easily with a fork.

Serve with fresh lemon.

—————— Mango Salad ——————

Salad

3 mangos, peeled and cubed
1 bell pepper, halved and thinly sliced
1 medium red onion, halved and thinly sliced
1 jalapeño pepper, seeded and thinly sliced
¼ cup thinly sliced fresh basil
¼ cup chopped fresh cilantro

Dressing

juice from 2 limes
zest from 1 lime
1 tbsp honey
1 tbsp extra virgin olive oil
¼ tsp salt (kosher or sea salt is best)
¼ tsp freshly ground black pepper

Combine all salad ingredients in a large bowl.

In a small bowl, whisk lime juice with zest and honey. Slowly whisk in olive oil until the mixture is emulsified. Add salt and pepper to taste.

Drizzle dressing onto the salad and gently toss. Serve immediately.

—————— Seasoned Rice ——————

2 tbsp extra virgin olive oil
¼ cup finely diced onion

1 clove garlic, minced
2 cups long-grain white rice
1 tsp salt (kosher or sea salt is best)
4 cups chicken stock
¼ cup unsalted butter
¼ cup chopped fresh parsley

In a large, deep skillet, heat olive oil over medium-high heat. Add onion and cook, stirring regularly, about 5 minutes or until translucent. Add garlic and cook another minute or two. Add rice and salt. Stir constantly for about 3 to 4 minutes, lightly toasting the rice in the oil and onion. Add chicken stock.

Bring to a boil. Cover skillet and reduce heat to low. Cook, without lifting the lid or stirring, for 20 minutes or until all liquid is absorbed and rice is tender.

Remove from heat and stir in the butter and fresh parsley. Serve.

Hallee Bridgeman is the *USA Today* bestselling author of several action-packed romantic suspense books and series. An Army brat turned Floridian, Hallee finally settled with her husband in central Kentucky, where they have raised their three children. When she's not writing, Hallee pursues her passion for cooking, coffee, campy action movies, and regular date nights with her husband. An accomplished speaker and active member of several writing organizations, Hallee can be found online at www.halleebridgeman.com.

ESCAPE TO A LUSH SETTING
AND SEEK REFUGE WITH
THE A-TEAM IN *HONOR BOUND.*

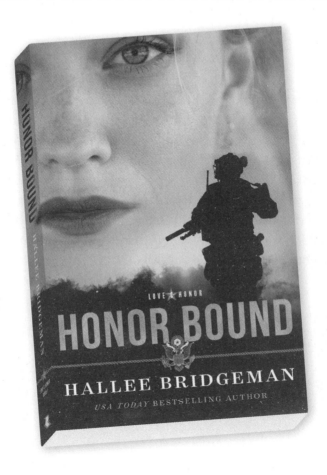

Medical missionary Cynthia Myers is trained to save lives.
Captain Rick Norton of the Special Forces A-Team is ordered
to take them. When Cynthia's past catches up to her,
they must learn to put aside their differences to make it out
alive from the jungles of a war-torn African country.

MEET
HALLEE BRIDGEMAN

HALLEEBRIDGEMAN.COM

- authorhalleebridgeman
- halleeb
- halleebridgeman